I0657255

Armand de Quatrefages de Bréau

The Pygmies

Armand de Quatrefages de Bréau

The Pygmies

ISBN/EAN: 9783337407162

Printed in Europe, USA, Canada, Australia, Japan

Cover: Foto ©Andreas Hilbeck / pixelio.de

More available books at **www.hansebooks.com**

BY

A. DE QUATREFAGES

LATE PROFESSOR OF ANTHROPOLOGY AT THE
MUSEUM OF NATURAL HISTORY, PARIS

TRANSLATED BY

FREDERICK STARR

WITH NUMEROUS ILLUSTRATIONS

NEW YORK

D. APPLETON AND COMPANY

1895

COPYRIGHT, 1894,

BY D. APPLETON AND COMPANY.

EDITOR'S PREFACE.

No apology is necessary for introducing any work of de Quatrefages to American readers. No man has done more than he to further anthropological study in France; no man was more respected than he over the whole of Continental Europe; no European anthropologist's works have been more widely read in America. Since the idea of incorporating *Les Pygmées* into the Anthropological Series was reached its learned and respected author has died. It seems proper, therefore, to present here a brief sketch of his life and work.

Jean Louis Armand de Quatrefages de Bréau was born February 10, 1810, in the Department Gard, France. Studying at the College of Tournon, and later at the University of Strasbourg, he received the degree of Doctor of Mathematical Sciences in 1830. Two years later he became Doctor of Medicine, and received a subordinate appointment to the Faculty of Medicine at Strasbourg. Shortly after, removing to Toulouse, he began the practice of medicine. For four years he remained in that city as a practitioner, and at the same time busied himself with scientific work, taking active part in several learned societies, and founding (with a colleague) the *Journal de Médicin et de Chirurgie de Toulouse.* In 1840 he removed to Paris, studying in zoölogy under Milne-Edwards, and taking the degree of Doctor of Natural Science. Particularly interested in marine life, he prosecuted important researches and published many papers, some of permanent value. In 1850 he was appointed Professor of Natural History at the College of Henry IV; in 1852, elected member of the Institute; in 1855, called to the head of the Department of Anatomy and Ethnology at the Museum of Natural History. Here he found his life-work, remaining until his death, busying himself with study, writing, and teaching.

A man of strong convictions and very conservative, de Quatrefages was ever ready to hear the other side, and ever candid and kindly in argument. He was one of the first to support the Society of Anthropology. Those who know the story of the early days of that great association understand what that means. When the claim for man's antiquity was generally derided, de Quatrefages championed the cause. A monogenist, a believer in the extreme antiquity of our race, he was never won over by any of the proposed theories of evolution.

The ethnographic works of de Quatrefages are many and valuable. From the list of nearly one hundred and fifty important papers or volumes, we select as most important *Les Polynésiens et leur migrations, Crania ethnica* (written in collaboration with E. T. Hamy), *L'Espèce humaine, Hommes fossiles et hommes sauvages,* The Natural History of Man, *Introduction à l'étude des races humaines,* and *Les Pygmées.* The Natural History of Man and a translation of *L'Espèce humaine* have been published in America.

To the very end of a long life our author lived happily and busily active among his books and specimens. Age touched him lightly. Only a few weeks before his death we visited him, and received from him that gracious, kindly assistance which he ever gave freely to all foreigners. At that time, although past fourscore years of age, and though, as he himself remarked, his hand trembled, and it was not as easy as formerly for him to write, he was engaged upon an important scientific work.

He died January 12, 1892, after a brief illness, and in his death France lost an eminent son and science a brilliant leader.

INTRODUCTION.

—

For a long time past the small black races have attracted my attention and my interest in a special manner. On several occasions, in my courses and in various publications, I have recurred to their history.*

It has seemed to me that it might be useful to gather and unite these materials in a book which should present a sort of monograph of this human type, very curious for more than one reason.

These little blacks are to-day almost everywhere scattered, separated, and often hunted by races larger and stronger. They are no longer found in certain parts of the globe which they formerly occupied, and they are disappearing from many others. Nevertheless they have had in the past their time of prosperity; they have played a very real ethnologic *rôle*. Finally, they have become the subject of legends which the poets have collected and which the most serious classical writers have not disdained transmitting to us.

To make known the scientific truth in regard to these

---

* See Gazette médicale, 1862 ; Revue d'anthropologie, 1872 ; Bulletin de la Société d'anthropologie, 1874 ; Comptes rendus de l'Académie des sciences, 1874 ; Crania ethnica, 1875–'79 ; Journal des savants, 1881–'82 ; Revue d'ethnographie, 1882 ; Hommes fossiles et Hommes sauvages, 1884 ; Matériaux pour l'histoire primitive et naturelle de l'homme, 1886 ; Introduction a la histoire des races humaines, 1887.

fables, to show what the pygmies of antiquity really are, is the principal purpose of this book.

I have carefully indicated in the footnotes the sources whence I have drawn my facts. But I must thank here Bro de Saint-Pol Lias, E. de la Croix, and Marche and Montano, who have kindly furnished me unpublished material, and to whom I owe the greater part of the photographs reproduced in the text. The figures of skulls are drawn from specimens in the collections of the museum.

Although Greek and Roman antiquity did not know either the Bushmen or the Hottentots, I have felt it my duty to devote a chapter to them. One cannot separate these two populations, and by its little stature the first well deserves to take its place by the side of the classical pygmies, from whom it is otherwise very distinct. Yet I have confined myself, so far as their physical and ethnographic characters are concerned, to simply indicating these. They are described in many works.

It is otherwise with regard to their religious characters, the importance of which, from many points of view, is more and more recognised. Those of the races of the Cape have remained little known until these last years. Therefore I have made a *résumé* of what Hahn has taught us on this subject, just as I have made known in some detail the discoveries upon this point made by Man among the Mincopies. The comparison of these two mythologies, spontaneously developed among savages located almost at the lowest steps of the social ladder, I hope may interest those who occupy themselves with these questions.

A. DE QUATREFAGES.

Paris, *May 24, 1887.*

CONTENTS.

LIST OF ILLUSTRATIONS.

THE PYGMIES.

CHAPTER I.

THE PYGMIES OF THE ANCIENTS, ACCORDING TO MODERN SCIENCE.

Homer and Aristotle: Pygmies of the Nile.—The Marsh of the Nile.
—Pliny: African and Asiatic Pygmies.—Buffon: The Apes.—
Roulin: Northern Populations.—Beloochistan: Brahouis.—
Ctesias: Asiatic Pygmies.—Pomponius Mela: East African
Pygmies.—Herodotus: West African Pygmies.—Voyage of the
Nasamones.—The Niger.—Negritos and Negrillos.

THERE is probably no nation, not a human population,
which has not believed in the existence of men of more or
less dwarfed stature and has made them play a *rôle* in
its legends.* One knows that the Greeks have not escaped the common law, and that Homer has borrowed
from beliefs, which were without doubt much older than
his time, the beginning of the third chant of the Iliad, -
" when under the orders of their chiefs they had arranged
themselves in battle array, the Trojans advanced noisily
like a cloud of birds, making their loud cries heard. So

---

   * I have no intention of here examining all that has been said on
the subject of the pygmies. It is understood that I shall not occupy
myself with puerile traditions, nursery tales, which some ancient
authors have transmitted to us on the subject. . . . 1 shall confine
myself to discussing that which has been said which is nearest true.
Readers who wish more may consult Banier.[12]

1

raises itself to heaven the outcry of storks when they flee from winter and the continual rains. They utter shrill cries, they fly over the ocean, they bear carnage and death to the men called pygmies; and from high in the air they give them dreadful combat."

The country of the pygmies is not mentioned in this passage. Yet Homer certainly knew of the migration of the storks; he knew that they passed each year from Europe into Africa and back again; and as, according to him, these birds met their enemies only after having crossed the sea in order to escape the severity of the bad season, it is evident that it is somewhere in Africa that the poet located the home of these dwarfs, supposed too small and too feeble to resist their winged invaders.

Although he has spoken of the pygmies in connection with the natural history of storks, Aristotle said nothing of the pretended combats which furnished Homer his term of comparison. One may say that he did not believe in it. Behold how he expresses himself: "The storks pass from the plains of Scythia to the marsh of upper Egypt, toward the sources of the Nile. This is the district which the pygmies inhabit, whose existence is not a fable. There is really, as men say, a species of men of little stature, and their horses are little also. They pass their life in caverns."[7]

Without being as explicit as one might wish, Aristotle here corrects exaggerations relative to the claimed height of the pygmies. There is a great difference between *men of little stature* and those miniature human beings among whom storks could *carry carnage and death*. Upon the other points the founder of natural science is, one might say, upon the line of truth such as it appears to us to-day.

It is toward the sources of the Nile that he placed the home of the pygmies. It is, in fact, in proceeding almost in the general direction of this river that Schweinfurth

discovered the little men of whom we shall speak farther
on. But Aristotle placed these sources in the midst of
swamps situated in upper Egypt. We know, but only
very recently, that there the course of the Nile was singularly cut short. The swamps exist in fact. All explorers
of these regions have insisted upon the difficulties which
they have experienced in traversing the inextricable labyrinth of canals encumbered by islands now fixed, now
floating, which form the *Sett*, a true vegetable barrier,
of which papyrus* and herminisria† form, so to speak,
the framework, and which more humble plants, particularly the pistia, compared by travellers to a little cabbage
which grows, in the manner of our water lentils, consoli-
date. But these swamps, which commence a little south
of Khartoum, become pronounced at about the ninth degree of latitude.[11] One knows that it is much farther to
the south and beyond the equator that the sources of the
Nile are found. It is in our hemisphere near the second
degree of north latitude, two or three degrees of longitude
west of the African river, and in a totally different basin
—that of the Welle—that Schweinfurth discovered the
Akkas, which are apparently the little men of Aristotle.[172]

Aristotle speaks of the little horses of the pygmies,
but no traveller mentions this quadruped as forming part
of the fauna of the country. One might be tempted to
see in this contradiction a motive for doubting the exacti-
tude of the facts conveyed by travellers to the Greek phi-
losopher. But it is easily explained. Baker tells us that

---

* *Papyrus domestica, L.* This so justly celebrated plant appears
formerly to have been very abundant over the whole of Egypt. However, Schweinfurth saw it first on the banks of the Nile, at 9° 30'
north latitude.[172]

† *Herminisria,* Adanson; *Ædemone mirabilis,* Kotschy. This
plant grows to a height of fifteen to twenty feet, with a diameter at
base of five to six centimetres; it is very light, more so than cork.

the animals of the Bari (a negro tribe of the neighbourhood of Gondokoro) are of very small size—"cows and ewes have dimensions truly Lilliputian."[11] Probably at the time of the Egyptian domination the horse had reached even into these districts; and, if it had been so, he must also have suffered the degeneration reported by the English traveller in the cases of the other domestic mammals.

Thus Aristotle has been very definite; that which he said is in part true, and in any case at least reasonable. With Pliny, we meet with uncertainties, exaggerations, and fables. He places the pygmies now in Thrace, not far from the shore of the Euxine Sea;[138] now in Asia Minor, in the interior of Caria. On two occasions he designates India as the country of these little beings; elsewhere, in speaking of peoples of Africa, which live at the extremity of Ethiopia, he says, "Some authors have also reported that the nation of the pygmies was among the marshes which were the source of the Nile."

One has reproached Pliny for the multiplicity of the habitats assigned by him to the pygmies; one has wished to see in this fact one more example of the haste with which he took his notes, and of the contradictions into which his manner of working led him. But has one not been too severe in this, and have his words not been misunderstood? In placing pygmies upon geographic districts so separated from each other, and so distinct, Pliny could not have intended to speak of one single population. He has evidently believed in the existence of these little men upon different parts of the then known world, and admitted in particular Asiatic and African pygmies. Upon this point modern discoveries have shown that he was right.

Pliny reproduces, however, without any reservation, all that which was said upon the subject of the combats sustained by the pygmies against the storks. It is these, so

the barbarians say, which have chased them from Thrace.
Thanks to the annual migration of these birds, the little
men enjoy each year an armistice. Finally he sums up
all this *ensemble* of beliefs in the following terms : " In
India, beyond the mountains, one speaks of the Tris-
pithames and of the pygmies, who are no more than
three spithames in height (twenty-seven inches, about
0·73 metres) ; they have a wholesome climate and perpetual springtime, protected as they are by the mountains against the north wind. Homer relates, on his
part, that the storks make war against them. It is said
that, borne upon the backs of rams and of goats and
armed with arrows, they descend all together at springtime to the seacoast, and eat the eggs and the little ones
of these birds ; that this expedition lasts three months ;
that otherwise they could not resist the increasing multi-
tudes of the storks ; that their cabins are constructed
of mud, feathers, and eggshells. Aristotle says that the
pygmies live in caverns ; as for the rest, he gives the same
details as the others."

We have just seen how inexact this last assertion of
Pliny is, and I need not emphasise the point. But the
reports collected by the celebrated Roman compiler suggest other remarks.

It is difficult to understand what has caused him to
locate the pygmies in Thrace or in Asia Minor. In these
countries neither the history of man nor that of animals
presents any fact which, twisted by ignorance nor by the
love of the marvellous, could have served as a basis for
the legends which are here considered. It may be, as M.
Maury has pointed out, that one may find the explanation of these mistakes in a general fact. The habitation
of beings more or less strange, whose existence was admitted by the ancients, was always placed by them at the
borders of the then known world, without their troubling

themselves concerning the precise point or the exact direction. From thence resulted, when one concerned himself with this fantastic geography, the vagueness and contradictions so often observed, and of which the history of the pygmies furnishes a striking example.

Unlike the countries to which the preceding reflections are applied, Africa and tropical Asia present certain facts which permit explaining in various ways what the ancients have said of their pygmies, and these facts proceed from the history of animals as well as from that of men.

In his History of Birds, and à propos to that of storks, Buffon has discussed the whole of the facts which I have just recalled in order to find out how much of reality they contain. But he too much forgot Aristotle, and only really concerned himself with the assertions of Pliny. Comparing what this latter reports of the annual expeditions of the pygmies with some facts in the habits related of monkeys, he saw in these last the dwarf men so celebrated among the ancients. "One knows," said he, "that the monkeys, which go in large bands in the greater part of the regions of Africa and India, carry on continual warfare against birds; they seek to surprise their nests, and without ceasing prepare ambushes for them. The storks, on their arrival, find these enemies, perhaps, assembled in great number to attack this new and rich prey with greater advantage. The storks, quite sure of their own powers, trained among themselves to battles, and naturally quite disposed to war, defend themselves vigorously. But the monkeys, anxious to carry off the eggs and the young birds, return constantly, and in bands, to the combat; and as by their tricks, their feints, and movements they seem to imitate human actions, they would appear to ignorant people to be a band of little men, . . . Behold the origin and the history of these fables!"[22]

This interpretation of the ancient legend is simple and

natural; it must have presented itself to many minds.
Supported by the authority of our great naturalist, it has
been generally adopted. Perhaps one should consider it
still to contain some truth. It may well be that, under
the sway of general beliefs, voyagers have really taken
some band of monkeys for a tribe of real pygmies.

But has not man himself supplied his share of facts,
true at bottom and only distorted, to these legends, which
have been transmitted since the time of Homer? Many
men of science have replied affirmatively to this question,
and proposed solutions quite diverse. One *savant*, whom
all the world has loved for his character as much as it
has esteemed him for his so varied and exact knowledge—
Roulin—adopted upon this point the opinions of Olaus
Magnus and of Paul Jove.[12] Unfortunately, the notes
traced by him on the margin of a copy of Pliny which
formed part of the library of the Institute are evidently
of very ancient date. They were written apparently long
before the discoveries of which I shall speak farther on.
The most precise and important information has come to
us only after the death of my colleague. He could not
then use them in order to explain the words of the author
whom he was commentating. Although we cannot accept to-day the theory at which he arrived, it is desirable
that I should refer to it. It is always interesting to know
the thoughts of an ingenious and fine mind upon a difficult subject.

For Roulin, at the period when he wrote his reflections, the pygmies of the ancients were our circumpolar
population. Although the notes say nothing of it, one
could not doubt that the little stature recognised among
several of these peoples has been the source of this interpretation. One knows, in fact, that the Lapps have long
been regarded as the smallest human race. Certain Eski-
mo rival them in this respect, and even go further. Hence,

to see in them the dwarfs of the ancient legends is but a
step. The question of country was no hindrance to the
partisans of this theory. Have not the pygmies been
placed in Thrace and in Scythia as well as in Asia and
Africa? Some peculiarities of customs lend themselves
to the identification. The author recalls the fact that
certain northern populations inhabit alternately each year
the interior and the seacoast just as Pliny said the pygmies did. It is also to eat the eggs of aquatic birds, of
which they destroy an immense number, that these tribes
go to the coast. That which the Latin author reports of
the huts of the pygmies is explained, moreover, without
much difficulty. Roulin wrote: " Perhaps in the original
tradition these huts, in place of being made of mud and
of the shells of eggs, were made in the form of hemi-
spheres (half eggshells) and of mud. Those of the Eski-
mos have this form, but are made of snow."

Finally, the tradition reports that the storks met their
enemies in their annual journeys from north to south.
Roulin replies: " In placing the migration of the storks
between these same two points, but making them proceed
from the marshes of upper Egypt to Scythia—i. e., towards
the frigid zone—it is there that the pygmies are found."

To discuss the ingenious corrections proposed by Roulin
is to-day useless. I will limit myself to observing that he
has neglected another passage, of great importance—in that
it permits determining with precision the point where the
author places the Asiatic pygmies. One reads, in fact, the
following phrase in his description of India: " Immediately beyond the nation of the Prusians, in whose mountains they say are the pygmies, one finds the Indus."
The mountains here considered were then west of the
river; and as the pygmies betook themselves each year to
the seacoast, from which they could not, therefore, be
very far distant, one sees that we are here dealing with

the most southern part of the mountainous district of
Beloochistan.

This region is situated at about 25° or 26° north latitude
and 63° or 64° east longitude. Travellers do not mention
in this district any population of particularly small stature,
but I have elsewhere shown that the most ancient inhabitants of this country, the Brahouis, who speak a Dravidian
language, belong to a great group of crossed races, of which
the Negritos form the black element.[150] At the time of
Pliny they were certainly less altered than to-day by the
mixture of bloods, and must have resembled those Dravidians, properly called, whose height descends below 1ᵐ50
and seldom rises to 1ᵐ62 or 1ᵐ63. Perhaps even at the
epoch when the facts were collected which were transmitted by the Roman writer there existed yet in the province of Loos, just where Pliny places his pygmies, some
tribe of Negritos similar to that of which we are about
to speak. However that may be, the Brahouis present a
peculiarity of customs which recalls exactly what Pliny
attributes to the pygmies. They change their dwelling
twice a year—at the beginning of summer and winter.
These annual migrations are compelled by the necessity
of procuring good pastures for their animals, which consist, as those of the pygmies did, of sheep and goats.

Everything concurs, then, to make us see in the Brahouis the descendants of the little men of whom Pliny
spoke. But long before him Ctesias had spoken of Asiatic pygmies, and had referred their habitation much
farther to the east. In the midst of fables, which he accepts without reserve, he has given some important and
true facts. Behold how he expresses himself : "There
are in the midst of India black men whom one calls pygmies. They speak the same language as the Indians, and
are very small. The largest are only two cubits (0ᵐ924 or
0ᵐ900, according to the value we give to this measure).

The greater part are only one cubit and a half high. Their hair is very long; it descends as far as to their knees, and even farther. They have a much heavier beard than all other men. When it has attained its growth they no longer wear any clothing; their hair and their beard take the place of such. . . . They are flat-nosed and homely. They are skilful in using the bow." [35]

Ctesias has no doubt diminished the height of his pygmies into fabulous proportions. Without doubt he was wrong in taking for hair or beard the mantles and other garments of long floating grasses which the women in the neighbourhood of Travancore still wear. [79] But what he says of the geographical position, of the colour, and of the use of the bow, does not permit doubt that he had knowledge of the Negritos or of proto-Dravidian tribes preserving in high degree the characters of the primitive type. It is, in fact, in the heart of India, in the Vindhya Mountains, that M. Rousselet has found the *Bandra-Loks*. [163, 164, 165] The name of this tribe literally signifies *man monkeys*. They are true Negroes of very small stature, who, in the midst of populations more or less crossed, have preserved unmixed the characters of the type, and are one of the evidences left by the black race.

Neither Aristotle nor Pliny mention the black colour and the woolly hair, as characters of the dwarfs of whom they speak on hearsay. Ctesias alone is very precise upon the first point. The memory of these peculiarities is evidently lost in the long journey which the informants, probably very few in number, must have made from the heart of Africa and from the extremity of India to Greece and Rome. This omission is, moreover, less singular than one would at first be tempted to suppose. The ancients attributed the dark colour and the woolly appearance of the hair of the Negro to the action of the sun, whose heat burned the skin and crisped the hair. They have not, then, been surprised to find in a hot country, by the side of other black men, such as their Indians and Ethiopians, tribes presenting these two characters. The diminution of the stature must have struck them much more strongly, and their very exaggerations show that it has been so. They have done in an opposite direction that which Pigafetti did with reference to the Patagonians.

Let us return now into Africa.

The contemporary of Pliny, Pomponius Mela, has also spoken of the pygmies. The very short passage which he has devoted to them has yet a decided interest. He places beyond the Arabic Gulf, at the head of a little bay of the Red Sea, the Panchiens, surnamed *Ophiophages*, because they ate snakes. "In the interior of the land," he says, "one saw formerly pygmies, a race of men of very small stature, which has died out in the wars which it has sustained against the storks in order to preserve its fruits."

The translator of Pomponius Mela regards the little bend of the Red Sea which is mentioned here as our Gulf of Aden. But it would seem to me strange that the Latin geographer should have employed this expression in order to designate the great expanse of sea which extends itself along the African coast from Cape Guardafui to the Strait of Bab-el-Mandeb. The Bay of Moscha, which almost buries itself in the lands southwest of the strait, seems to me to correspond much better and in every respect to the description of Pomponius. But this bay, situated at about the thirteenth degree of north latitude, lies consequently under the same parallel as the commencement of the grassy region of the Nile, but about four degrees farther north than the labyrinth, whence the river seems to proceed. Pomponious, moreover, does not speak of the Nile; no more does he say anything regarding the Abyssinian plateau interposed between it and the sea.

He seems, then, to place his pygmies entirely to the east of this portion of the continent.

Here again modern discoveries appear to support the wisdom of the ancients. The tradition of the eastern African pygmies has never been lost among the Arabs. Always the geographers of that nation have placed their *River of the Pygmies* much farther to the south. It is in this region, a little to the north of the equator and about the thirty-second degree of east longitude, that the R. P. Leon des Avanchers has found the *Wa-Berriki-mos* or *Cincallès*, whose stature is about 1ᵐ30.[8] The facts collected by M. d'Abbadie place the Mallas or Mazé-Malleas, with a stature of 1ᵐ50 at about the sixth degree of north latitude.[1] Everything indicates that there exist to the south of the country of the Gallas various Negro tribes of very little stature. It seems to me difficult not to refer them to the pygmies of Pomponius Mela, only they have retreated more to the south. Probably this change had already been effected when the Roman geographer wrote, and one understands how he might have regarded this race as having disappeared.

In sketching the history of these little men so celebrated in antiquity I have been obliged to insist first upon the traditions relative to those whose name Homer has immortalised, and to the populations located either in Asia or in the northeast regions of Africa, which one has connected with the pygmies of the Nile. But, about a century before Aristotle, Herodotus had also spoken of a kind of pygmies, without, however, using that name. Some one must have repeated to him the story of certain pilgrims of Cyrene, who had received their information from Etearchus, King of the Ammoniens. He had told them that a number of young Nasamones had conceived the idea of exploring the deserts of Libya. Five of them, selected by lot, started out supplied with food and water. "They first traversed the inhabited country, then the wild region, and finally entered the desert, where they made their journey, directing their way towards the setting sun. After having marched several days in the deep sands, they perceived some trees which rose in the midst of a field. They approached them and ate some fruits which the trees bore. Scarcely had they commenced to taste them when they were surprised by a great number of men very much below the average height, who seized them and dragged them away with them. They spoke a language unknown to the Nasamones, and did not understand theirs. These men conducted the five young men across a country intersected by great marshes into a town whose inhabitants were black. Before this town flowed a considerable stream, whose course was from the west to the east, and there were crocodiles in it."

In spite of the brevity of this story it agrees too well with modern discoveries for one to doubt the reality of the facts which it relates. The geographical districts indicated by the Nasamones are identifiable still, and the river whose existence they made known is our Djoliba, or Niger, which was alternately believed to be the Nile itself, or a tributary from Lake Tchad, before Mungo Park, Caillé, Clapperton, the Lander brothers, and others made us know its true course. One knows to-day that this river, whose source was discovered very recently by two young Frenchmen, takes its rise in one of the cañons of the mountainous plateau which, in the interior of the country, follows almost parallel the north coast of the Gulf of Guinea. Although Zweifeld and Moustier were not able, on account of having no instruments, to determine exactly the location of Mount Tembi, whence the source of the Niger proceeds, and although they have been able to contemplate it only from a distance on account of local superstitions, one may see, by the map which the Geographical Society of Marseilles has published, that this mountain is very close to 8° 35' north latitude and 12° 45' west longitude. The river, then a small streamlet, flows at first from south to north; but soon its general direction is due northeast. It remains the same as far as to Timbuctoo, a little beyond 18° (18° 3' 45" north latitude and 40° 5' 10" west longitude). There the river bends abruptly and flows almost directly from west to east as far as Bourroum,* over a distance of more than three degrees of longitude, before turning towards the south-southeast to reach the Gulf of Guinea. It is, then, between the first and fourth degree of west longitude that the Nasamones reached the Niger. One can no longer locate the town inhabited by Negroes whither the bold travellers were conducted. We are only sure that it could not possibly be the celebrated Timbuctoo, the founding of which, according to the annalist of those countries, Ahmed Baba, would date only from the fifth century of the Hegira, or about 1100 A. D.

Herodotus informs us that the young Nasamones found crocodiles in the stream visited by them. This again is a perfectly correct statement, more so than one at first might think. *A priori*, one would reasonably suppose that the great reptiles inhabiting two rivers so widely separated as the Nile and the Niger would be of different species. It is not so. The question has been specially studied as the result of discussions which arose between Cuvier and Geoffroy Saint-Hilaire—discussions to which the first of these great naturalists attached so much importance as to consecrate to it in his *Regne animal* a note of exceptional length. Cuvier admitted the specific identity of all the crocodiles of the great rivers of Africa. Geoffroy denied this identity, and admitted the existence

---

* Situated at the east bend of the River Niger (Barth).

in the Nile alone of four distinct species. Dumeril and Bibron restudied the subject with materials which were lacking to the two illustrious adversaries, and have proved that Cuvier was right.[44] The crocodile of the Niger, as that of Senegal, is the same as the crocodile of the Nile.

Finally, the Nasamones declared that they were led into a town all of whose inhabitants were blacks. Here also they have told the truth. Although Timbuctoo was founded by the Tuaregs; although these, the Berbers and the Peuls, dispute in our days the control of this city and the countries which are bathed by the middle portion of the Niger, it is known that these people are foreigners and have arrived there at an epoch relatively recent. According to Barth, in the tenth century the country of the Negroes extended still, on an average, to the twentieth degree of latitude. At this epoch all the region of which we speak belonged to the black race, and more truly was it so at the time of Herodotus.

From this it results that the black men seen by the Nasamones were true Negroes, and certainly had woolly hair. This point is nevertheless neglected in the recital of the travellers. This fact justifies, as one sees, the interpretation which I have given above of the omission of this peculiarity in regard to the little Asiatic blacks.

Thus, as regards the soil, waters, animals, and men, everything up to this point in the report gathered by the Greek historian is true. What reason have we to doubt that which he reports of the little human race met with by the Nasamones? None. And even if observation had not confirmed these reports, one should accept them. But modern discoveries have also, upon this point, confirmed the facts transmitted by Herodotus, at least in so far as relates to the existence of this race.

It is otherwise in regard to its geographical position. This position connects itself, as we have seen, with that of a well-determined portion of the river. But the most northern station of the western pygmies reported up to the present time is located in the heart of Senegambia, in the Tenda-Maiò, near the tenth degree of north latitude and the fourteenth degree of west longitude, that is to say, about eight degrees farther west than the point where the Nasamones were captured by the little men.[119]

We find again, then, in relation to western Africa, the same difference between tradition and modern observations which we have had to mention when we considered upper Egypt and eastern Africa. The dwarf race again shows itself farther from us than it must have been at the time of the Greeks. But in the two preceding cases we could attribute this disagreement to an imperfect knowledge, which would have reduced the distances. Here, however, this hypothesis is inadmissible. In view of the precision of Herodotus and of the agreement which his story presents with material facts of a fixed kind, it is necessary to admit either that the little human race seen by the Nasamones still exists to the north of the Niger but has not yet been discovered, or else that it has disappeared from these regions.

Without at all wishing to commit the future, this last hypothesis seems to me to have great probability. Without doubt it is also necessary to apply it to other countries where the ancients have located their pygmies. The Egyptians knew the Akkas under the name which they still bear, for Mariette Pasha has read this name by the side of a portrait of a dwarf carved upon a monument of the old empire.[74] But while admitting that they may have been able to explore the Nile Valley far beyond the barriers which lately arrested us, nothing, I believe, permits us to suppose that they reached the most southern tributaries of this river, or that they have passed to the west, crossing the divide which separates this basin from that of the

Welle.   It would seem to me far more reasonable to admit that at the time of Aristotle the Akka tribes stretched far more to the north, and even reached the swampy district of the great river.   Their being driven backwards towards the south and west would not be at all surprising.   In fact, wherever we follow this little race, whenever information regarding them is increased a little, they appear to us as having been in the past more prosperous than in our own days, as having occupied formerly a geographical area more vast and more connected than now.

It is not before the attacks of birds or beasts that these little men withdrew and that their communities broke to pieces.   We shall see, on the contrary, that there are among them peoples who know how to attack and conquer even the elephant.   But they were forced to yield to larger and stronger human races.   These are, in Africa and Melanesia, the African Negroes and the Papuans; in Malaysia, the different Malay races; in India, the races who, in crossing with them, have given birth to the Dravidian populations.   Wherever one meets with them to-day one sees them retreating, and often dying out.   This progressive diminution commenced many centuries ago. To-day there are true pygmies no longer upon many of the points where they formerly prevailed.   Very often some feeble tribes alone represent the pure type.   But, even in disappearing, these little blacks have left traces in the modern populations.   In western Africa, as in the Philippines and in the two Gangetic peninsulas, they have played an ethnological *rôle*, at times important, in crossing with superior races and in giving birth to half-breed populations.

On the whole, the ancients have had information more or less inexact, more or less incomplete, but also more or less true, concerning five populations of little stature from whom they have made their pygmies.   Two were located

in Asia, in the extreme southeast of the then known
world; the third, to the south, towards the sources of the
Nile; the fourth, more to the east, but not far from the
preceding; the fifth, still in Africa, but entirely to the
southwest, and in a region where the Nasamones alone appear to have penetrated. Two of these groups, more or less
reduced, more or less altered by crossing, are still located
in Asia. The three African groups in our days are
found at a distance from Greece or Rome greater than
the tradition states, but situated very nearly in the same
direction. All of them are, moreover, but fragments of
two human races well characterised as blacks, occupying,
the one in Asia, the other in Africa, a considerable area,
and both of them including not only tribes or distinct
peoples, but even subraces.

From the first years of my instructing at the museum
I have proposed to unite all the black populations of
Asia, of Malaysia, and of Melanesia, characterised by
smallness of stature and relative gracefulness of limbs,
into a *Negrito branch*, opposed to the *Papuan branch*,
to which I referred the Eastern Negroes of large size and
of proportions frequently athletic. The Australians, who
present in a high degree the characters of a *mixed race*,
and the Tasmanians, who form by themselves a distinct
race, remain outside of the two preceding groups.[142]   I
have reason to think that under one form or another this
division is to-day generally adopted.

On his part, Hamy first showed that, contrary to common opinion, there exist in western Africa some Negroes
distinguished from the classical type by the shortness of
their skulls.[73]   In pursuing this line of investigation he
recognised that this cephalic character coincided with a
noticeable reduction of the stature. Grouping together,
in this point of view, observations before scattered and
isolated, he showed that Africa, like Asia, possessed a black

subtype, of which one of the most striking characters was a remarkably reduced stature; that the little Negroes, African and Asiatic, so widely separated geographically, resembled each other in several other features, either anatomical or external; that these two groups are in reality two *corresponding terms*, geographically and anthropologically. Hamy proposed for these dwarf African tribes, taken collectively, the name of *Negrilles*.[74]* This name, which has the advantage of recalling one of the characteristic features of the group and the relations which unite it to the *Negritos*, will, I believe, be readily accepted by all anthropologists.

---

* English *Negrillos*.

CHAPTER II.

I HAVE just recalled the principal divisions to be established in the totality of the Eastern Negro populations. I only wish, however, to contrast the Negritos and Papuans, long regarded as one and the same race. It is easy to summarily characterise these two groups. Both have the more or less black colour and the so-called woolly hair of the true Negroes. But the Papuans are often large, muscular, at times athletic (Fig. 1); their skull is at once dolichocephalic and hypsistenocephalic—that is to say, it is relatively long from before backwards, compressed laterally, and very high (Figs. 2, 4). The Negritos are always of little stature, have rounded forms (Fig. 3), and their

---

* This chapter is taken almost *verbatim* from an article published by me in the Revue d'ethnographie, founded and directed by M. Hamy.[150]

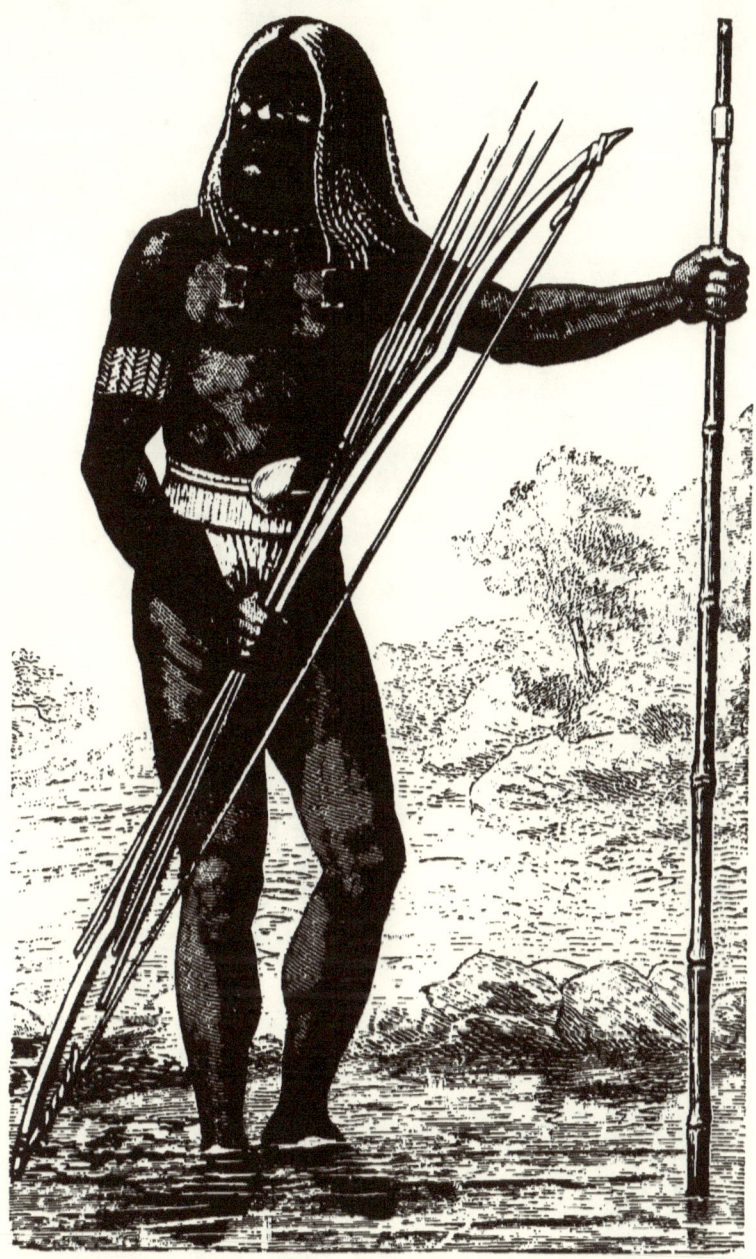

Fig. 1.—New Guinean, from the Strait of Bourgat. (After Van Vort.)

skull is brachycephalic or subbrachycephalic *—that is to say, it is relatively short and broad and of little height (Figs. 2 and 5). I published, fifteen years since, a general work upon this race—*Études sur les Mincopies et sur le race negrito en général.*[148] Later, M. Giglioli attacked the

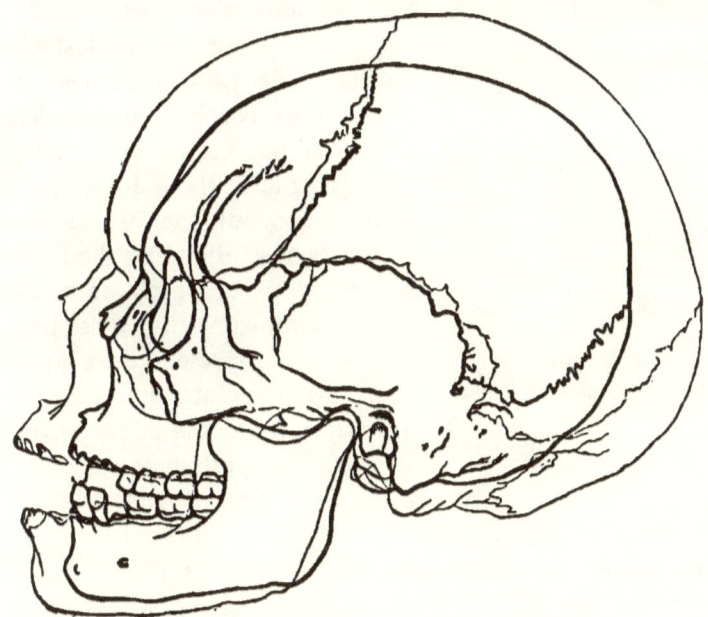

Fig. 2.—Skulls of Mincopy and Papuan superposed.

same subject.[60] But we do not give the same meaning to the words. The Italian anthropologist comprises in his Negrito race all populations of little stature—Asiatic, Oceanic, and African, including the Bushmen. The ques-

---

* It may not be useless to give the meaning of the words here employed to characterise these skulls. They all express a relationship established between certain diameters. This relation is called an index. When the degree of dolichocephaly or brachycephaly is desired, the relation existing between the maximum transverse diameter and the maximum antero-posterior diameter taken as unity is found. To measure hypsistenocephaly, the vertical diameter is

tion of the Negritos has also been treated in a general way by F. A. Allen.[3] The works of Logan, which will be considered later, although written from a point of view even more general, also touch upon most of the questions raised in this study.

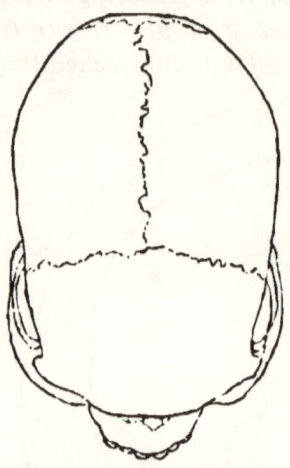

FIG. 4.—SKULL OF PAPUAN FROM TORRES STRAIT. One fourth natural size (Mus. d'hist. nat., No. 4771.)

The Papuans are exclusively insular. They form a mass of populations as continuous as that sort of a habitat allows. They occupy practically all of New Guinea and all the Melanesian archipelagoes, inlcuding the Fijis. But the type of which we speak is not confined within these limits; it has representatives upon many other points, and even to the extremity of the ocean world. Towards the west, conquest, emigration or slavery have carried Papuans to Timor, Ceram, Bouro, Gilolo, and even to the eastern shores of Borneo, and have scattered them over various other parts of the great Indonesian archipelagoes. Towards the north the same causes have carried

compared with the transverse diameter. A skull is hypsistenocephalic when the former equals or exceeds the latter. As to dolichocephaly and brachycephaly, Broca, reducing the numbers first adopted by Retzius to decimal form, and multiplying the transverse diameter by 100, prepared the following table of horizontal cephalic indices, in which the relations are represented by a fractional number :

Dolichocephals, 75 and below.
Subdolichocephals, 75·01–77·77.
Mesaticephals, 77·78–80·00.
Subbrachycephals, 80·01–83·33.
Brachycephals, 83·34 and upwards.

FIG. 3.—GROUP OF MINCOPIES.

them into some of the secondary groups of the Carolines. Towards the northeast they have reached the Sandwich Islands; towards the south-west, New Zealand, where they preceded the Maoris.*

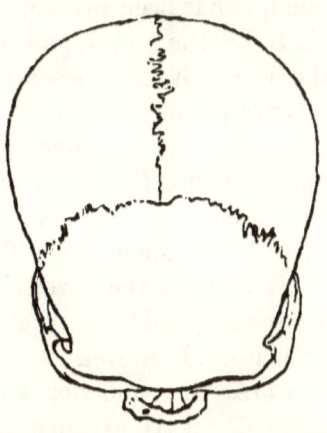

Pinart brought back with him from his voyages and gave to the museum a skull which he took from an ancient tomb on Easter Island, probably contemporaneous with the strange statues noticed by all travellers.[157] †

Hamy has shown that this skull in the totality of its characters belongs essentially to the type of those of the best authenticated Papuans. Finally, Ten Kate has brought

Fig. 5.—SKULL OF NEGRITO FROM THE NEIGHBOURHOOD OF BINAN-GONAN, LUZON. One fourth natural size (Mus. d'hist. nat., No. 3629).

a Melanesian skull gathered on the little island of Spiritu Santo, on the eastern coast of Lower California.

---

* The traditions of the Maoris gathered by Sir George Grey, the details given by various travellers and portraits, all witness to the existence of a black ethnological element in New Zealand, but crani-ology alone could permit the determination of its nature. A num-ber of skulls of perfectly determined origin have permitted the solu-tion of this curious problem. The museum possesses one skull from New Zealand which has all the characteristics of the Papuan, and con-trasts in a remarkable manner with Maori skulls, as well as two dried heads, whose tattooing in itself would be proof of their origin, which have the woolly hair of Oceanic Negroes. I will add that the most dolichocephalic skull known was brought from New Zealand and given to Mr. Huxley, who has described it.[78] The horizontal index of this skull is 63·54; its vertical index, 113·11. It is then, at once, extremely dolichocephalic and hypsistenocephalic.

† The reader who desires further details will find necessary references in the bibliographical notes accompanying the excellent

Thus the Papuan race has extended outwards in all directions, and has had its days of conquest. On the other hand, it has been pressed in upon at various points, especially by the Malay and Polynesian races; [154, 155] but on the whole it has preserved its area entire, and forms a relatively compact mass. Immigrations, either peaceful or warlike, have nowhere affected it in a very marked way, unless at the Fijis, and at the east end of New Guinea. On the contrary, it has by its migrations mingled its blood with that of some very different and remote populations.*

It is quite the reverse with the Negritos. The area occupied by this race is almost as extended as that of the Papuans. It is even greater, if one cuts off from the Papuan area the Sandwich Islands, Easter Islands, and New Zealand; it is at once insular and continental. But upon the mainland, as well as in the archipelagoes, the Negrito tribes are almost always isolated one from another, and as if submerged in the midst of populations of very different ethnic origin.

Moreover, wherever this contact exists one finds the little blacks located in the least favourable localities of the country where they live. I shall later return to this fact, and to conclusions which must be drawn from it.

From what I have just said of their habitat, the Negritos naturally fall into two geographical groups, one continental, the other insular. Let us first consider the latter.

---

monograph of Papuan skulls inserted in the work just quoted, a monograph entirely the work of M. Hamy.

* At the exposition which accompanied the Congress of Geographical Sciences of Paris, in 1875, M. Hamy exhibited a map representing the present distribution of human races in the Indian archipelago. He presented a *résumé* of the result of his studies in a communication made to the subsection of anthropology. The limits of the Papuan and Negrito races are shown upon it.[57]

FIG. 6.—PORTRAIT OF AËTA CHIEF FROM THE MOUNTAINS OF MARIVELES, LUZON. (From photograph of MM. Montano and Rey.)

When the Spaniards began to settle the Philippines they met in the interior of Luzon, by the side of the Tagals of Malay origin, dark men of whom some had smooth hair, while others possessed the woolly head-covering of the African Negroes.[139] These last alone were true blacks, whom the conquerors called *Negritos del monte* (little Negroes of the mountain), on account of their remarkably little stature and their habitat (Figs. 6 and 9). The local name was *Aigtas* or *Inagtas*, which seems to mean *blacks*, and from which is derived that of *Aëtas*, generally adopted. One shortly recognised that this same human race was met with at other points in the archipelago, and that it entirely peopled some small islands, among them the island Bougas, which is also called for this reason *Isla de los Negros*. In these different localities the Aëtas change their name, and are called Ates at Panay,* Hillrouas and Mamanousa at Mindanao,† etc.

As the archipelagoes of these eastern seas have become better known, our little black race has been found almost everywhere. Doubts upon some points left by the first information received on this subject have almost always been removed by later observations more and more exact. Thus the existence of Negritos at Formosa has been until recently denied, in spite of the direct testimony of various Dutch and English travellers. But in 1868 Schetelig presented to the Ethnological Society of London

---

* Rienzi has described, under the name of *Melano-Pygmees*, two individuals belonging to a race of Panay less than four feet ten inches in stature. Their hair not crinkled and their skin less black than that of Negroes, shows crossing; but the smallness of stature, without being extreme, shows us that this character persists in part in spite of the crossing.[162] Elsewhere Lafond assigns them a much less stature.[61]

† It is under this last name that Dr Montano has discovered Negritos in the peninsula, northeast, near Lake Maïnit.

two well-authenticated skulls whose characters leave no
ground for objection. There exists a skull,* also, which
has enabled Hamy and myself to confirm the testimony of
Rienzi, of Lafond de Lurcy, of the Bishop of Labuan, etc.,
and to affirm that true Negritos inhabit the interior of
Borneo.[72]

Finally, from the testimony of Earl and the various authors cited by him, it results that the Negritos inhabit the
mountainous parts of the Sandal Islands (Samba), Xulla,
Bourou, Céram, Flores, Solor, Pantar, Lombleu, Ombay,
the eastern peninsula of Celebes, etc.

I have elsewhere indicated the greater part of the
principal points where the actual existence of Negritos has been established.[155] I have at the same time
remarked that in this maritime world Sumatra and Java
are the only large islands where they have left no other
traces than some doubtful mixed breeds, and the remains
of an industry which appears not to have passed beyond
the age of stone.† It is in Java that the destruction has
probably been the most sudden and complete. These unfortunate little Negroes could but disappear before the
Malay races, who joined to arms more terrible and to
their murderous instincts a civilisation capable of erecting
the *thousand temples* and of carving the bas-reliefs of
Bôrô-Boudour.‡

---

* This skull forms part of the Museum of Lyons, and I am glad
to here thank M. Lortet for placing it at our disposition for description and illustration. It bears its own certificate of origin, for its
surface is covered with those arabesques and designs which the
Dyaks engrave upon the skull of their victims. (Crania Ethnica,
p. 195, Figs. 212, 213.)

† I now believe that I was too hasty in formerly considering as
true Negritos the *Althalo-pygmées*, seen at Sumatra by Rienzi. They
are probably only mixed-bloods.

‡ I cannot write this name without mentioning the magnificent
publication of the Netherlands Government so generously placed by

The Sunda Islands form the southern limit of the Negrito area. On the north, Formosa is the last place where the race of which we speak has preserved all its characteristics ; but it reveals its ancient existence beyond this island by the traces it has left among the present populations. In the little archipelago of Loo-Choo,* Basil Hall found at certain points " some men very black by the side of others who were almost white." Ancient traditions in Japan speak of formidable black savages who were subdued and driven away only with great difficulty.[143] Thanks to the more kindly instincts of the conquerors, these Negritos of the north were not exterminated, as in Java. Kempfer and Siebold have reported the differences in colour and hair which certain classes of the population present, and the latter mentions particularly the black colour and the more or less crinkly hair of the inhabitants of the southeast coast.

Long since, I mentioned these characters as confirming the opinion first propounded by Prichard relative to the intervention of a black element in Japan, and this element can only be referred to the Negrito race. The examination of a Japanese skull from the Broca collection has fully confirmed these conclusions. Studied by Hamy and myself, it has presented a mixture of features, of which the most characteristic clearly betray this ethnic origin.[148,73,157] † The details given by Dr. Maget have fully

it at the disposition of men whom it interests from any point of view—Bôrô-Boudour, in the Island of Java, by F. C. Wilson and C. Leemans, Leyden, 1874. This book has now even greater interest than at the time of its publication. The Bôrô-Boudour appears to have been, if not destroyed, partly ruined since the eruption of Krakatoa. The work of Dr. Leemans has preserved a faithful and detailed representation.

* Liou Kiou = Lieou Tchou, Liou Tchou, Licou-Tcheou, Riu Kin.[164]

† This skull, secured by Dr. Noury, of the navy, in a cemetery of

confirmed these conclusions. He has discovered and described veritable *Negrito metis* living in the midst of Japanese populations. I have found incontestable traces of Negrito blood upon various skulls from the Mariannes.[148] But in Micronesia the mixture of races seems to stop. The black element which recurs in the Carolines appears to belong essentially to the Papuan type.

The extension of Negritos in Melanesia is much more considerable. Here their tribes are mingled and in contact with those of Papuans probably through the whole of New Guinea. To the testimonies I have already cited I can to-day add others.

Beccari declares that it is not uncommon in New Guinea to meet natives of small stature who, judging by descriptions, might be taken for Negritos. It is true that he has not seen any tribe composed wholly of individuals presenting this character; * but the map published by one of his compatriots represents the Karons, or Karonis, as occupying a chain of mountains parallel to the north coast of the great peninsula of the northwest; and three skulls of these Karons, studied by Hamy, have shown him the essential characters of the Negrito head.[157]

M. Meyer, who has sojourned in these regions, has, however, supported the opinion of Wallace and Earl. He considers, with them, all the Eastern blacks as of one race. But the German traveller has brought from Kordo, in the island of Mysore, a magnificent collection of skulls, whose characters and measurements he has made known.[114, 115]

Hamy has discussed this mass of facts, and shown that in themselves the figures published by that author bring one more proof to the support of our common view. If

---

criminals at Yokohama, is of perfectly ascertained origin. Hamy has justly remarked that the very place whence it has been taken proves that it has belonged to an individual of the lower classes.

* Extract from a letter written at Ternate, March 6, 1876.[60]

the greater part of the skulls of Kordo are plainly Papuan, if others seem to show mixture, there are still others which show beyond doubt the presence of the Negrito element, pure or almost pure.[157] The study of the measurements taken by Dr. Comrie lead to the same conclusion.[31]

Moreover, as the materials become more numerous—thanks to the efforts of courageous travellers—the last defenders of the ethnologic unity of the New Guineans are themselves coming around to the opinion which Hamy and myself adopted years ago.[2, 103, 104, 105]

This mixture recurs in the islands of Torres Strait. The museum possesses a head brought from the island of Toud, or Warrior Island, by the companions of Dumont d'Urville, which reproduces the essential features of the Negrito. It was collected in a tomb where it was mingled with others presenting all the characters of Papuans. We find again, then, at the southern extremity of New Guinea, the juxtaposition of the two races which we established in the northwest.[148, 157]

Thanks to D'Albertis, we follow the Negrito type as far as to Epa, situated upon the eastern coast of the Gulf of Papua, and consequently even into the great elongated peninsula which terminates New Guinea on the southeast. There the Italian traveller saw an individual of mature years, well formed, elegantly proportioned, the body covered with woolly hair, and possessing head hair equally woolly. His skin was extremely black. He presented very little or no prognathism. His stature was, moreover, very small, and was not more than four feet nine inches. In the concurrence of these features it is impossible not to recognise an excellently characterised pure-blood Negrito. This individual belonged to a tribe of the interior, living probably among the mountains, represented upon the map as being located to the east of Epa.[2]

Finally, to the southeast of Epa, at Port Moresby,

4

Lawes shows us in the midst of real Papuan tribes a mountain tribe of little stature, decidedly dark, whose feet and hands are remarkably small. All these features are essentially Negrito, and it is more than probable that the Kolari belong to this race.[90]

Although not distinguishing the Negritos from the Papuans, Lawes has, like D'Albertis, the merit of insisting upon the variety which the human races of New Guinea present.

There the area of residence belonging to our little Negroes seems to stop. Pickering, who, perhaps, first clearly distinguished them from the Papuans, was mistaken in prolonging it farther to the southeast into the New Hebrides.[137] The eminent American anthropologist has probably taken account only of some external characters, particularly that of stature. He has not paid attention to the far more important osteological characters, of which one did not appreciate the full value at the epoch when he wrote. Hamy, in the craniological monograph which I have just cited, has studied one by one the skulls proceeding from the different Melanesian islands. Outside of New Guinea, when the Papuan type is altered it is not by a Negrito, but by a Polynesian element.[157] Nevertheless, it may perhaps be necessary to extend the southeastern limit of the Negrito area as far as to the province of Queensland, Australia. There, according to Odoardo Beccari, natives with crinkly hair are found who might indeed be ethnologic neighbours of the more or less mixed islanders of Torres Strait.[61]

The western element of the Oceanic Negritos is much more easy to fix than the preceding. It is in the Bay of Bengal, at the Nicobar Islands, and in the Andamans that we find it.[61] In the first of these two little archipelagoes the Negritos have undergone the same lot as in the ......ds. Attacked by the Malays, they have in part been exterminated, and inhabit at present only the mountains of the interior.[55,41] On the other hand, they have preserved complete independence, and have remained pure from all mixture in the Andaman Islands—above all, in the three islands which collectively were for a long time called the Grand Andaman—until the English chose this isolated archipelago as the site of one of their penal establishments. But even this has been of value to us in giving numerous and precise facts regarding the Mincopies.

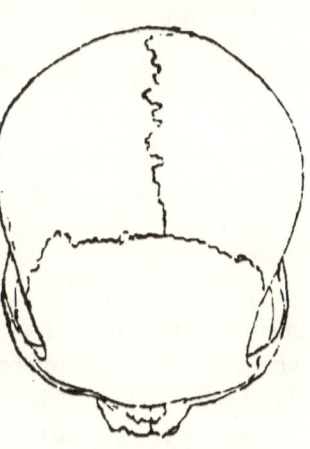

FIG. 7.—SKULL OF MINCOPY FROM THE GRAND ANDAMAN. One fourth natural size.

Let us now find the traces of these Negritos on the Asiatic continent whose island colonies stretch from Formosa to the Andaman Islands.

The existence of Negroes—that is, men with black skin and woolly hair—on the continent has been denied, even quite recently, by some eminent geographers, yet numerous witnesses, evidently trustworthy, do not permit a doubt of it. Since 1820, Macinnes and Crawford have described, as presenting the typical characters of the race, two natives of the little kingdom of Kedah, in the peninsula of Malacca.[71,157] Other travellers were not slow in confirming these details, and Prichard, while fighting a theory to which I shall have to return, admits that the Samangs, Simangs, and Semangs of this region are true Negroes.

The description which Anderson, former secretary of the government of Penang, has given of one of them is most characteristic. This individual, thirty years old, measured only 1^m441 ; his hair was woolly... .d, his skin

was jet-black and glossy, his lips thick, his nose flat, his
belly protruding. The author adds that he exactly resembled two natives of the Andamans whom he had previously seen.[4] These Semangs, then, are not only Negroes,
but true Negritos. This opinion is at present accepted by
all anthropologists who have occupied themselves with
this question. Reservation should be made, however, in
regard to their purity of blood, and it should be admitted
that the type of the Semangs, as well as that of analogous
tribes, has often been altered by crossing.

To the south of Kedah are other savage tribes, whose
characters have been variously described by travellers.
These variations explain themselves. Here, as well as
in the Philippine Islands and elsewhere, the Negro race
has been crossed with a population of a different origin,
which resulted in numerous half breeds. But even among
those tribes where this crossing has taken place there are
frequently found individuals who have preserved all the
characteristic features of the type. A photograph by
Alph. Pichon, former secretary of embassy, and two
other photographs kindly given to me by M. de la Croix,
permit affirming this. All three are now part of the collection of the museum.

The first one represents a group of Jakuns, five men
and two women, from the neighbourhood of Singapore.
One of the two women is essentially Malay, but her wavy
hair and some of her features would betray a slight crossing; the other woman is an out-and-out Negrito. One of
the men has perfectly straight hair; but that of the
others, and especially of a warrior and his son, is absolutely woolly, and the *ensemble* of their features reminds
one of an Aëta, drawn by Meyer.[71, 68]

The photographs of de la Croix were taken in the
province of Perak by M. de Saint-Pol Lias. They represent two groups of Sakaies, who individually vary in the

way which I have just indicated. Five out of ten individuals have straight hair (Fig. 9); two seem to have crinkly hair; that of the others is decidedly woolly (Fig. 8). We must add that M. Montano, who had just seen the Negritos at Luzon and Mindano, has found all the characteristics of this tribe in some of the Sakaies.

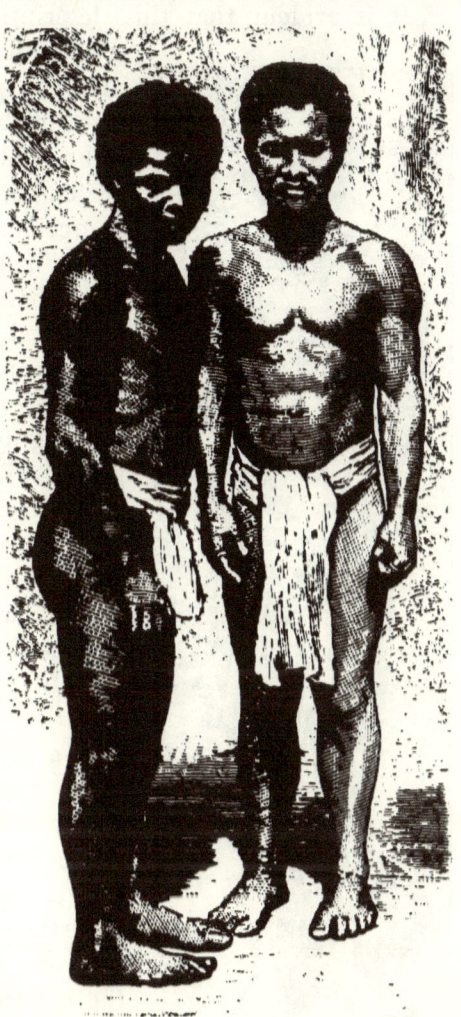

These three photographs are very important, because they testify to the variation in hair in one and the same tribe. This fact explains the differences between descriptions and between the opinions of different authors. For instance, in the note which I just quoted, Anderson describes three Sakaies belonging to a half-civilised tribe, and speaks of their complexion as being

FIG. 8.—SAKAIES OF PERAK. (After a photograph of M. Bro de Saint-Pol Lias, given by M. de la Croix.)

analogous to that of the Malays, of their hair as being

tufted, not woolly, and of a stature varying from I^m^657 to 1^m^474.⁴

It is evident that this description might lead into error, and make us fail to recognise the presence of the Negrito blood, which is testified to by photography.

Thanks to it, we can also appreciate at their real value other materials, such as the two photographs of Semangs published by Giglioli, after the photographs of Colonel Yule.⁵⁹ Neither of them, to judge from the engravings, were pure Negritos. The hair of the man, native of the province of Wellesley, seems to have been nearly straight or only wavy; that of the woman, falling almost to her shoulders, seems to be quite crinkly. But there is nothing in either one of them to indicate a truly woolly head, and these portraits could furnish an argument to those who deny the existence of true Negroes in these regions. To my mind, nevertheless, they testify to the presence of Negrito blood in the individuals represented by them; only the type has become changed by crossing.

The people mentioned before are crosses. But in the

FIG. 9.—SAKAIE. (After a photograph of M. Bro de Saint-Pol Lias, given by M. de la Croix.)

great highland region between Perak, Selangou, and Kelantan, in Malacca, there are still one or more witnesses of the ancient population which have remained entirely pure. There are tribes, which the Sakaies treat as savages, inhabiting caves and using only stone in making their utensils and weapons. These savages are black, have crinkly hair, are very short, and dress themselves with leaves hung about their bodies. They run away as soon as they perceive a stranger. De Morgan has seen fires lighted by these Negritos, but has not been able to approach them.[129] De la Croix has gathered identical information on the spot.

As the Malay, so has the Annamite peninsula its representatives of the Negrito type, known under the name of Moïs or Moys. Logan long since considered this fact as demonstrated.[94] The doubts so often expressed in regard to this seem to me scarcely tenable in view of the old proofs recalled by M. Giglioli himself,* of those which Earl obtained from the Annamites and Cochin-Chinese, and of the communications of two French physicians of the navy to Hamy. These last stated to my learned colleague that some Negro tribes live near the northern frontiers of the Cochin-Chinese province of Bien-Hoa.[70] The latest information furnished by Allen seems to me to remove the last doubts. One of the authors quoted by him (Tomlin's Geography) describes the Moys as having woolly hair, a truly black skin, and a face resembling that of the Kaffirs.† It seems to me strange that a writer should have been so explicit without reason. Everything indicates that the

---

* M. Giglioli[59] declares himself to be very sceptical as to the existence of true Negritos in Annam. The portrait of a Chong, native of Siam, published by Crawfurd, and which the eminent Italian anthropologist has mentioned, seems at least to justify conjecturing to the contrary.

† "Woolly haired, very black, and savage, and with faces resembling the Kaffirs."

black tribes of Annam must resemble those of Malacca, and side by side with the true Negro there are individuals deviating more or less from the pure type. Hence the diverse and apparently contradictory opinions that have been entertained for so long in regard to the Malay peninsula.[3]

We are much better informed on the subject of the populations of the peninsula this side of the Ganges. The Tamil books, says Logan, tell us that the original inhabitants had hair "in tufts," which can only refer to Negroes.[96] Evidence, the descriptions of a number of travellers, confirmed by photographs, drawings, busts, and skulls, explains everything that is true in these old texts. These various proofs show us in the whole of southern and central India peoples with a more or less black skin, among whom are individuals whose woolly hair testifies to their at least relative purity of blood, and clearly indicates the nature of one of the ethnic elements which have given rise to these peoples.

The same means of study permit us to specify to what branch of the Negro trunk this element belongs, and to affirm that it is essentially Negrito.

Justice Campbell holds that all of the tribes which he calls aborigines are physically related to the Negrito type.[25] He gives a *résumé* of their characteristics, and specially mentions their figure, short and slight;* their complexion, truly black; their hair tangled, at times curly, and even woolly. This latter characteristic is often seen in the drawings made after the photographs, although the au-

---

* "To the Aëtas and Mincopies has often been ascribed a protruding belly. I do not find this either in the photographs of forty-eight Negritos of the Philippine Islands taken at Luzon by M. Montano, nor in those of the seven Negritos which I owe to Colonel Tytler, nor in the sixteen individuals of the same race represented in the phototypes of Mr. Dobson.[42]

thor does not mention it in his description, and has even sometimes stated the contrary. Thus, in speaking of the Santals, who inhabit the basin of the Ganges east and west of Bhagalpore, Colonel Dalton mentions their straight hair.[38] But the drawing, which is reproduced from a photograph, shows two persons of this tribe whose heads are covered with tufts as rounded and tight as those of any Negrito, and one of them is a true Mincopy, while the other is nearer like the Aëta. What the same author says about the hair of the Oraons would leave room for much doubt; but of five figures of these tribes represented on his plate, one woman has all the features of the Negrito, and at least half-woolly hair.[38] * The same can be observed in the portrait of Dhoba Abor, of a tribe of the upper Brahmapootra. In the text, Dalton says nothing about the hair; in the drawing, copied from a photograph, it is that of a Negro of pure blood, although the Negrito type here has manifestly changed by crossing with Mogul blood. I will cite also the plate where Fryer has represented the Mulchers from the district of Coimbatore, in the province of Cochin.[54] These individuals are seen of very different statures, proportions, and features, but the woman to the right is a true Aëta; she has the hair which is characteristic of all of this race, and the features of the Philippine subtype.†

---

* Frontispiece. I am so much more certain that I am not mistaken in this opinion, as, in a note addressed to Campbell, Colonel Dalton declares himself to have seen woolly heads among the Oraons.

† It is to be seen above that my opinions are founded on the comparison which I have been able to make of these various drawings with seventy-one photographs. Therefore they may, I believe, be received with confidence. This abundance of materials has enabled me to establish certain differences between the Aëtas and the Mincopies. The former have coarser features; their nose is more flattened at the root, thicker and broader in general. They have

The Bandra Lokh or Djangal of the forests of Amarkantak of whom M. Rousselet has brought us a portrait,[164, 165] * are doubtfully referred to any subtype of Negro (Fig. 10). The features are not those of a Negrito.
There is something in them which reminds one of certain
Papuans. In his case, misery and hunger have altered his
form and discoloured his skin; but the woolly hair, which
our countryman has not forgotten to mention in his description, leaves no doubt as to the general type to which
this individual should be referred.

In the work which we have published with Hamy [157]
we have put the profile of a young Ghond, modelled by
the Schlagintweits, beside the profile of a Mincopy taken
from a photograph of Colonel Tytler and that of a young
Aëta girl drawn by Choris.[23] I here reproduce this drawing (Fig. 11). It will be easily seen that the Dravidian
is just about a mean between the two insular types, although coming nearer the Aëta than the Mincopy; and
Colonel Dalton has told us that the Ghonds have the hair,
the skin, and physiognomy of the Negro.

To these proofs, founded on their external characteristics, may be added those which result from the study of
the skulls. Among the Negritos generally the head and
face of the skeleton usually show very peculiar characteristics. In an excellent work Flower has pointed out
the extreme similarity of twenty-four skulls which he had
at his disposal, and declared that he would be quite sure

---

also thinner legs than the Andamanese. Altogether the latter are
endowed with a finer physique. The Negritos of India seem to be
connected more with the subtype of the Aëtas than with that of
the Mincopies.

* The appellation Πô, used here, must be a general term, which
may be applied to very different races. Hodgson uses it in speaking
of a people of Singhbhum, whom he describes as being remarkable
for their clear complexion and beauty of features.[77]

FIG. 10.—DJANGAL OF SIRGOUDJA. (From a drawing by Rousselet.)

never to confound the head of an Andaman with that of any other race.[51] Hamy and I have shown that the Aëta head possesses all its most characteristic features. These features are of such a nature as to be easily recognised even when attenuated or brought into relation with others as the result of crossing.[148, 157] They make it possible to

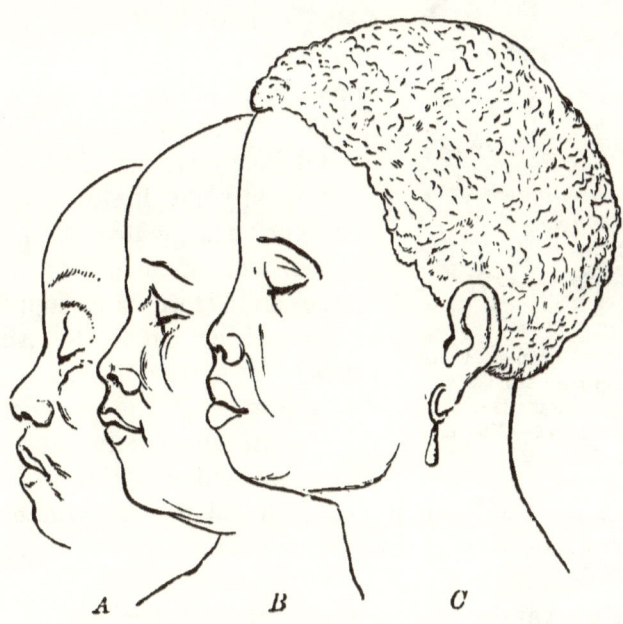

Fig. 11.—PROFILE OF BODA, GHOND OF SCHAGPORE *A*, compared with that of a Mincopy woman, *B*, and an Aëta woman, *C*. (¼ natural size.)

follow and recognise the Negrito type even when disguised, as it were, by mixture of blood, change of language, religion, or customs. Behold some examples: A French traveller, Leschenault de la Tour, collected about 1820, in the mountainous region of Cattalam, south of Madura, a skull which was deposited in the museum.[181] Besides some entirely individual characteristics, it presents all the features of the Mincopies (Fig. 12).

In his excellent work on the ethnology of India, Campbell declares that he does not quite know what to do with the Bengali. A skull which I owe to Dr. Mouat enables me to solve this problem.* It is that of a pariah woman, twenty-five years old, from the neighbourhood of

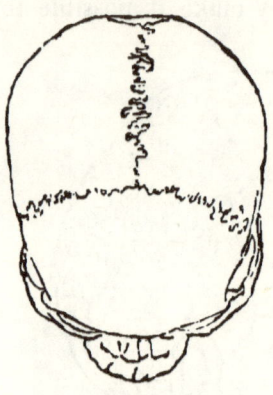

the capital of Bengal. Compared with the skull of a Mincopy man which Colonel Tytler sent me, I find that in reality it does not differ from it at all, except in sexual characters. The fundamental characteristics of the type are not only not diminished, but sometimes exaggerated, so that if one were not sure about the origin of the skull it would be supposed to have come from the Andamans.† This craniological observation testifies to the presence of the Negrito element in the heart of Bengal, and confirms and explains the traditions gathered by Allen in regard to the ancient existence of dwarfs, supposed to be cannibals, in these regions.[3] ‡

Fig. 12.—Skull of Female Negrito of the Cattalam Mountains. One fourth natural size. (Mus. d'hist. nat., No. 3502.)

Almost at the other extremity of the Ganges basin, in the district of Malwar, the Coorumbas are living, who in the

---

* Dr. Mouat has published several most interesting works on the Mincopies. I will only mention his classical work, Adventures and Researches among the Andaman Islands, 1863.

† I have said a few words about this skull in my Études sur les Mincopies. It is given in front view and of natural size in the Atlas of Crania Ethnica, pl. xvii.

‡ A number of times the Negritos have been accused of man eating. As they became better known it became evident that they were not. Yet it would be possible that when they were pursued by

jungles of Wynood seem to have preserved the purity of their Negrito blood. Samuells, in the short note which he devotes to them, tells us that they are black, very short, and have woolly hair. These little Negroes are remarkable for their activity and their courage, which causes them to be in demand as *shikaris*.[169] But not only in the heart of India can the type that occupies us be found. It can be traced farther north, and even to the base of the Himalayas. I have already mentioned a portrait of one, Dhoba Abor, published by Colonel Dalton. These tribes live in the eastern extremity of Assam, on the banks of rivers which empty into the upper Brahmapootra. Quite a good deal to the west, an English traveller, Traill, has found in Kamaon, by the side of Brahman castes and Rajpouts, a class entirely different from all the others. These are the Doms, of whom it is said that they are extremely black, and that many of them have hair more or less woolly.* The Doms live west of the Kali River. Still farther west live the Chamangs, Chamars, or Kalis, who seem to possess the same characters.[36]

Certainly neither the Tibetans nor the Aryans could have given the Doms and their western neighbours this truly black skin, and hair which reminds one of wool.

---

pitiless invaders they would have been compelled by misery to feed on human flesh. It is known that similar things have happened in Africa among tribes previously pastoral, as a consequence of the devastation of Chaka and Dingaan.

* Many having curly hair, inclining to wool, and being all extremely black.[182] These exact details, given by a traveller who has seen them himself, are the more important, as Campbell, in his remarkable Memoir on the Ethnology of India, declares himself as not knowing any people in these regions which could be connected with those that he calls aborigines, and whom he considers as all having more or less Negrito blood.[25] Prichard quotes the preceding passage twice. Once he reproduces it exactly; the other time he replaces *extremely* by *nearly*, which is quite different.

This latter character is of the greatest importance. In the crossing of two races of which the one has elliptical and the other round hair this latter character very soon becomes preponderant in the half breeds. The observations made by Semper in the Philippine Islands agree with those made before in America and in eastern Russia on this point. The same traveller, confirming the oldest descriptions, has recognised that the black skin still continues after the hair has already been greatly modified. A somewhat woolly head, then, announces the presence of Negro blood hardly attenuated.[173]

As regards Negritos and their half breeds, another characteristic is of the greatest importance. This is their stature. All pure Negritos are very small. Travellers are unanimous upon this point. I shall later give some exact measurements of individuals of this race, both pure and mixed. Here I limit myself to remarking that in mixed races the stature decreases in the same measure as the other characters by which the individuals examined approach the Negrito type become more pronounced.

Thus Roubaud has given as the mean stature of Dravidians with straight hair and chocolate-coloured skin, 1^m64 for men and 1^m56 for women, while the stature of the Pouleyers, with nearly black skin, and hair sometimes straight, sometimes curly and even crinkly, has decreased to 1^m61.[146]

So also, in speaking of the Bhils, with straight hair and skin of the colour of slightly burned coffee, Rousselet says that they are of average stature.[164] But Colonel Sealy, who has come in contact with Bhils having very dark skin* and curly hair, adds that they are small.†

---

* "Of very dark complexion."
† "Of short stature" (quoted by Prichard).[139]

The Gounds, darker and uglier than the Bhils, rarely measure 1ᵐ62 or 1ᵐ63. With the Puttouas the stature descends to 1ᵐ57 in men and 1ᵐ291 in women.*

The stature of the Mintiras of Johore, in the south of

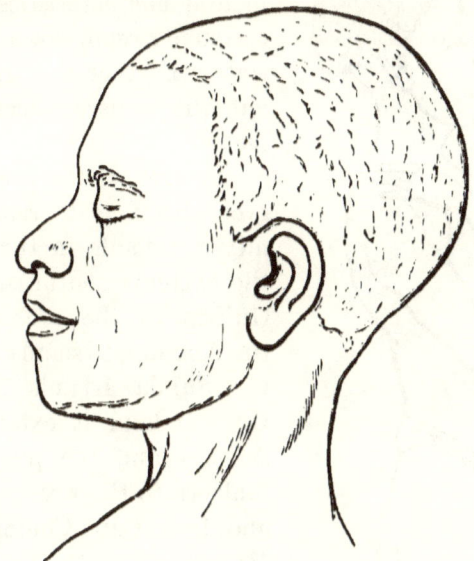

Fig. 13.—Bust of Orion, Negrito-Papuan of Tidore—Profile. ¼ natural size. (Mus. d'hist. nat., No. 880.)

Malacca, who have sometimes straight and sometimes curly hair, varies from 1ᵐ62 to 1ᵐ47, and the average is 1ᵐ58.[97]

Wallace attributes to the Semangs a stature of 1ᵐ266 to 1ᵐ416.

I think I have said enough to demonstrate that, in the

---

* I must remark that another element, very different from the Negritos, may shorten the stature. It may be supplied by some small though very robust Tibetan peoples; but in this case the skin should become lighter instead of darker. This seems to be the case with the Touleous, studied by M. Ronband, who in connection with a yellowish-white skin and thick-set forms, have an average height of 1ᵐ62.

5

midst of these mixed peoples of the great peninsula this side of the Ganges and in the adjacent countries, the Negrito type betrays itself at every step by some one of its fundamental characteristics, and occasionally reappears in its pure state. Farther on I shall point out the consequences of this fact.

FIG. 14.—NEGRITO-PAPUAN. (After Crawfurd.)

In fact, at the present time even the Negrito race, pure or mixed, extends in the sea from the extreme southeast of New Guinea to the archipelago of the Andaman Islands, and from the Sunda Islands to Japan. On the land it extends from Annam and the peninsula of Malacca to the western Ghauts, and from Cape Comorin to the Himalayas.

The race whose history we are sketching has not remained the same throughout the immense area to which it fell heir. External characters vary considerably between some Negritos of New Guinea and the Indian archipelago on the one hand, and those of the Philippine and Andaman Islands on the other.

We know the former by the description and full figure which Crawfurd has published,[33] the accuracy of which has been attested by Earl, and which I here reproduce (Fig. 14); also by a bust modelled by Dumoutier, of which I give the profile (Fig. 13).[157] As to the latter, the old drawings of Choris and numerous photographs of the present time furnish everything desirable in the way of

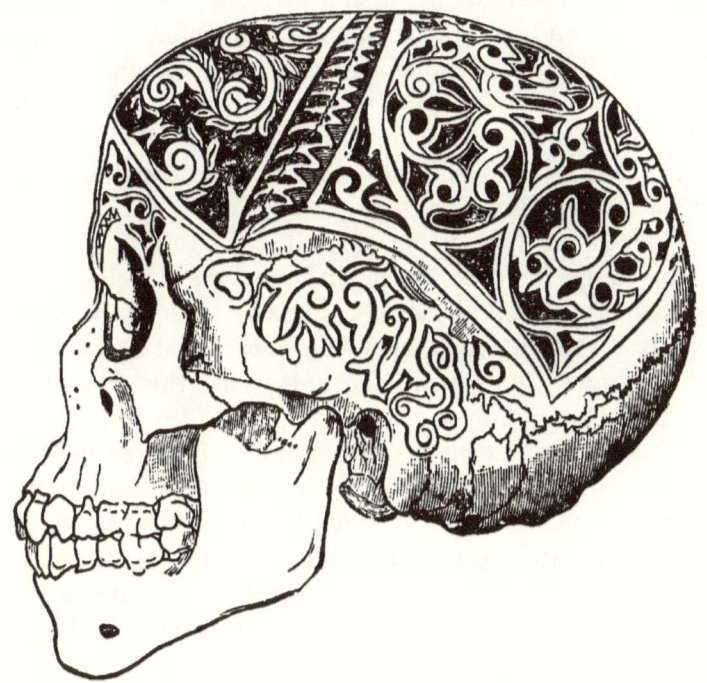

Fig. 15.—Skull of a Negrito-Papuan of Borneo, forming part of a Dyak trophy.

materials. These two secondary types present a strongly marked contrast. The Negrito of Crawfurd has a much lighter skin than the Aëtas and Mincopies; his nose is flatter, his chin more retreating, his loins are not so well formed, his thighs and legs are not so rounded.

These differential features have seemed to me sufficient to justify the division of the Negrito race into two branches, the Oriental and Occidental branches. The study of the skull has since confirmed this view. The Oriental Negrito has a little longer skull than his brother from the West, although very far from possessing the absolute dolichocephaly which characterises the Papuan.* Hamy and I have considered it necessary to emphasise the distinction just established, and we have considered each of these secondary types as constituting a subrace. For us, the little Oriental Negroes are the Negrito-Papuans ; those of the West are Negritos proper. As to the latter, the differences mentioned above between the Aëtas and the Mincopies are too slight to render it necessary to form them into two distinct groups.

The centre of population of the Negrito-Papuans seems to be in New Guinea and its dependencies. The Mincopies, as well as the Aëtas, belong to the type of the Negritos proper, which seem to have occupied a great part of the Indonesian archipelagoes ; it is also this type which we found again on the continent.

The limit between the two groups is, however, difficult to trace. On the one side, the Negrito whom Earl had as a companion, and who reminded him of Crawfurd's drawing, was a native of Gilolo (Moluccas) ; on the other side, Hamy has traced as far as Timor the indubitable evidence of Negritos proper ; † and the decidedly black skin

---

* In the Negrito the horizontal index varies from 80–84 ; in the Negrito-Papuan of New Guinea, from 78·85–79·87 ; and in the Papuans of the same island, from 69·35–78·23. The latter very high figure was found in the skull of a woman, and suggests suspicion of the influence of crossing. I have already pointed out elsewhere these craniological differences, and I must recall the fact that the Papuans are also taller, stronger, and more athletic than the Negritos.[144]

† " All these cranial traits, eminently those of the Negrito, make of the Timorese, whom we are studying, an excellent type of the race. . . . All the characteristic features of the Negrito face can be found in our specimen. The shapes of the various cavities are the same, and the bones which surround them have the same curvatures." [69]

of individuals seen by D'Albertis at Epa and by Lawes at Port Moresby seems to indicate that they are found again at the eastern extremity of New Guinea. One sees that the two divisions of the race have interpenetrated, and very likely are bound to each other by connecting links.

However that may be, to judge from the proofs collected up to date, the area of the Negrito-Papuans is entirely pelagic; the Negritos proper inhabit both islands and the continent. The presence of our little Negroes over so large an extent of the eastern maritime world has especially attracted the attention of anthropologists. To explain this distribution, Richard Owen has considered it necessary to recur to the hypothesis, too often invoked, of an ancient continent, at present partly submerged, and which has left as traces of its existence plateaus and mountain chains, which alone project above the water.* I believe it possible to account for these facts in a more simple manner.

The history of the peopling of Polynesia shows how it has been possible for a seafaring people to reach the farthest extremities of the ocean world.† Without going nearly as far in the art of navigation as the Polynesians, we know that the Negritos, entirely by themselves, have invented canoes the nautical qualities of which astonish

---

* This hypothesis would lead us to extend this continent over the whole Negrito area, and to consequently attach to India not only the islands of the Sunda and Indonesian archipelagoes—which might be reasonable—but also New Guinea and divers adjacent archipelagoes, which it is impossible to admit.

† See Les Polynésiens et leurs Migrations. I have given in this work a *résumé* of the principal facts relating to the peopling of Polynesia and a chart of the Polynesian migrations, completing that of Hale. I returned later to the subject, and have given a second edition of the chart in 1877.[147] I have just published a third, more complete one, which shows the migrations of the Papuans beside those of the Polynesians.[156]

the English sailors. Where they have been left in possession of their shores they have remained bold fishermen. It is not difficult to admit their migration from island to island, and their scattering by winds and tempests in these waters, where the islands are larger, more numerous, and nearer to each other than in the Pacific.

The taking possession of these archipelagoes must have been all the easier for the Negritos, as they apparently have been the first inhabitants. This conclusion results from a quantity of details given by travellers, which may be generalised into a fact already mentioned, viz., that these unfortunate little Negroes have been surrounded almost everywhere by people superior to them either in physical strength or in civilisation, and who seem to have considered it their task to exterminate them.* If, in some rare cases, and owing to exceptional circumstances, an inferior race might succeed in slipping into a country already occupied by stronger enemies, and in maintaining themselves there, it is impossible to admit that this fact would be repeated on a multitude of points, everywhere under identical circumstances. In seeing these Negritos almost always confined to the mountains of the interior of islands of which other races occupy the plains and shores, it is difficult not to consider them as having been the first occupants.

The continent presents similar facts in Annam and at Malacca. We will not consider the former region, regarding which we have but incomplete information. At Malacca the greater number of Negritos are more or less crossed. Less ferocious or more feeble, their invaders have crossed with them ; but the Negro blood still shows itself with all appearances of purity in a great number of

---

* At Borneo the Dyaks chase the Negritos like wild beasts, and shoot with the blowgun at the children—who take refuge on trees— as they would at a monkey.[45]

individuals, and we have seen that there are still little groups in existence which seem to be exempt from mixture. Analogous facts are also found in India. Yet the crossing here probably dates further back, and has been accomplished under more complicated conditions.

The results of crossings in India cannot always be traced with anything like the same regularity which I have pointed out above. With man, as well as with animals, crossing, unregulated and at haphazard, seems to have its caprices. Sometimes the opposing characteristics modify each other, sometimes they remain in juxtaposition. Some are more easily effaced than others. Thus, woolly hair often disappears, while the colour of the skin is little or not at all changed. For Montano, as well as for Semper, the straight-haired Negroes of Luzon, spoken of by old Spanish authors, are nothing but crosses of Aëtas and Tagals, such as are seen at the present day. All the other characters may present analogous facts.

What•has happened at Luzon must have happened more markedly in India, where the crossing is more ancient, and has been carried on on a greater scale and between more numerous and diverse ethnological elements. There, also, the woolly hair must have disappeared in a number of tribes, leaving as the evidence of the fundamental type—sometimes on the whole of the population, sometimes on a more or less large number of individuals—certain features of face, the colour of the skin, the small stature, or the shape of the head.* Successive crossing

---

* The first three characteristics are reported among a large number of the Dravidian populations, and are found in the same degree in others which do not come under the same denomination, as they do not speak a language of that stock. The lack of specimens for study does not allow certainty as to the fourth. It was shown above that the Negrito head is found in Bengal among peoples speaking an Indo-Aryan tongue. Mouat has found everywhere that

with different types and the varying proportion of eth-
nical elements have necessarily produced among the
crosses predominance now of Negrito characteristics, now
of features derived from some other source. Atavism has
never lost its rights in the midst of this confusion of
blood, and has many times revived ancient types which
one might think had been effaced.

These very simple considerations account for all the
facts reported by travellers. They explain the extreme
diversity of characteristics so many times reported in one
population, and, consequently, the contradictory opinions
of authors so well summarised by Latham in regard to
the Rajmalis mountaineers: " Some say their physiognomy is Mongolian, others say it is African." [85]

As concerns mixed populations, everything depends
on the individuals whom the observer has met, as is so
clearly shown by photographs. But these apparent contradictions cannot longer mislead us as to the general
fact, and this fact can be expressed in a few words. In
India and its dependencies all or almost all peoples of
short stature and black skin are more or less crosses of
Negrito; there are some in which the type is preserved, or
where, by force of atavism, it reappears almost in a state of
purity; and, lastly, there are groups which have remained
pure.

The facts becoming more numerous and better established each day, lead then to an order of ideas which Logan had already supported by serious arguments,[94,96] which
I think I have been one of the first to develop, and to

---

the peoples with whom most of the Dravidians are connected are
divided into dolichocephales, subdolichocephales, and mesatice-
phales. Only some tribes of Assam and one Mishmi alone reach to
subbrachycephaly.[127] These facts are easily explained by the multiplicity of races which have successively crossed with the primitive
Negro population.

which Hamilton Smith,[174] Campbell, Dalton, Giglioli,[60] Allen,[3] Flower,[51] etc., have more or less agreed.*

I cannot present here in detail all the facts and considerations which have led me to these general conclusions regarding the past of the various Negro races. They will be found in a book the first part of which has already appeared.[156] But I can give a summary of this mass of data in some propositions formulated from the standpoint of modern study.

The Negro type was originally characterised in southern Asia, of which, no doubt, it was the sole occupant for an indefinite period of time. From there, the various representatives of the type have migrated in various directions, and, in passing some to the east and others to the west, have given rise to the black populations of Melanesia and of Africa. In particular, India and Indo-China have belonged at first to the blacks. Invasions or infiltrations of various yellow and white races have separated the Negro populations, which formerly occupied a continuous area, and, in mixing with them, have profoundly altered them. The actual condition of things is the final result of struggles and mixtures, of which the most ancient date back to prehistoric times. The Negrito subtype is one of the oldest of the race, and was at least predominant in India and Indo-China when the crossing began.

It would evidently be impossible to even approximately fix the time of the first crossings, but we can establish some of the more recent ones. The Malays had settled at Luzon before their conversion to Mohammedanism, as

---

* It is more than a quarter of a century since I propounded at the museum ideas founded on facts then known, similar to those which I express here, and which have only been confirmed and expanded since then.[142] I gave in that lesson a *résumé* of my course of the preceding year.

they were still pagans on the arrival of the Spaniards. To all appearances they must have arrived there before the conquest of Madjapahit by the Mohammedans, which takes us back at least to the middle of the fifteenth century.*

But this settlement must have been quite recent, since the first Europeans could collect traditions according to which the Indians with straight hair—that is, the Malays or their crosses,—already masters of the plain, had nevertheless to pay a certain tribute to the pure blacks.[162]

This itself shows that the latter had been the first occupants. It is, moreover, very probable that the movement of expansion, determined in Malaysia as in Arabia by the triumph of Islam, must have been fatal to our little Negroes, who must have seen themselves encroached upon in many islands where, up to that time, they had lived in peace.

In India, the legend of Rama may suggest some conjectures. The history of the Aryan hero, though disfigured by fable, surely contains a nucleus of truth. The account of the services which he receives from Hanouman is very simple, if we see in this one and his monkey people a Negrito chief and his tribe. This interpretation gains from modern discoveries a character of probability. If it is well founded, as one may believe, it would result that in the heroic times of the Aryan conquest the Negritos still formed flourishing populations, whose assistance the newcomers did not disdain, although regarding them as creatures of inferior rank.†

Race pride and the differences of religion and customs

---

* The conquest of this city may be considered as marking the advent of Mohammedanism in Malaysia. It took place in 1478.[160]

† I recognise, however, the fact that the legend of Hanouman may be equally applied to any of the Dravidian tribes which had already emerged from savagery.

have never prevented the Europeans,—the Anglo-Saxons
no more than others—from crossing with the lowest of
savages.* The Aryans were no more reserved. We see
their heroes of the oldest times, the Pandavas themselves,
set the example of these unions. Bhimasena, after having
vanquished and killed the *rakchasa* Hidimba, at first re-
sists the solicitations of the sister of this monster, who,
having become enamoured of him, shows herself under
the form of a charming female. But upon the represen-
tations of his oldest brother, Youdhichshira, the *King of
Justice*, and with the assent of his mother, he yields, and
spends some time in the enchanted dwelling of this Dravidian or Negrito Armida.[134]

Thus ever since the heroic times of the Aryan race it
has mixed its blood with that of local populations. But
these mixtures certainly date farther back, and have con-
tinued ever since. One well knows how numerous invasions have been, generally from the west or northwest.
The inevitable result was the more and more marked
effacement of the Negrito type. Thus all these mixed
races have arisen, within which the white, yellow, or
black type predominates alternately, and which are comprised under the common name of Dravidians. But the
fundamental type persists, nevertheless, in a sometimes
very curious and significant manner.

The Dravidian races have, from the point of view that
occupies us, an interest easily understood. They teach us
regarding the ancient extension of the Negritos. We can
with almost absolute certainty say that this race formerly occupied all the territory where at present we meet the
Dravidians. Here I must make an important remark.

---

* Witness the English and Australian crosses. The Tasmanian
race is only represented now by the half breeds of the seal fishermen,
and we know from Bonwick that there were often many children in
a family.

Until now, only those groups have been considered Dravidians who speak one of those languages to which linguists have given the name Dravidian, and the characteristic feature of which seems to be that they are intimately related to the Australian idioms. Physical characteristics were not taken into account. Hence all tribes speaking an Aryan or Iranian language have not been considered as belonging to the *ensemble* of peoples occupying us, and, consequently, as not being related to the Negritos. This exclusively linguistic point of view could only lead to serious ethnological errors.

For example, Jauts, who are in the opinion of Elphinstone, the first possessors of the soil, are, according to his description, small, black, and ugly. Nor are their women any more beautiful.[48]

But this short characterisation gives all the essential traits attributed by different travellers to some tribes which have been considered as typically Dravidian. Bishop Heber particularly speaks of the Bhils in this same manner.[76]

Elphinstone's Jauts then are by their physical characteristics related to all these populations, in the composition of which the Negrito element has played a more or less important part. In the Punjab they are considered as the oldest inhabitants of the country, just as in central India the Dravidians are universally considered the predecessors of the Aryans. But the Jauts do not speak Dravidian; their language is related to the Sanscrit stock, and Prichard and the linguists in general have made them Hindus. The physical characteristics, much less easily modified than language, religion, or customs, have for all anthropologists preponderating value, and I can only see in the black aborigines of the Punjab representatives of the race which farther south has likewise preceded the others, and shows the same characteristics.

The Jauts of Elphinstone especially inhabit the lower parts of the Punjab, and consequently the neighbourhood of the Indus. The Dravidian type, then, still extends at least as far as the neighbourhood of the eastern bank of that river. But we must go one step farther, and carry the habitation of Dravidians to the western bank of the river.

Very high up the Indus, and from the point where the river makes a bend towards the South, is the Damân. This province lies between the Sinde, or upper Indus, the Soliman Mountains and the Salées Mountains, and the Indus itself. It is, then, entirely on the right bank. One of its subdivisions, the Mackelwand, occupies the whole plain along the river. There lives a population which Elphinstone considers a mixture of Belutchis and Jâts. But at the same time he informs us that the inhabitants along the banks of the Indus are "people of dark complexion, and lean and meagre form."

We have here in four words the characteristics of the Jauts of the Punjab. But the true Belutchis are large and well made. So are the Jâts.[110]

Neither of them are nearly black, or the travellers, and especially Rousselet, would have spoken of it. They cannot, therefore, have given rise to the population of Mackelwand. This is evidently only a remnant of the black peoples of Ctesias, a branch of the Jauts of Elphinstone, who have crossed the river. They are Dravidians.

At the other extremity of the Indus, and always on the right bank of the river, we meet with entirely different facts, but facts which lead, nevertheless, to conclusions analogous to the preceding. They are supplied by the Brahouis, of whom I have already spoken, but to whom it may be useful to return.

The Brahouis live in Beluchistan, side by side with the Belutchis. While the latter have an aquiline nose, deep-set eyes, and a clear complexion, the former have a very brown skin, flat nose, and flat figure, but large, well-formed eyes, which denote a very mixed origin. These latter features, which so plainly recall various Dravidian types, belong essentially to the mountain Brahouis, who are, besides, shorter than the Belutchis proper. Let us add, above all, that the Belutchis and the Brahouis differ in language as much as in their external appearance. The former speak an Iranian language; the latter, a language of which Maury tells us that "it is related to the Dravidian tongues, and forms a transition between them and the Iranian languages."

It is evidently impossible to admit that a Dravidian language should penetrate from east to west into an Iranian or Turanian population, which had remained pure, and that it should have been adopted by them. No more can it be supposed that Dravidians should have come to settle, by force or otherwise, in the midst of these races, whom we everywhere see to be their superiors and to push them back more and more. It must be admitted, then, that the Iranian Belutchis, in coming into these regions, found there Dravidians, Brahouis who, more or less altered and elevated by crossing, still in part preserve their physical characters and a characteristic language. This is, moreover, shown by the traditions of the two races. The Brahouis consider themselves aborigines; the Belutchis admit that they are of foreign origin.[85]

The Brahouis are very likely the most western branch of those Koles, Khôles, Côles, or Coolees which are already quite numerous beyond the Indus delta, still more so in Guzerat, and tribes of whom extend more or less scattered across almost all central India into Behur and to the eastern extremity of the Vindhya Mountains.[163] Placed thus, under such diverse conditions, these tribes have either preserved their primitive characteristics or else have changed in varying degrees. The eastern Khôles, withdrawn to the mountain passes of Nerbuda or on to high plateaus, are at times inferior to the Bhils, and resemble some Dravidian groups. The western Khóles, inhabiting open countries, in contact with the conquering races, have been strongly influenced by them. "One can find among them," says M. Rousselet, "a series of types from the pure Bhils to the pure Rajpoot." What has happened in Rajpootana must still more have happened in Beluchistan, where the Dravidian population, even more exposed to invasions, could not recruit itself from tribes which had remained more or less protected against the new mixtures.

Thus the black races of India have passed the Indus. But how far did they extend west of that river? It is a question difficult to answer.

Hamilton Smith admits that true Negroes have existed within historic times, or still exist in Laristan, in Mekran, in Persia proper, and on the banks of the Helmund, which rises in the mountains of Cabul and empties into Lake Zerrah.[174] Elphinstone has somewhere said that there are Negroes along the borders of this lake.

We can easily admit that the Dravidian tribes of the province of Lous formerly extended farther west along the seashore. But did they reach the Persian Gulf? Could the existence of groups more or less like the Negro in Laristan not be easily explained by the importation of African Negroes as slaves? The examination of some skulls will remove all uncertainty.

What travellers report in regard to the inhabitants of the shores of Lake Zerrah would not, it seems to me, be interpreted in that manner. They represent, we are told, the first inhabitants of the country, and differ from the other inhabitants of Seistan in features as well as in habits. They are really black and ugly.* None of the

---

* They are big, black, and ill-featured (Latham).

races from the west or northwest who have invaded Afghanistan could have brought in either these features or this complexion. On the contrary, it is quite easy to understand that Dravidian tribes from the upper Indus might have gone up the Cabul River and crossed the barrier which separates it from the sources of the Helmund, and by following the course of the latter have arrived at the lake.

The facts just indicated permit us to solve the ethnological problem which an oft-quoted passage of Herodotus has long since propounded. It is known that in enumerating the different peoples which figured in the army of Xerxes, the ancient historian expresses himself in the following manner:

" The Eastern Ethiopians (for there were two kinds of Ethiopians in this expedition) served with the Indians. They resemble the other Ethiopians, and only differ from them in their language and their hair. The Oriental Ethiopians have, in fact, straight hair, while those of Libya have more crinkly hair than any other men."*

Here again we find the *Negroes with straight hair* of Luzon. The father of history expresses himself exactly as P. Bernardo de la Fuente. Only when India or the adjacent countries are spoken of we can affirm, taking into account all known facts, including the observations of Semper and Montano, that it must be a Dravidian population that is considered. The *Ethiopians* of whom Herodotus speaks were probably the Jauts of Elphinstone, less altered than they are to-day, and having preserved intact the fundamental colour of the type.

---

* Herodotus, liv. vii, § 70.

CHAPTER III.

A RACE spread over so vast a space as that spoken of
in the preceding chapter could not remain everywhere
identical. I have stated above how I have been led to
refer all the small Oriental Negroes to two secondary
types—the Negritos proper and the Negrito-Papuans.

It is not easy to determine the respective limits of
these two groups. It is possible that there are none in
reality, and that they mutually penetrate and give rise to
peoples with mixed characteristics. At all events, we
know that the Andaman and Philippine Islands, and, according to the recent researches of Montano, Mindanao also,
belong to the Negritos. The Negritos of the continent
seem to belong to the same type. New Guinea appears to
be the centre of population of the Negrito-Papuans,[157]
who, according to Earl, extend as far as Gilolo in the

6   59

Moluccas. Hamy has traced the pure Negrito type as far as Timor,[69] and the individual seen by d'Albertis at Epa seems also to have had all the exterior characteristics of the Negrito proper, among others the perfectly black skin and the absence of prognathism.[2] On the other hand, the Hindu Negritos of Amarkantak are, as it seems, only dark brown.[164] Altogether, we know little enough about the Negrito-Papuans. This ignorance is largely due to the fact that they have been and still are too often confounded with the Papuans. Both Wallace and Earl have committed this error.[155] Many more recent travellers have made the same mistake. Meyer, who has tarried in New Guinea and brought back a magnificent collection of skulls, has adopted the opinion of Wallace, and opposed the idea that the Negrito type is represented in this island by two distinct types.*

Beccari himself, although struck with the resemblance of certain New Guineans to the Aëtas, does not dwell on this question,[14] and the few words quoted by Giglioli[60] from a letter of this traveller do not teach us much more. D'Albertis, while maintaining great reserve, which he justifies by saying that he does not know the Negrito type, at least understood that he had under his eyes at Epa an individual entirely different from any he had seen so far, and that the question deserved to be studied. Such was also the opinion of Lawes in regard to the mountain tribes of Port Moresby.[90]

The most complete description of the Negrito-Papuans which has yet been published we certainly owe to Crawfurd. Notice how this author expresses himself: " I do not think I have seen any whose stature exceeded five

---

* Meyer.[114, 115] Making use of the same numbers published by the German traveller, M. Hamy, in his monograph on the Papuans, published in our Crania Ethnica, has shown that Meyer had brought new proofs to the support of the very idea opposed by him.

feet (1ᵐ25).* Moreover, their forms are lean and poor; their skin, instead of being dark black, like that of the Africans, is soot colour." From Everard Home he quotes: " The skin of the Papuan is lighter than that of the Negro. His hair is woolly, and grows in little tufts; each hair forms an entangled spiral. The forehead is higher than that of the Negro, the nose is more projecting, the upper lip longer and more prominent, and the lower lip is thrown forward in such a way that the chin disappears and the mouth is the lowest part of the face. The buttocks are much lower than those of the Negro, whence results a very striking distinctive feature; but the calf is also high, as in the African." [33]

To the support of this description Crawfurd borrows from Raffles the drawing of the young Papuan (Negrito-Papuan) of New Guinea, which I have reproduced above (Fig. 14).† To be sure, the subject is only a child of ten years, and its youthfulness may call forth criticism. But we must not forget that the physical development of these races is completed at an earlier period than among European populations. This single thought will make us understand how Earl, so good a judge in such matters, could affirm the resemblance of this portrait to adults whom he saw. He tells us that on one of his trips he had as a companion a Negro from Gilolo, who had all the features of Raffles and Crawfurd's Papuan. He thus testifies to the accuracy of the English writers, as well as to the extension of this type in the Indian archipelagoes.

---

* Beccari attributes to the small New Guineans. whom he calls Alfourous, a stature of 1ᵐ61 to 1ᵐ63. According to Leon Laglaise, the Karons never exceed 1ᵐ60.[82] This tribe may, however, have gained in size by crossing.

† In this plate the author has placed side by side his young Papuan (Negrito-Papuan) and a native of Bali, taken as a Malay type. The figure of the Negrito has been reproduced in the History of Java, by Raffles and Crawfurd.

We see that this type does not shine by beauty of features; and when we observe it in its native country, the proportions of its body harmonise only too well with its face. But Earl tells us further that these Papuans, transported as slaves to the Malay Islands, and placed in comfortable circumstances, such as they have never known, gain rapidly. Their scrawny limbs become more regular, rounder, and as if polished, and their vivacity and grace of movement compensate for their ugly faces.

The lamentable confusion to which I have just called attention is the reason why the differential features which might distinguish the Negrito-Papuan from the true Papuan in regard to social state, customs, beliefs, and industries have not been sought. Wallace and Earl go so far as to say that, great or little, the Papuans have only one mode of life. It has always seemed to me a little difficult to admit this assertion, and the information which begins to come to us more and more justifies my doubts. Yet, in the actual state of our knowledge, it would be very difficult for us to define with certainty what belongs to each of these two races, the more so as they surely must have crossed often and given rise to mixed tribes.*

---

* This seems to be the case with the tribes visited by Comrie, in the neighbourhood of Astrolabe Bay. Of fourteen skulls collected, only one was subbrachycephalic; the others were dolichocephalic. But the average stature of twenty individuals measured was only 1ᵐ553, and one measurement was as low as 1ᵐ321. These dwarfs can neither be Papuans nor crosses of Polynesians. Only Negrito blood could have decreased the stature to such a degree. Dolichocephaly connected with such small stature is an example of that juxtaposition of characteristics to which I have often called attention in a general way, and which Montano has confirmed among the half breeds of Negritos, as I shall state further on.[81] Among the works to be consulted on all of these questions, I would call attention particularly to two memoirs of Mantegazza.[103, 105] In the first of these memoirs Mantegazza still supported the idea of the ethno-

The Negritos proper we know much better than the Negrito-Papuans. Since the middle ages the Arabs, and no doubt the Chinese before them, knew that the Andaman Islands were inhabited by black men with crinkly hair.[161] On their arrival at the Philippine Islands the Spaniards found there the Aëtas, whom at present we know to be of the same race as the Mincopies.* Since that time, as the Malay Islands and the two Indian peninsulas have become better known, and the points which these little Negroes inhabit have been seen to multiply and extend themselves, more accurate information in regard to them has been gathered, and to-day it is possible to gain a general idea of the race, as well as of the variations which its tribes the most distant from each other present.

Let us state, first, that these variations are very slight in the character which interests us most, on account of the special consideration which has led us to these studies. Everywhere the stature of the Negritos is so reduced as

---

graphic unity of all New Guinean Negroes. He has since been converted to the duality of the races merely by the sight of the craniological collection brought back by D'Albertis, and in a note addressed to the Société d'Anthropologie de Paris announces his new convictions.[104]

* This name, given to the inhabitants of the Andaman Islands, has given occasion for many hypotheses. In my first publications I thought to find its origin in the vocabulary collected by Colebrooke. This traveller asserts that the inhabitants of the islands called their country Mincopy. It seemed to me evident that from the islands the name had passed to the inhabitants.[39] But Man asserts that this word does not exist in any of the dialects spoken on the islands. He tells us that the only utterances the sounds of which resemble that of the generally adopted name are *kámin kápi* (which he translates by *stand here*) and *min katch* (*come here*). The natives often use the latter words; the Europeans might have adopted them to designate those who used them.[101]

to place them among the smallest human races. The unanimous testimony of various travellers can leave no doubt upon this point. It has, however, usually been vague and general in expression. But we have now accurate measurements in sufficient number from the three principal stations of the race, viz., Luzon, the Andaman Islands, and the peninsula of Malacca.

Two French travellers—Marche and Montano*—have visited Luzon and measured the native Aëtas; the former at Binangonan de Lampon on the Pacific coast, the latter in the Sierra de Marivelès.

		Maximum, metre.	Minimum, metre.	Average, metre.
Marche	7 men..............	1·472	1·354	1·397
	3 women...........	1·376	1·310	1·336
Montano	18 men.............	1·575	1·425	1·485
	12 women	1·485	1·350	1·431

These figures seem to indicate that the mountain population is, on the average, a little taller than that of the

* Marche and Montano received from the Secretary of Public Instruction two scientific missions for the Philippine Islands. Both of them have acquitted themselves in a remarkable manner. Marche has limited his explorations to Luzon. The collection which he brought back is of great zoölogical and anthropological interest. What has been exhibited of it in the rooms of the Geographical Society has attracted great attention by the variety of its objects and by the ethnographical importance of several among them.

Montano, after having stayed for some time about Manilla, went to Mindanao, where he explored some of the least known regions. He also has brought back collections interesting from various points of view. Among other things, he sent to the Société de Géographie a mass of observations, notes, itineraries, and charts which have won for him the Logerot prize (a gold medal), awarded to him at the public meeting of April 28, 1882, in consequence of a report made by Hamy.

coast. But perhaps the difference is due to the fact that Montano, having been able to measure a greater number, has come nearer the truth.* However that may be, it can be seen that the general average of the Philippine Aëtas, men and women, is about 1ᵐ413.

Let us now pass to the other end of the maritime area of the Negritos.

When I published my first studies on the Mincopies there had been only five measurements taken of these islanders, the maximum of which was 1ᵐ480, the minimum 1ᵐ370, and the average 1ᵐ436. Since then Flower has tried to determine the stature of the Mincopies from an examination of nineteen skeletons of men and women.[51, 53]

The results have been confirmed in a remarkable manner by direct measurements taken by Brander upon fifteen men and as many women.[59, 17] Finally, Man has published detailed measurements taken upon forty-eight men and forty-one women.[101]

The following are the figures obtained by these two methods:

		Maximum, metre.	Minimum, metre.	Average, metre.
Flower	men	1·600	1·385	1·448
	women	1·481	1·302	1·375
Brander	15 men	1·562	1·408	1·476
	15 women	1·441	1·308	1·366
Man	48 men	1·598	1·367	1·484
	41 women	1·496	1·343	1·397

One sees that the difference is slight. In the means, it rises only to 0ᵐ036 for the men and 0ᵐ031 for the women.

* In a note which he kindly gave me, Montano remarks that among the eighteen men which he measured only five surpassed 1ᵐ500.

Besides, in the maxima and the minima the extreme numbers mingle with each other. They relate, then, to a real difference of the statures, and not to the inductive method followed by one of the authors. Nearly the same value may be placed, then, on the figures of Flower, Brander, and Man.*

If we leave the sex out of consideration and calculate the general average, we find that the stature of 1ᵐ358 of the Andamans, taken all together, exceeds that of the Aëtas only by 0ᵐ055.

The first accurate information relative to the stature of the Negritos of the peninsula of Malacca was given by Major Macines and reproduced by Crawfurd.† Much more recently the celebrated Russian traveller Micluko-Maclay has published a work on these peoples which I regret knowing only through the analysis which Giglioli has given of it.[61, 116] Finally, Marche and Montano have collected new measurements, the more interesting as these travellers took pains to give the names of the tribes which furnished them.‡

The following table represents all but the observation of Macines, which, referring only to one individual, has now lost its former importance

According to these figures, the general average stature of these tribes would be 1ᵐ507—0ᵐ094 above that of the Aëtas and 0ᵐ149 above that of the Mincopies. The latter are the smallest of the Negritos.

---

* The English anatomist has not given the number of skeletons for each sex.

† Crawfurd.[33] The stature assigned by Macines to the only individual measured by him is 1ᵐ445.

‡ Marche has not, as far as I know, published the figures which he kindly gave me. Those collected by Montano have appeared in a memoir.[121]

		Maximum, metre.	Minimum, metre.	Average, metre.
Mieluko-Maclay	Men *.	1·620	1·460	1·540
	Women	1·480	1·400	1·440
Marche—10 Sakaies †		1·705	1·462	1·584
Montano ‡	12 Manthras	1·580	1·330	1·461
	8 Knabouis	1·578	1·455	1·517
	2 Udaïs	1·545	1·390	1 467
	2 Jakuns	1·550	1·525	1·537

It is interesting to compare, in regard to their statures, the different human races who merit the name of dwarfs. The Laplanders have long been considered the smallest of men, but Capel Brooke, who stayed among them for a long time and measured several of them, ascribes to them a mean stature of 1ᵐ550—greater, as one sees, than that of the Negritos.[20, 21] On the contrary, that of the Bushmen measured by Barrow descends to 1ᵐ370 among the men and to 1ᵐ220 among the women, thus being inferior to that of the Mincopies. Let us add that this traveller measured one woman, the mother of several children, who was only 1ᵐ140 in height.

It can be seen that in regard to stature the three races spoken of form a scale in the following order: Bushmen, Negritos, Laplanders; but perhaps the Negrillos of the Congo are still smaller than the Bushmen. Dr. Wolff,

---

* The analysis of Giglioli gives neither the number of individuals nor their sources. The means are not taken, as before, from the entirety of the observations, which I do not know. They only express the numbers intermediate between the extremes.

† The observations of M. Marche were collected at Nogen-Bara, in the province of Perak. They refer only to adult men.

‡ I have combined in this table the measures taken upon both sexes. Montano has published another, in which the figures of men and women are given separately as regards the Manthras and Knabouis. Of the Udaïs, he measured only one woman and none of the Jakuns.[120]

who has just rediscovered them under the name of *Batouas* in the country of the Bahoubas, asserts that none of these dwarfs exceed 1ᵐ400, and gives as their average height only 1·300.[58]

In the study of these little peoples we must always take into account the influence of crossing. One of the photographs, which I owe to M. de la Croix, is instructive in this respect.* It represents seven Sakaies, standing. Three of them have straight hair, while that of the others is more or less woolly. But the latter are much smaller than the former; the difference between the two extremes is nearly one tenth. This teaches us that the Negrito type has been altered in this tribe by mixture with another ethnic element with a much greater stature.

This fact, which can be seen at a glance, explains the difference which Marche and Montano have found between the maximum and minimum stature of the tribes just mentioned and among the Manthras. This difference is 0ᵐ243 among the first, 0ᵐ250 among the second. Nothing like it is seen among the Aëtas and Mincopies, who have remained pure, or nearly pure. Here the same difference only reaches 0ᵐ117, 0ᵐ118, 0ᵐ150, 0ᵐ133, and 0ᵐ154, according to measurements taken upon living subjects.

Finally, in all these tribes, insular or continental, the minima are much the same, and the smallest stature has even been met with among the Manthras. The difference between these and the Aëtas, measured by the French travellers, and the Mincopies, measured by Brander and Man, is only 24, 95, 67, and 78 millimetres.

The conclusion to be drawn from all these facts is, evidently, that the primitive Negritos at Malacca were no taller than the Aëtas and the Mincopies.†

---

* The two photographs which I have from this traveller were taken by M. de Saint-Pol Lias, whose companion he was.

† In order to have more precise terms for comparison, I did not

Our knowledge in regard to the Negritos of India is much more limited. Here crossing has caused the primitive stock to disappear over such large areas that many *savants* have, until lately, denied the existence of true Negroes in this country. The observations of several English travellers,* and those of Rousselet,[164] should have removed our last doubts. They teach us that some rare representatives of this primitive type still exist in a state of purity, and even form entire tribes, but only in the most inaccessible and unwholesome places. Unfortunately, the information gathered in regard to them is very little. The individual interviewed by our countryman, and whose portrait he brought back, ran away during the night, terrified by the commencement of the study of which he was the object. The English observers, who have been able to examine them more at leisure, have only brought back a few details. Sometimes they even say nothing of the hair, and the plates only give us information in regard to it.

Rousselet, on the contrary, has not failed to call attention to the *woolly curls* which partly hid the forehead of his Bandar-lokh.† This character, the most important of all when we consider the Negro race, testifies to the

---

take into consideration the measures calculated by Flower, the women measured by various observers, nor the Udaïs and Jakuns, of whom Montano measured only two individuals.

* I will mention particularly the works of Justice Campbell,[26] Dalton,[38] Fryer,[64] etc. Among the plates in these works reproducing photographs, are several which represent individuals whose Negrito characteristics are striking at a glance.

† Literally, *man ape.* This is the name which the neighbouring tribes give to the Negritos. They also call them Djangal, or *men of the jungles*—a term which they apply to all peoples more savage than themselves. Finally, the village visited by the English officer belonged to the Puttouas, or *leaf people.* They are so called by the more or less civilised Indians from the fact that their women use

purity of blood of the individual, even though the skin was a reddish black.*

The stature of this individual, says Rousselet, hardly reached 1ᵐ500. The Puttonas, measured by an English officer, attained 1ᵐ570, but their women were only 1ᵐ291.

According to Dalton, the stature of the Jouangs with black skin and curly hair is 1ᵐ525 among the men, and 1ᵐ416 among the women ; the maximum with the Oraons is 1ᵐ570 ; it falls to 1ᵐ525 among the Bhûihers, who in the entirety of their characteristics reminded him of the Andamans. This last figure recurs often in the descriptions of other more strongly crossed tribes. The average of all these numbers is 1ᵐ488 at the most. One sees, then, that this *ensemble* of populations takes us back to the same figures as the preceding groups.

The differences in height, which can be expressed in figures, can be made plain to every one. It is not so with other characteristics, such as the general proportions of the body and the features of the face.

I have by me the photographs which I owe to Col. Tytler, and which represent the full-length portraits of seven inhabitants of the Andaman Islands ; † the photo-

---

as their entire dress two bunches of fresh leaves, the one suspended in front and the other behind (Rousselet). This custom is also found in the Andamans among the Mincopies.

* This fading out of the black colour is easily explained by the sad conditions of life under which these tribes have existed since time immemorial. It is known that the complexion of the African negro becomes paler by disease.

† These two photographs represent one adult man, one young boy, and five women or young girls. In one, all the individuals are naked ; in the other they are dressed in a blouse closed at the neck and bound by a belt at the waist. This dress, however simple, is sufficient to partly take away the strange appearance which these persons present in a state of nudity, in spite of their closely shaved heads.

types published by Dobson, which reproduce in full figure and grouped in various ways, sixteen natives of the
same islands; *[42] those published by Man, representing

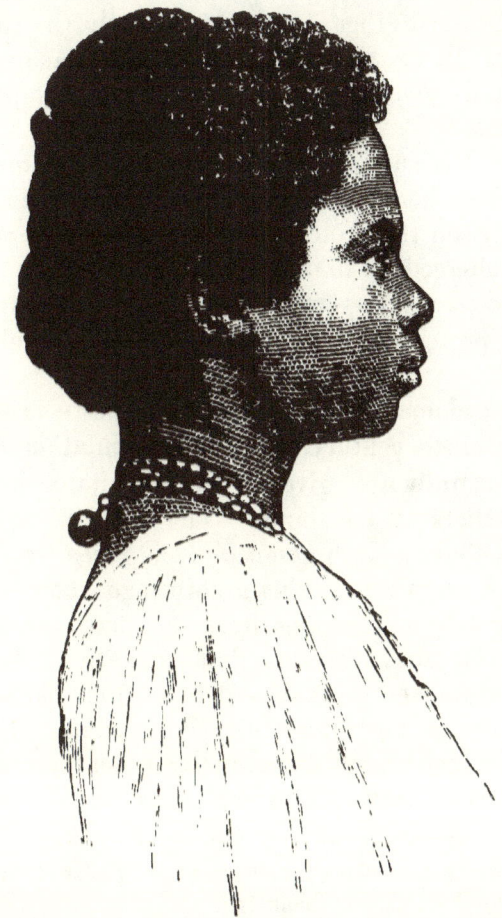

FIG. 16.—YOUNG AËTA GIRL. (After a photograph of M. Montano.)

* These phototypes represent five men, seven women, and four
young girls. The original photographs, like those of Col. Tytler, were
taken in the southern part of what was for a long time called the

twelve individuals;[101] twenty photographs of these same Mincopies, which the museum owes to Maxwell; and thirty-six photographs by Montano, showing the features of forty-eight Aëta men and women, young and adult, pure and mixed (Figs. 16 and 17); finally, the two photographs of M. de Saint-Pol Lias, of nine Sakaies of Malacca, kindly given to me by his travelling companion, M. de la Croix.*

Never has such a mass of authentic material been brought together. In discussing it I shall take as a term of comparison the Mincopies, who, in consequence of isolation prolonged up to our times, have certainly preserved an ethnic purity very rare even among people apparently the best protected against the infiltration of all foreign blood.

The Andaman Islands have been known to the Arabs since the ninth century,[101] but the reputation of barbarism and cannibalism given their inhabitants has always kept travellers at a distance. The same influence—and, no doubt, above all, the absence of the cocoa tree, which is · not found anywhere in this archipelago—have prevented the Malays from invading it, as they have the Nicobars. Marco Polo, whose voyages date back to 1273–'95, had heard of them, and gives some details which contain nothing but errors regarding their inhabitants. From the time of the celebrated Venetian traveller to the end of the eighteenth century I do not think mention was made

---

Great Andaman, and which is now known to consist of three islands separated by three narrow channels.

* M. de Saint-Pol Lias and M. de la Croix had been charged with a scientific mission by the Secretary of Public Instruction. M. de la Croix intends shortly to publish his observations on the peoples in question. I have to thank him all the more for having put at my disposal those photographs and notes of which I shall make use later on.

of these islands. In 1790 the English tried to found there
a naval establishment (Fort Cornwallis), which was soon

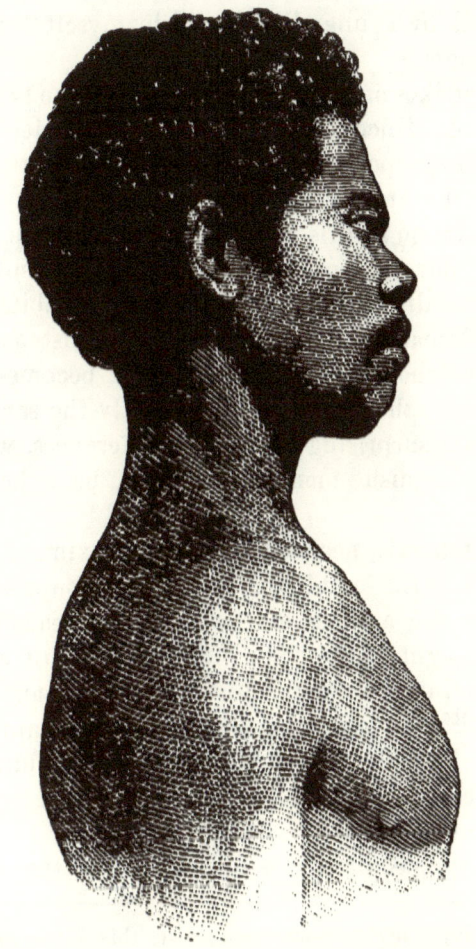

Fig. 17.—Aëta. (After a photograph of M. Montano.)

given up. The project was revived and carried out only
in 1857. The new establishment (Port Blair) brought
thither numerous observers, among whom it is only just

to mention especially Dr. Mouat [124] and Mr. Man. Charts, drawings, photographs, skulls, and whole skeletons arrived in Europe and were studied by R. Owen [131, 130] and Busk [24] in England, by Pruner-Bey [140] and by myself [148] in France, and by others.

What strikes one at once in examining the twenty-three portraits of Mincopies is the great similarity they present in the proportions of the body, the features of the face, and the almost identical physiognomy. There is nothing strange in this fact. Isolated from the world for centuries, marrying only among themselves, subjected to the same conditions of existence, these inhabitants of the Great Andamans have become uniform, just as a race of animals watched by a careful breeder becomes uniform. As, moreover, the two sexes lead exactly the same kind of life, it is not surprising that many differences, which elsewhere distinguish men and women, have here disappeared.

Measurements, necessarily only approximate, upon the young girl in the middle of one of the groups of Dobson have given me a little more than seven heads lengths as the total height of the body. The same result was gained from studying the portrait of John Andaman, published by Mouat.[126] In this respect the Mincopies approach the Egyptian Hercules measured by Gérard Audran;* and as their head is also broad, it results that it is large in proportion to the rest of the body.

The same peculiarity is found among the Aëtas. It

---

* According to this celebrated artist, this Hercules measured 7$\frac{18}{?}$ heads. The Pythian Apollo, which represents the other extreme of measurements taken by Audran, was 7$\frac{12}{?}$. It is known that Audran divided the head into four equal parts, which he again divided into twelve minutes. To make this result more readily comparable, I have reduced all these fractions to a common denominator.

is true that I have only been able to measure one of the individuals photographed by Montano, the others having too great an abundance of hair covering their heads. In this individual the total height would hardly equal seven heads. So far as it is possible to judge, it is nearly the same among the Sakaies of M. de Saint-Pol.

There is nothing surprising in this. Quételet has well shown that among ourselves the proportion spoken of varies with age and with the stature. The proportion of the head to the entire body is much larger in the child and the dwarf* than in the adult and the giant.[159] This is a result of the operation of morphological transformation which begins after birth. We must, then, expect to find among the Negritos a relatively larger head than among ourselves.

Among all Mincopies, men or women, the body is nearly of uniform width, and scarcely enlarges around the hips and the trochanters (Fig. 4).† With this exception, both sexes are well proportioned. The breast of young girls is very small and conical; in women it remains full, and falls very little. The chest and shoulders of both sexes are large, the pectorals very strong, arms and forearms muscular but well rounded, the hands rather small than large, have long fingers, well separated, at times of very elegant shape, terminated by long and narrow nails.

---

* The question is here only of true dwarfs, and not of microcephalic individuals, too often confounded with them. I have insisted upon this distinction in a note relating to the true dwarf known under the name of *Prince Balthazar*.[145]

† See [155], Fig. 114. From the cut we can easily form an opinion of the anatomical characteristics. I have already made this remark in my first memoir. Giglioli urges against me that one of the women observed by him is quite large around the hips. If it is so, this woman is not represented in the engraving which he has published.[59, 60]

7

The abdomen is not very prominent. The lower limbs have the same general characters as the upper ones. The thigh and leg are, however, often less fleshy than the arm and forearm, and the calf is usually a little high, at least in the women. This latter characteristic, to which I called attention in my first work as recalling what exists among African Negroes, is lacking in the only man whose legs can be well seen in the phototypes of Dobson. In him the calf, very pronounced, is perfectly well-formed.* The foot, finally, in the rare cases where it is placed so as to be easily seen, is small, high-arched, and the heel does not project behind.†

Montano's photographs of the Aëtas show almost entirely similar characteristics in the whole upper part of the body (Figs. 6 and 17). Here also chest and shoulders are large, the pectorals well developed, the arms fleshy and likewise without any conspicuous muscular protuberances. But the waist line of a certain number of men and women is conspicuous, and narrows in; above all, in both sexes, with the exception of two or three women, the lower limbs are much less fleshy than the upper ones, and sometimes are really thin. From this, and also from the pose adopted by the operator, the feet—at least of a part of them—seem to be much thicker and larger than those of the Mincopies (Fig. 6).

It is quite different with the Sakaies, particularly with those whose hair indicates them to be true Negritos. Their

---

* [42] This same individual is remarkable in his whole appearance. Everything about him indicates strength. His chest is large, the pectorals very well developed, as is, however, the case with all the men; his thighs are very fleshy. And yet we find again that roundness of contour and absence of muscular prominences which occurs among so many savages, and particularly in America.

† Colonel Fichte had already called attention to this feature as distinguishing the Andamanese from the African Negro.[50]

lower limbs are quite as well developed as the upper ones (Fig. 8). One of them particularly is remarkable for the thickness of his legs and arms without the roundness of contours being lost. All have the calves situated where they should be according to our European ideas, and the feet seem to resemble those of the Mincopies. At all events, the heels do not markedly project.

The resemblance of the Mincopies to the African Negro is really limited to their hair and complexion. In all my photographs the head is shaved, but the unanimous testimony of travellers can leave no doubt as to the woolly quality of the hair. Fichte, Mouat, etc., have added that the hair seems to grow in tufts, and that it forms curious little round balls, so often described by various travellers among the Papuans. Giglioli has established the accuracy of this information by two photographs.[60] The portraits of Aëtas and of certain Sakaies show that this characteristic is exactly the same with them. There results from this, in crosses, wavy, curly, or even crimpy hair (according to the degree of the mixture of blood), very different from that of the Malay peoples. On his part Flower has discovered that the cross section of this hair often presents a more elongated ellipse than that of any other human race.

All travellers affirm that the Aëtas, like the Mincopies, have a skin pronouncedly black.* As to the more or less crossed tribes of Malacca, their skin seems to have generally become lighter by the mixture. Montano describes, in one of the notes kindly written to me, those he observed in the neighbourhood of Kessang † as having frequently

---

* Only Symes and Colonel Fichte have spoken of a *sooty black*. I have already remarked that this opinion, no doubt, is based on their having seen individuals who still had on them traces of the yellowish soil with which these islanders are prone to cover themselves in order to protect themselves against mosquitoes.

† North of Malacca.

an almost sooty skin.* To judge from the photographs,
the tint seems at times to be darker. A statue of black
bronze would not give any other photographic result
than the robust Sakaie of whom I have already spoken
(Fig. 8).

Despite the resemblance of hair and colour, it would
be impossible to confound a Mincopy with a true African
Negro. The shape of the head and the features of the
face are too different. The head of the former, seen from
the front, looks almost round, instead of being compressed
and lengthened; the forehead is large, and often arched,
instead of being narrow and receding.† The face becomes
much broader at the cheek bones, which gives the cheeks too
much breadth; the ears, which stand out markedly on these
shaved heads, are small, and elegantly shaped; the nose,
very much sunken at the root, is straight and rather short,
and the nostrils, generally little separated, are sometimes
narrow.‡ The lips, without being very fine, are not thick,
and have nothing recalling those of the Negro; above all,
they are little or not at all sticky at the edges. The chin
is small, round, and little or not at all receding; there is
no prognathism, or scarcely any. The men rarely have
any trace of beard.#

In examining the numerous photographs which I have,
many individual differences can be recognised, and yet it
is impossible not to be impressed by the uniformity of
physiognomy common to nearly all. This is no doubt

* Unpublished note, communicated by Dr. Montano.

† This feature is very striking in the only woman, seen in profile
in the photographs of Colonel Tytler, of whom I have given a sketch
(Fig. 3). All the individuals represented by Dobson have been
taken full face; also those in the engraving of Giglioli.

‡ For instance, in the chief figured by Dobson, pl. xxxi.

The body is equally free from hair, except in the usual places
(Fig. 4).

partly due to the fact that the features in general really
differ but little, but perhaps particularly to the shape
and position of the eyes. These organs, quite protruding
and round, are well to the sides, and separated by a very
noticeably larger space than our own,* which makes the
expression of the face somewhat peculiar and strange.
Their eyes, however, are brilliant and very good, as is the
case with almost all savages.

This separation of the eyes is not found so generally,
nor to the same degree, among the Aëtas. It is not surprising, then, that the physiognomy of these two populations differs. Moreover, although the features may be variations of one type, they are usually coarser among the Philippine blacks. The forehead is broad and arched, as can
be seen when not covered by the hair; but the root of
the nose has become flatter, the nostrils are wider, and
spread more; the lips have become thicker, but do not
equal those of the Negro, and their commissure is somewhat clammy, as with the latter. The chin, finally, re-
treats, without, however, being as receding as that of the
Negrito-Papuan (Figs. 16 and 17). The Aëtas seem,
moreover, to be as smooth as the Andamanese, unless
changed by crossing.

The photographs of M. de Saint-Pol show that the
Negritos of Malacca in features resemble more the Aëtas
than the Mincopies. Behold how the traveller expresses

---

* This characteristic is well marked in the photographs of Tytler
and in the phototypes of Dobson; it is, on the contrary, lacking in
almost all the individuals in the engraving published by Giglioli.
Moreover, the physiognomy of these engraved faces does not at all
resemble that just spoken of. The shape of the head also sometimes
differs absolutely from that in my photographs and from the description given by the author (p. 249). I will mention particularly
that of the large individual standing at the left. Are these individuals crosses, or is it the fault of the artist, who has badly reproduced the photograph?

the impression made upon him by the sight of about
forty Sakaies: "In closely examining all these faces,
generally sympathetic, animated, and laughing, one can
soon distinguish characteristics of two races, of which the
one is plainly the Negro race, in spite of the colour of
the skin. The nose is straight, but the nostril is very
broad and the wing very spreading. Some have very curly,
crinkly, or even woolly hair, although the majority have
long, straight, or wavy hair. There is no prognathism
among them.[168] It would be so with the Negritos of
India if the individual figured by Rousselet should be
placed in this group. But it is necessary to admit at the
same time that the type had been much deteriorated by
the deplorable conditions of existence of the Djandals of
Amarkantak (Fig. 10). The forehead is depressed; the
nose has grown larger; the lips have become thicker, but
not elongated, as those of the Negrito-Papuan; the chin
has remained fairly receding. Despite this physical degeneration, these unfortunate blacks have not taken on
the well-known physiognomy of the African Negro, much
less that of a monkey or any other animal. I have already
said that they rather seem to incline toward the Papuan
type, of which it would not be at all strange to find some
representatives on the continent. On the other hand, the
Oraon and the two Santals figured by Dalton incontestably recall the Negrito type, as do also some of the Mulchers figured by Fryer.

This description would be incomplete if I did not say
a few words about the skeleton. But here I shall be brief,
and shall refer the reader to the technical works. The
skeleton of the Mincopies, in spite of its being so small,
shows no sign of degeneration or weakness. The bones
are relatively pretty thick; the muscular impressions, always well marked, are sometimes remarkably conspicuous.
The proportions of all the bones compared with each

other, the shape of the pelvis, etc., resemble, on the whole, those of the Australian or the Negro. Nevertheless, the discussion of the measurements published by Owen has led Broca to make a curious observation. If the length of the humerus is taken at 100, that of the radius is 81·53, and that of the clavicle 42. By the first proportion, the Mincopy differs from the European more than the Negro does; by the second, he differs from the Negro more than the European himself does.[18] It is quite different with the head. The Australian and the true African Negro are dolichocephalic. All Negritos are more or less brachycephalic, as I have already stated (Figs. 2, 5, 12, 15, 18). The Mincopies are found to have this characteristic.* It is connected with others which give to the skull quite a special character, and often enable us to distinguish it at a glance. Moreover, individual differences are as little marked in the skeletons as in the living. Flower has called attention to this uniformity, and declared that among no other race, without making intentional and systematic choice, would it be possible to find such a large number of heads so like each other. It is clear that the causes suggested above have rendered the osteological as well as the exterior features very uniform.

The head of the Mincopy, although large in proportion to the body, is absolutely very small.† Seen from

---

* Hamy and I had found as the horizontal index of the Andamanese 82·38 for the man and 84·00 for the woman. The measurements of Flower, taken upon a larger number of heads, reduce it to 80·50 and 82·70. It is seen that the difference between the two sexes remains nearly the same, and that the woman is more brachycephalic than the man.

† The cranial capacity of the men, according to Flower, is only 1.244 cubic centimetres; that of the women, only 1.128. Broca had found higher figures, but he had only seven heads at his disposition. The latter observer gives, as the average cranial capacity of one hundred and twenty-four modern Parisians, 1,558 cubic centimetres of

the front, but *particularly* from behind, the skull is noticeably pentagonal. The face gives an impression of being massive, owing mainly to separation of the zygo-

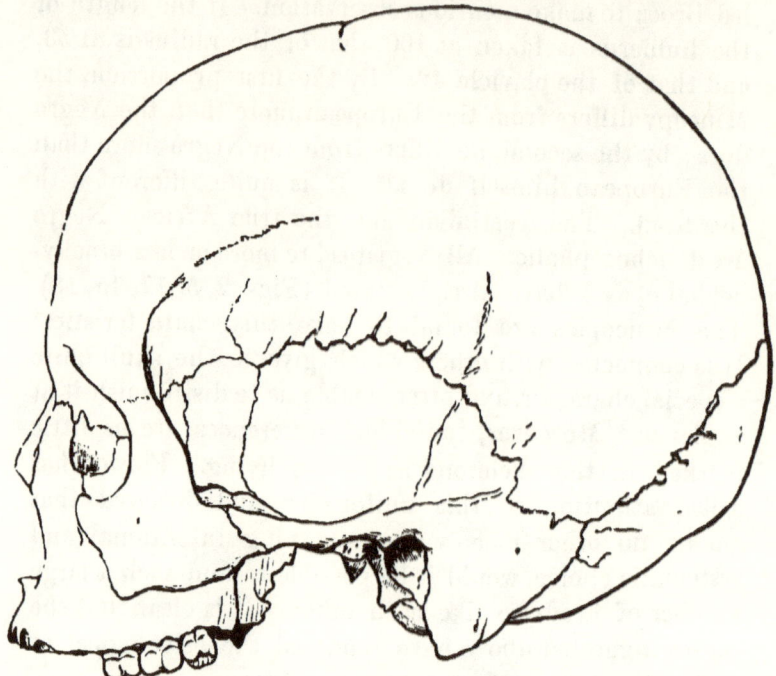

Fig. 18.—SKULL OF A MINCOPY OF THE GREAT ANDAMANS.

matic arches, to the little depth of the canine fossa, and to the direction of the ascending apophysis of the maxillary. Instead of hollowing in such a manner as

men and 1,337 of women. The lowest average he found was that of the Nubians (1,329 and 1,298 cubic centimetres). One sees that the Mincopies, as Flower thinks, would rank among the lowest of human races in this respect; but the observers have only given the rough numbers which they found, without taking the stature into account. But it is known that the weight of the brain increases and decreases almost in proportion to the stature, and it can hardly be otherwise with the case which encloses the brain.

to raise and narrow the skeleton of the nose, it rises directly upward. Consequently the interorbitary space is considerably enlarged, and the bones of the nose can only unite in a very obtuse angle. It can be seen that the form and disposition of these bony parts necessitate and explain the external characteristics pointed out above. Flower has insisted, as I did earlier, upon the peculiar features of the skull. They are just as marked among the pure Aëtas as among the Mincopies.

After having long and minutely studied twenty-four skulls of Mincopies, Flower wrote : " My actual impression is that I should never fail to recognise as such the skull of an Andamanese of pure race, and that I have never seen a single skull coming from any other part of the world which I could ascribe to any of these islanders."* These words of the eminent English anatomist make us understand how it is possible to follow up and recognise this type even very far from the places where it has preserved its purity. Craniological characteristics are very persistent. When crossing intervenes, they sometimes modify each other; but often, perhaps ordinarily, a sort of exchange takes place, and the two types are each represented on the head of the half breed by a certain number of perfectly well-marked features. When these characteristics are very peculiar, as those which I have just pointed out, they can at once be recognized. Thus, at a time when our opinion must have seemed somewhat paradoxical, Hamy and I were able to assert that the Negrito element had a more or less considerable part in the formation of the populations of Bengal and of Japan.

From the physiological point of view, we have hardly

---

* The same traits, though less accentuated, are found among the Negrito-Papuans.

anything to say about the Negritos but what a number
of travellers have reported in regard to almost all savage
peoples. Nevertheless, the Mincopies, who have been
most seriously studied in this respect, have some peculiarities which it will be interesting to point out.

Although true Negroes by the colour of their skin, the
Mincopies do not exhale that repulsive odour which seems
to characterise all the African Negroes, and their breath
is sweet unless they have eaten something which makes it
unpleasant. Man particularly mentions the flesh of the
turtle as producing this effect.

But, in spite of their tiny figures and round forms, the
muscular strength of these islanders is relatively great.
They use with ease bows which the strongest English
sailors could not even string.*   Man observes, with justice, that habit counts for a good deal in this practice.
But more than skill is necessary to shoot an arrow
pointed with shell, so that it pierces the clothing of
Europeans and enters deep into the flesh, at a distance
of forty to fifty metres.

In speaking of the rapidity of their running, Mouat
uses the ball, the bullet, as terms of comparison. The details given by Man would lead us to think that there was
some slight exaggeration here. But one point on which
the two observers agree is in regard to the acuteness of
the senses. Mouat tells us that the Mincopies distinguish by their odour fruits hidden in the thick foliage of
the jungle. Man asserts that they recognise by means of
smell only on what flowers bees have gathered the honey
which they seek. Sight and hearing are also extremely
delicate. The first of these senses, however, is more developed among the tribes who live in the jungle, and the
second among the inhabitants of the coast. The latter

* Mouat.

during the darkest night pierce with their harpoons the turtles which come to breathe at the surface of the water, guided only by the very feeble noise which these make at such a time.

The life of the Mincopy is short, although the length of the period of development is nearly as great as with us. Men reach puberty at about sixteen, women at fifteen; but the average duration of life is only about twenty-two years, and fifty is for them extreme old age.

The pathological history of the Mincopies presents some features which deserve our attention. A Sepoy deserter who lived long among them, and from whom Mouat and Owen have received much information, has mentioned the diseases from which these islanders suffered before the arrival of the Europeans. He gives asthma, rheumatism, diarrhœas, intermittent fevers, etc. He formally declares that he has not observed either syphilis or eruptive diseases; he does not even mention phthisis, and from his silence we may conclude that during his stay this disease was as unknown at the Andaman Islands as it formerly was in the archipelagoes of the Pacific, which to-day are depopulated by it.* The founding of the penal establishment has sadly changed this state of affairs. Man gives precise details on the subject. Some Hindoo convicts brought syphilis, which was rapidly propagated among the whole population, owing to the custom of the women of giving the breast to all sucklings

---

* I have long accounted for the strange mortality among the Polynesians by phthisis.[141] I have been more affirmative in a work published under the title Les Polynesians et leurs migrations. I can to-day be still more so, as recent studies have demonstrated that phthisis not only causes the death of the individual, but also his sterility. Thus the extreme mortality and the singular decrease of births which concur in the extinction of the Polynesians can both be explained.

of the tribe. Smallpox, it is true, had not appeared at the Andaman Islands before the departure of our informant, but in 1877 the greater part of the population were stricken by the measles, imported by convicts from Madras, and about one fifth of the sick died.

FIG. 19.　WILLIAM LANNEY.

Man gives phthisis as one of the diseases that he observed, but I have just given the reasons which lead me to regard it as being recently introduced. This conclusion seems to me confirmed by the fact which Ellis has recently pointed out.[47] The painful phenomenon found in Oceanica wherever Europeans have arrived is found again at the Andaman Islands. Here, as well as at Tahiti, at the Marquesas Islands, and at New Zealand, mortality has considerably increased, while births have at the same time decreased. The number of deaths far exceeds that of births.

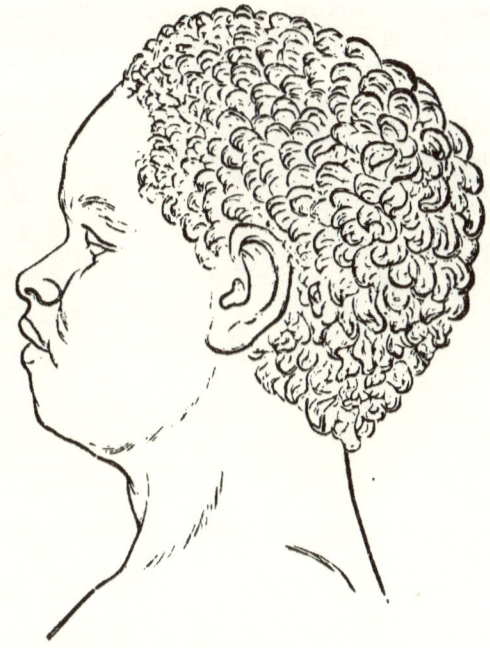

Fig. 20.—Truganina, or Lalla Rookh. (After the bust cast by Dumoustier.)

The population of the South Island, which at the time it was taken into possession numbered fifteen hundred souls, was reduced in 1882 to five hundred. In twenty-four years it was diminished by two thirds. It is evident that phthisis is at work in this little archipelago; and although there has not been there any *black war*, and the English have treated these islanders in an almost paternal manner, yet the Mincopies are destined to disappear within a few years, just as the Tasmanians have disappeared.*

---

* The race which used to people Tasmania is at present represented only by a few mixed breeds. The last man of pure race, William Lanney, died in 1869 (Fig. 19); the last woman, Truganina, the heroine of the *black war*, died in 1877 (Fig. 20). The English colonists have been considered responsible for this total extinction of a human race, and surely their conduct towards the natives has furnished serious reasons for this accusation. But I have shown elsewhere that the principal cause of the disappearance of the Tasmanians has been what I then called *le mal d'Europe*, which at present is, for me, nothing but phthisis.[144, 155]

CHAPTER IV.

INTELLECTUAL, MORAL, AND RELIGIOUS CHARACTERS
OF THE MINCOPIES.

Intellectual Characteristics of the Mincopies.—Language.—Translation of the Lord's Prayer.—Relation of the Mincopy to the Dravidian languages.—Poetical dialect.—Diversity of languages. —Numeration: Remarkable poverty.—General intelligence.— Social state: Tribes.—Hierarchy.—Family.—Monogamy.—Horror of incest. The *Guardian of Youth.*—Nuptial ceremonies.— Nursing of infants.—Adoptions.—Names.—Initiations.—Delicacy in social relations.—Property.—Hospitality.—Quarrels.— Wars.—Funerals.—Mourning.—Preservation and use of bones. — Industries.—Fire.—Drawing.—Music.—Dwellings.—Pottery. —Weapons.—Utensils.—Comparison with the Tertiary man of Thenay.—Dress: Ornaments.—Food. *Moral Characteristics.* —Ideas of crime and sin.—Shame.—Corrupting influence of Europeans. *Religious Characteristics.*—A supreme God.—His family.—Evil divinities.—Sun and moon.—Triple nature of man.—Hell and paradise.—Migration of the soul.—Resurrection.—The first men.—The Deluge.—Legends.—Various superstitions.—Elevated religious ideas among savages.—Binouas.— A supreme God and Shamanism or Fetichism.—Various examples.—Conclusions.

So far as physical characters are concerned, I have been able to compare the Mincopies and the other Negritos point by point. In passing to the intellectual, moral, and religious characters, it is very difficult to do the same, because too often we lack information on the subject now among one, now among the other of the black populations of the continent and the great archipelagoes of the extreme East.

The Mincopies only, are at present well known to us, thanks particularly to the publications of Mr. Man. Connected for eleven years with the penal establishment at the Andaman Islands, charged for four years with everything that concerned the government and the direction of the natives, this man of intellect and heart became attached to these islanders, learned their language, gained their confidence, and endeavoured to make us acquainted with them from every point of view. He has placed at our disposition a veritable monograph.

I have thus been led to take them again as a type and to give first their history exclusively, only putting at the end of this sketch—which would be quite complete in itself—the little that we know about their brethren.

INTELLECTUAL CHARACTERS.

Language.—Linguistic studies being entirely foreign to me, I can only present here the information obtained by travellers and linguists without discussing it, although allowing myself to make a general observation thereon.

Of all the languages used by the Negritos, that of the Mincopies would without doubt be the most interesting to study. Owing to the almost complete isolation in which these islanders have lived, particularly on the islands of the Great Andaman,* their language could not

---

* It is well known at present that the lands until recently spoken of as the Great Andaman consist in reality of three islands separated by narrow channels.[101] In my first Étude sur les Mincopies et la race negrito en général, I showed that some signs of mixture are found in the Little Andaman, lying south of the former.

have altered except by natural evolution without foreign influence. But this language surely dates very far back, and has probably preceded all those at present spoken at Malacca, at Siam, and perhaps even in India. Under these circumstances a knowledge of it would certainly be of the greatest interest from the ethnological as well as from the linguistic standpoint.

Man seems to have comprehended this. Before him, Symes, Colebrooke, Roepstorff, Tickel, and others, had contented themselves with collecting brief vocabularies. Being in daily contact with the natives in consequence of his official duties, Man learned their languages, as I have already said; he has made them the subject of several publications; * he has collected a vocabulary of about six thousand words; † he has translated into one of them the prayer which all Christians repeat, and has published it with a commentary and notes by Lieutenant R. C. Temple.‡ Colonel Lane Fox has reproduced this translation [83] in two communications, and has given, altogether too briefly, the general conclusions of the authors. I translate literally what he says on the latter, and believe myself to be useful and agreeable to readers engaged in linguistic studies in transcribing the document which has served as a starting point for this study. This translation is in the language of the tribe occupying the south of the Great Andaman, where Port Blair, the English establishment, is situated.

---

* Independently of the work which I especially quote here, Man has given elaborate details in his book,[101] pages 49, 195.

† It is principally upon this vocabulary, and upon entire phrases given by Man in the appendix F of his book,[101] that Ellis has based his work which I quoted above.

‡ The Lord's Prayer, translated into Boyig-ngi-ji-da by E. H. Man, with preface and notes by R. C. Temple. Calcutta, 1877.

8

He Maw-rô kŏktâr-len   yâtĉ   môllâdûrû   Ab-Mâyôla.
Oh Heaven   in   (is) where our (lit. all of us of)   Father.
Ngîa ting-len dai-î-î-múgû-en-inga îtân.   Ngôlla-len môllâdûrû
Thy name-to   be reverence paid   let.

You (to)   we all
meta mâyôla ngenâke ab-chanag iji-la bêdig Maw-rô kŏktâr-len tegî-
our chief wish for supreme only and Heaven in   is
lut-malin yatê ngîa kânik,   kū-ûbada   ârla-len ârla-len
obeyed which thy will, in the same way ever (daily always)
êrem-len îtan.   Ka-wai môllâardârû-len   ârla-nackan
earth on let.   This day   all of us   to daily (lit. daily like)
yât man.   Môllârdûrû   mol-oichik-len   tigrel yatĕ ôloichik-len
food give.   We all   us (to), i. e., against offend who   them
ârtîdûbû.   Môllârdûrû-len ôtig-ûjûnba îtân ya-ba dôna môllârdûrû-len
forgive.   Us all (to)   be tempted let not but   us all (to)
abja-bag-tek ôtrâj.   Ngôl kichi-kan kânake.
evil from   deliver. (Do) thou thus   order (i. e., Amen).

The study of the vocabularies alluded to had led Latham to admit some relation between the Mincopy and
Burman languages.[86] Pruner-Bey has pointed out some
features common to the Mincopy and the New Caledonian.
Hyde Clark thought he discovered in the Andaman language affinities with those of several peoples of Asia, Africa, and both Americas.[29]

In their first publications Man and Temple admitted
that certain relations exist between the Mincopy, Dravidian, Australian, and Scythian languages. In returning to the subject the latter of the two collaborators has
developed and systematised his opinions, which I briefly
repeat.[101]

For Mr. Temple the Mincopy languages are, above all,
purely and simply agglutinative. They form, however, a
special group, perfectly distinct from all others, in that
they at the same time make large use of affixes and suf-
fixes. In the use of the former they do not differ from
other agglutinative languages; in the use of the latter they

follow, the author says, the well-known principles of the South African languages. This complete development of the use of two kinds of particles is, in Temple's view, a unique exception. To the presence of certain prefixes he attributes the ability of the Mincopies to frequently form long compound words of an almost polysynthetic nature, and which sometimes represent a complete sentence.

In view of these divers opinions it is difficult not to think of the relations pointed out by so many linguists, among others by Maury, as existing between the African and Australian Dravidian languages.* To those mentioned, Man and Temple add a third linguistic group, but the latest recognised has probably preceded the other two in time. Everything tends more and more to demonstrate that the Negrito race, of whom the Mincopies are the purest representatives, form the fundamental Negro element of all, or of almost all, Dravidian tribes, and also of those who, without speaking a language of that name, resemble the Dravidians in physical characters. If this is so, would it not be allowable to expect that the *substratum* of this linguistic family would be found in Mincopan languages? At all events there is an interesting problem for solving, and we can only hope that Man and Temple may pursue their researches, which have already led to such curious results.

Independent of their usual language, the Mincopies have a poetic dialect which they use in their songs. Here, says Man, everything is subordinated to rhythm, and the composer enjoys the most perfect liberty. He modifies not only the form of words, but also the grammatical construction. The example quoted by our author seems

---

* Maury [112] is, moreover, inclined to connect these two groups of languages with the Medo-Scythian, probably spoken, he says, by the native tribes of Media and Susiana.

to me to justify his claims, although I am a judge of no great competence.*

Man several times states an important fact—viz., that there are in the Andaman Islands as many distinct languages as there are tribes. "The difference," says he, "is such that it would be as utterly impossible for an inhabitant of the North Andamans to make himself understood by a native of the South as it would be for an English peasant to make himself understood by a Russian." [83]

Mr. Man enumerates eight tribes in the four islands constituting the Great Andaman, and these four islands scarcely equal in size one of our ordinary departments.† There are four tribes in the Middle island alone, which contains not quite half of the total territory. The number of these languages, spoken by peoples of incontestably the same race, themselves admitting their common origin, and located side by side in such a limited territory without being separated by any real barriers, is certainly one of the most curious facts, contrasting strangely with what exists in Polynesia.

One knows that here (Polynesia), in spite of space and extended migrations, the original language has given rise only to dialects; so that inhabitants of Tahiti, Easter Island, or New Zealand can at once understandingly talk to each other. Moreover, the Mincopies have preserved

---

* The usual phrase *Mija yadi chebalen la kachire* (who missed the hard-backed turtle?) becomes, in the refrain of a song, Cheklu ya laku mejra.

† The lands long known as the Great Andaman have been recognised as four distinct islands separated by narrow channels, and have been named North, Middle, and South Andaman and Rutland. These islands extend almost directly north and south, and are together not more than two hundred and fifty kilometres long, and at their maximum about thirty-two kilometres wide. (Map of the Andaman Islands, illustrating the distribution of the tribes.[101])

the memory of a time anterior to the division of the tribes and separation of the languages. I shall return to this point in speaking of their traditions.

Mr. Man has thoroughly learned only one of these languages, and has taken care to announce that all details given by him apply only to the one spoken by the Bojigngijida of the South Andaman Island.* I cannot follow the author in this subject, and limit myself to calling attention to the multiplicity of words used to express possessive pronouns and adjectives, according to whether the object is inanimate, a human being, parts of the body, or relatives of a certain degree. Man enumerates seven different words relating to the head, to the limbs, to the trunk, etc., and eight words applicable to the mother, son, older or younger brother.

The preceding remarks, although very incomplete, are sufficient, I think, to show what a mistake it was to represent the Mincopan languages—as has been done quite recently—as being in a rudimentary stage and comprising only a small number of words, most of them monosyllabic.

Numeration.—This at least relative richness of the language in general makes its excessive poverty as to numerals all the more striking. The Andamanese has cardinal numbers to express only *one* and *two*. From these he counts to ten by touching his nose with each of his fingers successively, and adding each time the words *this one also.* But further he does not go, and for any

* In his first communication Mr. Man wrote this name Bojingijida (Journal of the Anthropological Institute, vol. vii. p. 107). The syllable *da* at the end of both of these names is a particle added to most substantives or adjectives, and to several adverbs when they are isolated or at the end of a sentence. Its use being, however, arbitrary, Man habitually puts it into a parenthesis and writes Bojingiji (da).

higher numbers he has only the general terms *several,* *many.*

He has, however, six ordinal numbers. Furthermore, the words expressing these numbers are not always the same. They vary at times with the kind of individuals or objects spoken of, but beyond the sixth order general terms only are used. It is evident that the poverty of language in this respect betrays a gap in the intellectual functions of these islanders. The lack of numerical ideas has often been observed among various savage peoples, but I do not think that anything so complete has been stated in this direction. In this regard the Mincopies must be placed in the lowest rank of mankind.

They are scarcely more advanced as to astronomy, and are in this respect inferior to the Tasmanians and Australians, who distinguish various stars and constellations, with which legends are connected. The Andamanese have only given names to the belt of Orion and the Milky Way, which they call the Road of Angels. They have, however, known enough to recognise the four cardinal points and the phases of the moon in their relation to the tides, and they have divided the day of twenty-four hours into thirteen periods, each of them having a special name.

General Intelligence.—In spite of this inferiority of the Mincopies in regard to ideas which might be called scientific, other weaknesses which one may observe in their intellectual manifestations cannot be considered as due to a radical incapacity. Dr. Brander, for several years in charge of the hospital at the Andaman Islands, has very well remarked that their mind seems to be asleep in consequence of their savage life, but that it can be easily awakened. Experience has shown that up to the age of twelve or fourteen the little Mincopies are as intelligent as children of the same age among our middle classes. One of them, educated in the orphan school, read, wrote,

and spoke fluently English and Urdu, without having
forgotten his mother tongue. He had also learned arithmetic very well. Mr. Man adds that this is not an exceptional case ; that he could quote other examples of the
same kind, and among them a young man even superior
to the pupil spoken of by Dr. Brander. It may then be
fully admitted that a suitable education would soon place
the Mincopies on the level of peoples who at present are
much superior to them.

Social State—Tribes.—Meanwhile, until that time shall
come their social organisation already elevates them somewhat. Hitherto exclusively hunters or fishermen, they
have been subjected to the necessities imposed by their
mode of life. The population has been scattered about
in bits, so to say. We have seen that there are eight
tribes in what is called the Great Andaman. A ninth
inhabits the whole of the Little Andaman, and has, furthermore, sent colonies to Rutland and South Andaman
Islands, where they live in a state of continual hostility
with the tribes of local origin. The following are the
names and distribution of these nine tribes, according to
the last memoir of Mr. Man :

North Andaman : Aka-Chariar (da), Aka-Jaro (da).

Middle Island : Aka-Kol (da), Aka-Kédé (da), Oko-
Juwai (da), Aka-Bouig-Yab (da).

South Andaman and Rutland islands : Bojigngiji
(da).

Little archipelago : Aka-Balawa (da).

Little Andaman : Jarawa (da).

All the tribes of the old Great Andaman and of the
little archipelago adjoining it have the same customs and
the same industries, and recognise each other as sister
tribes. The inhabitants of the Little Andaman, as yet
slightly known, seem to be somewhat different, owing,
perhaps, as Man thinks, to the influence of the Nicobarese.

I have elsewhere called attention to a fact from which it results that this southern extremity of the archipelago has suffered some of those accidental minglings which it is almost impossible to avoid, which the Great Andaman seems to have entirely escaped.

It has been repeatedly affirmed that the interior of the Andaman Islands was not inhabited and was not inhabitable on account of the density of the jungles and the absence of fruit trees. These assertions have no foundation whatever.

It is a fact which Man has established beyond a doubt. As I have said above, each tribe comprises inhabitants of the coast (*aryoto*), and inhabitants of the interior (*eremlaga*), forming two great divisions, each having a great chief independent of the other (*maïaigla*). These two divisions are again divided into an indefinite number of little groups or communities of from twenty to fifty individuals, each with a secondary chief (*maïola*), who recognises the authority of the principal chief. But this authority does not amount to very much. Its privileges consist mainly in regulating the movements of the tribe or group and in organising their assemblies and feasts. Moreover, neither the great nor the secondary chief can punish or reward. Their influence, then, is entirely moral; but, for all that, it is none the less real and considerable, principally over the young unmarried men, who zealously serve the chiefs and do their hardest work for them. The office of chief is elective, but generally passes from father to son if the son has the desirable qualities.

The wife of the chief occupies among her companions a position analogous to that which her husband occupies among the men. She keeps these privileges when a widow, if she has children; otherwise she loses her lofty position.

Marriage, Family.—However simple and rudimentary

this social organisation may be, it answers all the needs of these little societies. It contradicts certain exaggerations, too easily accepted, regarding the Mincopies. What Man tells us relative to the constitution of the family shows still better how much these islanders had been calumniated by those who have accepted without investigation the reports of some travellers. Duradawan claimed that mother and daughter had been given to him in marriage. Brown and Sir Edward Belcher stated that the union of husband and wife ceases with the weaning of the child, and that the parties then become free. It was added that marriage as we understand it was unknown to them, and that there existed among them a veritable promiscuity. Basing my opinion upon some facts collected by Mr. Day,[40] I long since expressed the strongest doubts regarding these assertions and the consequences drawn from them. One will now see how far I was right.

Among the Mincopies, as among many other savages, the young people of both sexes enjoy equal freedom before marriage. But, Man adds, in spite of this liberty, the young girls preserve the strictest modesty in their manners. Various precautions are, moreover, taken to make too intimate relations difficult, or to stop them. When, however, a young girl becomes pregnant, the *guardian of youth* makes a sort of legal inquiry to discover the father of the child; he never refuses to make the reparation demanded, and marriage properly adjusts the position of the lovers.

The Mincopies are strictly monogamous. Bigamy and polygamy are unknown to them, and marriage is a serious matter with them. Children are often betrothed by their parents at a tender age, and, no matter what happens, this contract must be carried out soon after the young people have attained the required age. The young *fiancée* is considered as being already a wife, and any weakness on her part would be considered a crime.

Marriage between relatives is absolutely interdicted to the last degree of relationship recognised by these islanders. This rule extends to relationship by adoption, but not to relationship by marriage. Our marriages among cousins german are highly immoral in the eyes of the Mincopies, and they reproach us with it. Thus they justify again the general observation made by an English author, that it is " among the least civilised people that the greatest horror of incestuous marriage exists."

When a marriage is in question it is not the interested ones themselves who take the first steps. This duty falls upon the *guardian of youth* who also has to watch all relations among his subordinates and to recognise which ones may promise a permanent attachment. If a young man or widower is found sleeping in the hut of a young girl, marriage necessarily follows. But this union is considered irregular, and has a particular name—*tigwanga*; there is no ceremony connected with it, and it entails a certain loss of respect and consideration.

Marriage is purely civil. On the appointed day the company assemble in the hut of the chief. The bride remains seated, assisted by some women ; the groom stands, surrounded by the young men. The chief approaches him and leads him to the young girl, whose legs are held by several women. After some pretended resistance on the part of both, the groom sits down on the knees of his bride. Then torches are lighted, so that all present can attest that the ceremony has been regularly carried out. Finally, the chief declares the young people duly married, and they retire to a hut prepared in advance. There, Man says, they spend several days without speaking to or even looking at each other, receiving provisions and presents of all kinds, which friends busy themselves to bring to them, and soon their housekeeping equipment is complete. Finally, the young couple resume ordinary life, and then only is the marriage celebrated by a dance, in which the whole community, with the exception of young married people, takes part.

These marriages are happy. "The women," says Man, "are models of constancy, and their husbands do not yield to them in this respect." The woman is far from being a slave, as has been said, and the two live on a perfectly equal footing; their mutual relations are marked by courtesy and affection; each has particular duties, but is always ready to help the other if necessary. Altogether, Man concludes, the consideration and respect with which the Mincopy women are treated might advantageously be imitated by certain classes of our own populations.

To marry a second time is not forbidden, and the marriage of a widow with a younger brother of her husband is almost obligatory. Yet profound respect is shown to the widower or widow, who proves affection to the defunct by chastely living alone. It is not rare to see even young men remain faithful to the memory of their companions for several years, or even for their whole lives.

The mother nurses her children as long as she has milk. Consequently the function of lactation, kept up by practice, becomes, as it were, chronic, and not rarely two younger brothers may be seen sharing the breasts of the mother.

These children are tenderly loved, and yet they rarely stay with their parents after their sixth or seventh year, by reason of the custom of adoption, which has been developed to such a degree in these islands. Every married man received into a family requests, as an expression of gratitude and proof of friendship, the privilege of adopting one of the children of the family. The request is usually granted, and the adopted child changes his abode. The parents often go to see him, but they cannot take him with them, even temporarily, without permission of the foster father. He, moreover, can dispose of his adopted son as he can of his own, and may pass him over to a new adopter.

It has been said of the Mincopies that they have no proper names. Quite to the contrary, they have a somewhat complicated system of appellation.

As soon as a woman is pregnant the parents, as with us, begin to choose a name, which the child receives at birth. This name is always followed by a qualificative common to the individuals of the same sex, varying with the sex, which is kept until the age of two or three years. At this time the first qualificative is replaced by a second, which the young men keep until their initiation, which is described farther on, and for which the young girls substitute the name of a tree, the blossoming of which coincides with the appearance of signs of puberty. Eighteen kinds of trees have the privilege of thus decorating with flowers the young Mincopies, and Man has given the names of some of them. Once married and become the mother of a family, the woman loses her flower name. She takes the title of *chana*, which Mr. Man translates by *madam* or *mother*, and which is added to her name, like the preceding qualificatives.

From the age of eleven to thirteen begins for individuals of both sexes a period of abstinence, called *akayaba*, which for the young girls extends nearly to the time of their marriage, and for the young men to the time of puberty. While it lasts they cannot eat turtle, pork, fish, or honey—that is to say, the food forming the staple of their usual diet is forbidden to them. They must also abstain from the use of certain delicacies, such as the meat of the iguana, the larvæ of a large beetle, etc. They may, however, satisfy their hunger with any other native dishes. This kind of *taboo* can only be removed by the chiefs, who keep it in force until the time when the candidates have given sufficient proof of their perseverance.

The *akayabu* comprises three periods, named from the three principal kinds of food tabooed : the meat of the turtle, honey, and the fat of pork kidneys. At the expiration of each a feast is celebrated, during which the neophyte must observe silence, deprives himself of sleep for twenty-four hours, and then with ceremony eats one of those dishes, the use of which is henceforth permitted him.   The ceremony closes with a special dance, reserved for these kinds of initiations.

Everything concerning family relations is to the Mincopy of prime importance.   His language expresses this sentiment in a striking manner.   Mr. Man has given a list of seventy-one terms, each indicating a degree of relationship, and specifying at the same time the relation of age existing between the speaker and the person in question.

The practice of frequent adoptions adds greatly to this complication, from which comes also the idea that relationship does not extend to more than three generations.   Father and mother use different words in speaking of a son.   The former calls him *he whom I have begotten ;* the latter, *he whom I have borne.*   This in itself shows us what part these islanders attribute to each sex in the act of generation.

The distinction of ages is always observed.   In speaking to an older relative, the title *maïola*, which we have seen to be that of the secondary chief, is added to his name ; in speaking to a younger relative, he is called by his name only.   The same distinction is observed in regard to women, but the terms are different.

Within families the relations between the individuals

of the two sexes show great delicacy. The man observes the greatest reserve toward the wife of a cousin or younger brother. He can only address her through a third person, and can never marry her. The wife of an older brother, on the contrary, receives from her brothers-in-law tokens of affection and respect such as are shown to a mother.

Property, Hospitality.—The preceding is no doubt sufficient to show that the Mincopies are anything but those barbarous and intractable creatures, nearer to brutes than to man, too often described. A mass of details, given by those few travellers who had seen them closely in their daily life, and particularly by Mr. Man, puts an end to these unjust assertions. I limit myself to point out two characteristic facts.

The rights of property are recognised and respected by these islanders. Territories of tribes are only bounded by rather undefined limits—a chain of hills, a belt of jungles, etc. ; nevertheless, they are rarely crossed without a formal invitation or special permission. Violations of this rule, though not frequent, entail almost always a bloody fight. Individual property is equally respected. " No Andaman Islander," says Mr. Man, " would take or disturb a weapon or utensil belonging to a neighbour." On the other hand, it is customary that the proprietor of a canoe, a vessel, or a plank drum should put them at the service of his community if he should be asked to do so.

Hospitality is one of the characteristic virtues of the Mincopies. Children, from their most tender age, are taught to respect guests and friends. In each family there is constantly kept a certain amount of food for visitors who may arrive. Strangers introduced by mutual friends are always warmly received by the whole community. They are the first served ; the best dishes that the camp contains are offered to them ; they are accompanied at their departure; before separating they clasp hands, and, instead of embracing, they blow at each other's faces; then they engage in an affectionate dialogue. Finally they separate with mutual promises of meeting again.

Quarrels, Wars.—Nevertheless, no more in the Andamans than elsewhere does life always preserve this idyllic character. Here, as everywhere, quarrels, strifes, and wars arise. The Mincopies are sensitive and quick-tempered. In such a case the one who considers himself damaged manifests his irritation usually by shooting an arrow near the offender; but at times he tries to hit him. Sometimes he is seized by a sort of frenzy, and begins to break and destroy everything that he can lay hands on, without sparing even his own property. In such a case he is considered as being *possessed*, and not responsible for his actions. This is, as can be seen, a sort of *amuck*, but less dangerous than that of the Malays, as it vents itself on things, and not on persons.

The bad instincts of the savage appear again in the war which sometimes breaks out among the tribes in the midst of an entirely peaceful feast. Of course all the property of the vanquished is carried off or destroyed. The wounded are massacred. Women and children suffer the same fate. The latter, however, are sometimes spared and kindly treated, in the hope of making of them so many members of the victorious tribe.

The Mincopies have always been accused of killing strangers thrown upon their islands by shipwrecks. They seem to have deserved this sad reputation. Duradawan, the Sepoy spoken of above, had not escaped alone; but all his companions were killed. These acts of ferocity are easily explained by the facts to which Lieutenant Blair,[15] one of the first explorers of these islands, called attention. The Malays and Chinese have for centuries frequented these islands in order to gather edible swallows' nests;

but on various occasions they have laid traps for the
natives, to catch and make slaves of them. It is natural
that a general spirit of distrust and hatred towards strangers should be the result of these treacherous and violent
acts. The English also were at first received by arrows
shot at them; but when the Mincopies saw that there
was nothing to fear, they quickly attached themselves to
these newcomers, and wherever the explorers went, accompanied by natives to introduce them, they were well
received.

Funerals.—Death, according to the slanderers of the
Mincopies, does not cause these islanders to manifest any
grief. On the contrary, these manifestations are usually
most lively, and the whole community takes part in them.
The funeral rites—for it is proper to use this expression—
are nearly the same for children as for adults. The former, however, are always buried in the midst of the camp,
while the latter are transported to the thickest part of the
jungle, where they are either buried, or exposed on a platform built at the bifurcation of two large branches.

On the death of a child the relatives and friends for
hours weep by the little body. Then, as a sign of mourning, they paint themselves from head to foot with a paste
of olive-coloured clay. Moreover, after having their heads
shaved, the men put a lump of the same clay just above
the forehead, and the women place a similar lump upon
the top of the head.

Eighteen hours are usually taken in making the toilet
of the dead. The mother shaves the head and paints it, as
well as the neck, wrists, and knees, with ochre and white
clay. Then the limbs are folded and wrapped in large
leaves held by cords. The father digs the grave under
the fireplace in the hut. When everything is ready the
parents say a last farewell to their dead by gently blowing
two or three times upon his face. Then one finishes the

wrapping in leaves, and places the corpse in a sitting position in the grave, which is immediately filled. The fire is lighted again, and the mother places upon the grave a shell containing a few drops of her own milk, that the *spirit* of her child may quench its thirst. The Mincopies believe, indeed, that one of the two principles which animate the body will haunt for some time its old abode. In order that it may not be troubled, the community leave their camp, after having surrounded the hut, or even the whole village, with a garland of rushes (*ara*), the presence of which informs any visitor that death has stricken one of the inhabitants and that he must depart.

During the period of mourning the village is abandoned. At the end of about three months they return, the funeral garland is removed, and the body exhumed. The father gathers the bones, cleans them carefully, and divides them into small fragments suitable for use in necklaces. The skull is carefully painted yellow, covered again with a sort of network ornamented by little shells, and the mother puts it on a string round her neck. After a few days the father in his turn wears this relic. The other bones are used to make necklaces, which the parents distribute among their friends as souvenirs. At the same time the lump of clay, which was worn until then as a sign of mourning, is removed, and the usual painting and ornaments are resumed.

However, all the ceremonies are not yet accomplished. On a day agreed on, the friends of the family gather about the hut. The father, holding in his arms the children left to him, chants some ancient song, the refrain of which is taken up by the women, while all assistants express their sympathy by noisy lamentations. Then the parents, after having executed the *dance of tears* (*titolatnga*), retire to their hut, while the dance goes on for several hours longer.

9

The manifestations of grief at the death of an adult are nearly the same as those just described. He also is buried in a sitting position, with his face turned towards the east. A fire is lighted on the tomb or under the platform which bears the body; a nautilus shell full of water and divers other objects are placed about him. The village is abandoned and surrounded by the *ara*. At the fixed time the bones are cleaned and distributed, to be used in necklaces. The skulls preserved in the camp are carried in turn for several hours by all the members of the community.*

Industries.—In regard to industrial achievements the Mincopies have been at once belittled and overpraised.

Let us first state the fact of one remarkable deficiency. It seems to be demonstrated by the researches of Mr. Man that these islanders know no means of making fire. They only know how to keep it alive. Man thinks that they must have originally taken it from one of the two volcanoes situated on islands near their archipelago. They themselves say that they obtained it directly from their supreme god, but in their traditions relative to it there are some facts which, it seems to me, would allow us to conjecture that their ancestors knew how to obtain fire by the process so common among all savages—of rubbing two kinds of wood together. However that may be, their

---

* The Mincopies are of existing peoples the only one among whom these singular customs in rendering homage to the dead have been found. But they may, perhaps, have existed among some of our Quaternary tribes. This hypothesis would explain the repeated discoveries of broken human bones and isolated skulls, since many other circumstances tend to do away with the idea of cannibalism. Perhaps it might be added that traces of these old practices could be found in the custom existing in some of our provinces, of distributing among relatives and friends objects which belonged to the deceased as reminders of the loved one.

present ignorance in this respect places them below all other human races—perhaps below all known peoples.*

It is evident that the preservation of fire must be the object of special cares. Man gives upon this point some details which it is needless to reproduce. He deprives the Mincopies, however, of the credit of an invention which Mouat had attributed to them.[125] According to this traveller, they preserved in the interior of large trees chosen for this purpose a perpetual fire. The fire, burning out the trunk downward, would have formed a kind of vertical furnace, where the glowing cinders were preserved almost indefinitely. Man sees in this description only a fable invented no doubt by Duradawan.

One may say that the Mincopies are unacquainted with the first rudiments of the art of drawing. Their masterpieces in this line consist of simple zigzag lines engraved upon their bows, pottery, or oars, the effect of which is sometimes quite pleasing.[101]

They seem never to have attempted to reproduce the form of an animal or a plant. In this respect they are below the Bushmen, or even the Tasmanians. Consequently there cannot exist among them anything resembling pictography. They have no means of communicating at a distance or of perpetuating their thoughts; only, when they want to indicate the way to follow in the jungles, they break or bend some branches in the direction to be taken.

The music of the Mincopies is also very rudimentary. It is a short musical refrain, which, indefinitely repeated, recalls somewhat those of certain dances still in use in

* The same ignorance has been ascribed to the inhabitants of some islands of Micronesia, but these casual observations need to be confirmed. It is known that the Tasmanians also were long represented as being incapable of producing fire, and this assertion was disproved later.

lower Brittany. To accompany these melodies our islanders have no instrument but a little board in the shape of
a truncated ellipse, which serves to mark time for the
dancers.[101] They are, then, inferior to all other savage
peoples, who have at least invented the drum.

The manner of life of the Andamanese tribes necessi-
tates frequent migrations within their territories. This
fact, poorly observed, has led to their being represented
as absolutely nomadic, without having any fixed dwellings, and as knowing how to construct only the simplest
shelter as a protection against rain or wind. Nothing of
the kind. The Mincopies have in reality three kinds of
huts; the simplest, of which they make use in their ex-
cursions, represent, so to speak, the tents of our soldiers.
They are quickly put up at each stopping place, and the
task is incumbent upon the women; but the men construct more substantial huts when a longer sojourn is projected. Finally, in the villages proper their dwellings are
made with great care, and are of considerable dimensions.
In the tribe of the Jarawas they are thirteen metres by
twelve. Poles set in the ground, cross-pieces attached to
them so as to form the framework of the roof, and palm
leaves artistically adjusted, make up the material of these
buildings, which can brave the most terrific rain storms.
Let us add that in the interior there are always mats or
leaves serving as beds. These huts are generally placed
around an elliptical space intended for dances. At one
end is what might be called the public kitchen. The boys
and girls sleep in special huts, to separate them from the
married people. This separation of the young people of
both sexes is observed even in the interior of the huts, and
this fact in itself contradicts certain assertions, too readily
accepted, in regard to these islanders.

Thus, as regards dwellings, the Mincopies show themselves superior to the Fuegians, and at least equal to the

most advanced tribes of Tasmania and Australia. In one other matter, whose importance is universally admitted, they are very superior not only to these peoples, but also to the most advanced Polynesians. They make pottery which stands the fire, and vessels in which they cook most of their food. These pots, generally with rounded bottom are made by hand, and are decorated on the outside with wavy or various cross lines, engraved by means of a wooden style. Their dimensions vary; the largest hold ten litres and more. The Mincopies also know how to make wooden vessels, to which they sometimes give the form of a double bamboo knot.

These islanders are not inferior in most primitive industries to any fishing or hunting populations. For instance, they make nets more than twenty metres long by five metres wide, with which they bar narrow creeks and the curves in streams. They have also arrows and harpoons, whose points are fastened to the shaft by a long cord. The animal struck unwinds this cord in trying to get away, and, hindered and stopped by the shaft which it drags along, it is easily caught. Nothing similar exists among many savages considered superior to the Mincopies.

Their bow also deserves a special mention. At the Little Andaman this weapon has the usual form, but at the Great Andaman it is entirely different. Here the middle, serving as a handle, is thick and cylindrical. The two side pieces are flat, relatively very large in the middle, and tapering towards the ends. They are, moreover, curved in contrary directions in the strung bow, so that it then resembles a much elongated S or a large integration sign. This arrangement results in protecting the hand of the archer from the shock of the string, which is stopped by the convexity of one half of the bow. The lack of symmetry in this weapon does not impair either its force or its surety. With a bow two metres long a Mincopy can at a distance of thirty to forty metres pierce a pine board four centimetres thick; at about a hundred metres he can still inflict a serious wound. It is a curious fact that the Mincopy bow has only been found elsewhere in some parts of eastern Melanesia, among others at Malli-colo—that is, among a population connected at least in part with a type of Negro very near the Andamanese.

Utensils of the Mincopies—Application to the Problem of the Existence of Tertiary Man.—The Mincopies have only the most rudimentary instruments with which to hew the trees and cut the poles which form the frame-work of their huts, or to shape their bows, hollow their vessels and canoes, and to carve the, at times complicated, designs with which they are decorated. In every way this part of their history is of special interest. It touches, moreover, the vigorous controversies in regard to our Euro-pean fossil races, and particularly those in reference to the existence of Tertiary man. I therefore consider it neces-sary to enter here into more elaborate details, and to repeat in part what I have elsewhere said upon this subject.[151]

The Abbé Bourgeois, in 1868, presented to the Con-gress of Prehistoric Anthropology at Paris flints which he believed to have been chipped by man. These flints had been collected by him in a deposit belonging to the Lower Miocene, in the village of Thenay, near Pontlevoy (Loir-et-Cher).[16] He concluded from this fact that man existed in Europe from the Tertiary epoch. This commu-nication was the starting point of discussions which are still going on. Three great objections were made to the conclusions drawn by the learned abbé from his discov-ery. The number of chipped flints seemed excessive; the fracturings which many showed were attributed to vari-ous causes entirely independent of the intervention of man; one emphasised the predominance of flints bearing no traces of human labour, and the *retouches* which the abbé and his adherents attributed to such labour were explained by the action of natural forces. Objections were also raised by some geologists, based upon the distribution of the flints in the layer in which they were found.

The history of labour among the Mincopies answers all of those objections which do not depend upon geology.

The Mincopies, to judge from one of their legends, have known iron for a long time; but before the arrival of the English they had to content themselves with what they could get from the few ships wrecked upon their coasts. Whenever they could procure any they hammered it cold between two stones into arrow points or hatchets, or rather that kind of adze which was their principal tool. But we can understand that this metal was very rare, and the Mincopies had, in fact, remained in the stone age. Although iron has become more abundant among them since the advent of Europeans, yet the quantity scattered among the natives is far from being sufficient for their daily wants. Man tells us that those tribes at a distance from the English establishment still are at the same point where their fathers were, and know even now scarcely any other tools. Even those close to the colony use by preference the first three kinds of stone instruments in the list which I am about to reproduce.

It is a singular fact that the oldest traditions of these islanders do not mention any stone as having served as blades for their hatchets or as points for their arrows. They used different shells for these purposes. Man mentions the *Perna ephippium* as having particularly been used to point arrows, and a kind of *Pinna* as having been employed as material for adzes. A species of *Cyrena* also was largely used in these tools. Bamboo and the bones of large fish and the spine of the tail of certain rays were also utilised in various ways.

Stone nevertheless played an important part in the industry of the Andamanese, and five tools or instruments made out of it are distinguished by particular names. I shall translate literally what Man says on the subject, adding some short reflections.

" 1. *Rarap*, the anvil."

From details given elsewhere it appears that this anvil consisted of a block of hard stone, more or less rounded.

" 2. *Taili-bana*, the hammer (smooth, rounded fragment of dolerite or fine-grained basalt).

" 3. *Talug*, whetstone, fragments of sandstone slightly micaceous."

Lane Fox has given a drawing and cross section of one of these whetstones.[101] It closely resembles certain of our prehistoric knives. These knives seem to be used exclusively to whet the edge of the points of javelins or of arrows.

" 4. *Tolma-loko-tug* (*quartz tooth*). These are small blades and splinters used for shaving and tattooing."

They are taken from veins of quartz, sometimes opaque and sometimes transparent, like crystal, or from semitranslucent pebbles of a bluish-white colour (Man).

" 5. *La*, cooking stone. These are common pebbles, about two inches in diameter, which are heated, and with which the foods to be cooked are covered."

Here we find a curious variation of the oven used throughout Polynesia. The Mincopies had not thought of scooping out the ground to utilise heat better and preserve it longer, but one sees that stones in the Andaman Islands play a similar *rôle* to that which has always been reported from New Zealand, the Sandwich Islands, Tahiti, and Tonga.

Mr. Man adds the following remarks, which I translate, italicising the passages relating particularly to the question which I have especially in view:

"When a new whetstone is needed, the Mincopies, not knowing the art of chipping stone, choose a block of sandstone. If it is too large, *it is put in the fire until it breaks.* The operator chooses the fragment corresponding best to his purposes, and shapes it by means of his hard, smooth, stone hammer. At the end of a little time the edge of the stone becomes blunted, but it serves for several months to give a finer edge."

In this passage Mr. Man contrasts the *whetstone* and the *fine stone.* It is to be regretted that the author here is too chary of detail. But it seems to me, from the *ensemble* of passages relating to this subject, that these stones are essentially used as *scrapers* (*racloirs* or *grattoirs*). As will be seen, these *knives* are the only stone utensils at the Andaman Islands which are really fashioned. There is there, it seems to me, a suggestion which might be applied to those found in our own country in such large numbers.

"*The small blades and splinters are never used more than once.* In fact, quite often several are used for a single operation. The sharp-edged splinters are used for shaving; those with a sharp point are used for tattooing or for sacrificial purposes.

"When the operation is finished, *these instruments are thrown away upon some pile of débris, or they are disposed of in some other manner.* Whoever happens to step on one of them, even unintentionally, runs the risk of great suffering. The manufacturing of these little splinters is considered one of the duties of the women, and there are those who habitually devote themselves to it.

"Two pieces of white quartz are necessary to obtain the small blades. They are neither pressed against the

thighs nor surrounded by a tight string to determine a
line of least resistance to the blows ; but *one of the stones
is first heated and then exposed to the cold* ; then, holding
it firmly in one hand, it is struck squarely with the other
stone. By this process the number of fragments desired
is obtained in a short time. A certain knack is no doubt
necessary to obtain the kind of splinter desired. The
smallest are made in the same way, without even using
pressure.

" No superstition is attached to these cutting stones.

" *The whetstones are never used to cut wood or bones.*
These last are habitually broken with the hammer to get
at the marrow. Before the introduction of iron, *little
holes were pierced with a fragment of bone or shell, perhaps rarely, if ever, with a stone. No instrument has
ever been found which might be supposed to have served as
a stone saw or scraper.* Shells, no doubt, were used for
this purpose."

I call the close attention of archæologists to the formal declaration put at the head of this paragraph. I have
said above that the whetstones absolutely resemble our
Quaternary knives. Could they have been used in the
same manner ? I am tempted to believe it. By the word
scraper Mr. Man certainly wished to designate the utensil
to which European archæologists have given the names
grattoir, racloir, and which is surely known to our readers. But, as I have already said, the brief allusions which
the English author makes show that the *whetstones* are
particularly used to scrape and smooth the blade, the edge,
or point which the Mincopies wish to sharpen. It is evident that they would do so if they had only shells, bones,
or a long point of wood hardened in the fire to point their
hunting weapons, and they have preserved the same process since they have possessed iron.

" In his note on the *Kjoekkenmoeddings of the Anda-*

man Islands, the late Dr. Stoliczka speaks of a *celt*, found in one of those heaps of refuse, as *a small but typical arrowhead*, and describes it as being made of Tertiary sandstone. *The Andamanese, however, maintain that never, even when iron was very rare, have they used stone for arrowheads, hatchets, adzes, or chisels.* They assert, besides, that the fragments found in the *kjoekkenmoeddings* and regarded as being one or the other of these instruments, were only quartz splinters or broken fragments of *cooking stones* or *whetstones*, which formerly as well as at present were thrown among refuse objects when they were no longer of any service."

But Dr. Stoliczka found more than this arrowhead.[178] He also found an axe, about two and a half inches long, which it would have been impossible, he says, to distinguish from celts of the neolithic period of Europe and Asia. He also mentions a real chisel, three inches long, with a sharp edge at one extremity. It is difficult to suppose that an educated man, even if not very familiar with such objects, should be misled in this regard so as to mistake a quartz splinter or the fragment of a knife for an axe or a neolithic chisel. I shall accept, then, the facts mentioned by Dr. Stoliczka as exact until more fully informed.

But these facts do not in any way affect the information gathered with so much care by Mr. Man.* They only teach us that the ancestors of the present Mincopies were more advanced than these, and in possession of industries now lost. It would be easy to cite analogous examples of degeneration. It is, moreover, evident that a people

---

* Several times Man dwells upon the care which he took to secure his information from those islanders whose customs had been least modified by the neighbourhood of Europeans, and from individuals who were regarded by their countrymen as being the best versed in their traditions.

capable of forgetting the means used by their ancestors to obtain fire could also more easily have forgotten the art of polishing, and even of chipping stone except by the rudest methods.

However that may be, we find at the Andaman Islands men who, as far back as their memory goes, and indeed probably for many centuries, have used stone in various ways, *but never to make from it either hatchets, chisels, saws, scrapers, piercers, lance points, or arrowheads.* The whetstones, razors, and lancets of the Mincopies do not need any retouching, and surely Mr. Man would not have failed to speak of it if this were practised. Evidently there is nothing to indicate any intentional chipping, except in the first-mentioned of these instruments.

But the Mincopy tribes, though knowing how to build substantial huts and having settled villages, are habitually wandering about in the territories belonging to them. They go from camp to camp, the length of their sojourn depending on the success of their fishing or hunting. Everywhere, Man tells us, they find the stones which they are in the habit of using. Consequently they scatter over the whole island, *among the stones that have never been used*, their cooking stones, more or less altered by fire ; the *débris* of the blocks broken in the fire ; fragments of whetstones no longer of value, which also show the action of the fire ; small blades and fragments of quartz showing no secondary chipping, and of which some, no doubt, bear also evidence of having undergone the action of heat.

And now let us return to Thenay. If we admit that in Tertiary times the plains of Beauce were inhabited by tribes leading the life of the Mincopies, having analogous industries, using stone as these islanders do, without, however, having yet developed the special art of chipping whetstones—that is to say, *knives* (*couteaux*)—almost all the facts which I mentioned at the beginning of this note are explained very naturally.

But in the midst of the most savage people, as among the most civilised nations, we always meet some men superior to their contemporaries. To these individuals I would attribute the small number of objects from Thenay which to my mind bear incontestable evidence of being shaped by an intelligent hand. Such are the scraper which the Abbé Bourgeois has shown me, and the piercers which at Brussels caused Tertiary man to be accepted by many eminent judges, among them D'Omalius, Cartailhac, Capellini, Worsaae, Engelhardt, De Vibraye, Franks, and others.

Thus we can very simply explain the existence and the small number of these exceptional specimens. If I am not mistaken, the ethnographic history of the Mincopies answers all the objections that can be made to the existence of the Tertiary man of Thenay, as far as these objections concern this man himself and his manner of life. I fully recognise that it does not remove all difficulties, but those remaining are exclusively in the domain of geology. They are not within my field, and I can only ask specialists for their solution. I hope they will find it.

Moreover, we fortunately have other proofs that man lived in Europe during the Tertiary period. The chipped flints of Puy-Courny, discovered by Rames in the Upper Miocene of Cantal, the incised bones found by Capellini in the Pliocene of Monte Aperto, would leave no doubt as to that. Finally, Ragazzoni has been so fortunate as to unearth the bones of a whole family buried in the Lower Pliocene of Castenedolo, and we know, thanks to him, that Tertiary man already possessed all the characteristics of the human species and belonged to the Canstadt race.

After this digression, let us return to our Mincopies.

Dress, Ornament.—The children of both sexes are

entirely nude. At the age of five or six the little girl
adopts the small apron of leaves (*obunga*) which constitutes her only garment, which she never thereafter leaves
off. The men usually have only a narrow belt (*tachonga*)
made of a cord, to which is attached a tuft of pandanus
leaves. Certain ideas of decency, or perhaps of simple
convention, seem to be connected therewith. Moreover,
here as everywhere, the women cover themselves as much
as they can with ornaments, which here consist of necklaces and girdles. One of these girdles, made of pandanus leaves (*rogun*), can only be worn by married women.

Both sexes tattoo their entire bodies in a very simple
way, by little horizontal and vertical incisions in alternat-
ing series. Man seems to think that no special signifi-
cance is attached to this practice. Some of the details
which he gives, however, would lead us to think the contrary. The women are generally charged with the operation, and, as instrument, employ a piece of quartz or glass;
but the first three incisions, made low on the back, can
only be made by a man, and with an arrow used for hunting wild pigs. Moreover, while these wounds are open
the patient must abstain from the meat of these animals.
These are, one sees, indications of a sort of initiation, or
of a rite, consecrated at least by usage.

Besides their tattooing, the Mincopies trace on their
bodies designs in clay of three different tints, the colour
and arrangement of which vary, according to whether the
individual is sad or gay, in mourning or preparing for a
feast. Finally, at certain times they cover their entire
body with a sort of clay paste, which, when dry, forms a
kind of crust or shell. This is one of the things they
have been reproached for doing. It was said that men
who covered themselves with mud could only be some
kind of pigs. In reality, the purpose of this practice is,
according to Mouat, protection against the bites of mos-

quitoes, and, according to Man, protection against the burning heat of the sun. To this antihygienic practice are perhaps largely due the frequent rheumatisms and diarrhœas reported among these islanders.

The Mincopies have long been considered one of the most miserable of populations, scarcely finding enough about them to support existence. Their imputed cannibalism was attributed to this cause. Day had already done partial justice to these assertions, when Mr. Man confirmed his statements and added precise details from which it appears that these islanders, so far as food is concerned, are in conditions far better than most tribes which have remained at the same social stage. The sea which washes their coasts is full of fish, and abounds in turtles; the jungles are filled with wild pigs; the bees furnish abundance of honey. To these three articles of food, which furnish the staple of their diet, are added some mammals and reptiles, more rarely captured, various birds, and several fruits and edible roots. This abundance of wild food readily explains how this population, so intelligent and industrious, has yet never felt the necessity of domesticating an animal or cultivating a plant; how it does not even know that rude form of gardening and farming met with among its sisters of the continent and of the Eastern archipelagoes.

To this matter of food supply are attached a number of superstitions really amounting to a veritable *taboo*. I have already mentioned some facts of this kind, but there are others yet more striking. Thus there are certain fruits and roots from which the Mincopies at set seasons abstain, in order to obey the commands of their supreme god, *Puluga*. We have here, then, a real religious practice.

The flesh of the dugong and of the porpoise is forbidden to every one who has not yet undergone the initiatory

ceremonies already mentioned. The pregnant woman
and her husband must also abstain from certain foods.
Moreover, every person is forbidden during his entire
life the use of some one definite food (*yattab*). A similar practice has been mentioned among some American
tribes.

MORAL CHARACTERS.

Notions of Crime and Sin.—The Mincopies have a
word—*yubba*—which Mr. Man translates as *sin, wrong-
doing*. This word, according to him, is applied to lying,
theft, grave violence, murder, adultery. All these acts
are regarded as arousing the wrath of Puluga, the creator. But more, in these little societies as in our greater
ones, they interfere with good order; and perhaps for
that reason they are ranked as misdemeanours and civil
crimes. There are other acts which, indifferent in themselves and only shocking religious ideas, are true *sins* in
our sense of the word. Such, for example, is the throwing of beeswax into the fire. The odour it gives out in
burning is most offensive to Puluga, who manifests his
anger by raising a tempest. Thus, when a Mincopy desires to damage some enemy who he knows is about to
take part in a hunting or fishing party, he burns some
beeswax in the hope of causing his foe to perish, or at
least of putting him to much distress. One sees that
these islanders have veritable wizards.

Thus these little Negroes, isolated through so many
centuries in mid-ocean, have moral ideas similar to our
own, and are attached to religious beliefs like those of
the most civilised peoples. Their conduct is generally
in accord with their principles. The crimes of rape, se-
duction, and unnatural vice appear to be unknown to
them.[102, 123] Adultery is very rare. In case of its occur-
rence, the injured party takes summary vengeance, without the intervention of a chief.

Some of the details already given show that modesty exists among the Mincopies. Man several times speaks upon this point. The woman who removes one of her girdles in order to make a present to a friend does it with a shyness which almost amounts to prudery. She never changes her apron before a companion. To do so, she always retires to some secret place. She acts like a European woman who removes her last article of dress; apparently she obeys the same instinctive impulse.

Mr. Man denies to the Mincopies that sort of courage which leads one to court danger for the pleasure of meeting it. In their wars they operate, so far as they can, by surprises, and only attack when they feel certain that they are the stronger party. In their first encounters with the Europeans, however, they conducted themselves gallantly, and displayed a great contempt for death. The Jarawas, the only tribe which has refused itself friendly relations with the English, still show the same warlike virtues. Mouat has brought into prominence the courage with which some of these islanders had braved firearms, and the expression of dignity which marked the face of a chieftain falling under a mortal blow. Man, however, sees in all this bravery only the consequence of ignorance of the power of our arms. But here he seems to me little just towards these islanders. It is plain that to-day the Jarawas must pretty well know the character and effect of European arms. All that our author relates of the mode of warfare among the Mincopies is much like what authors recount regarding the redskins; and who has ever denied the bravery of the Hurons and of the Delawares?

What precedes is applicable only to the islanders who have not yet come into close relation with Europeans. The contact of these savages with our compatriots has been not at all helpful. They have borrowed from the foreigners vices before unknown among them, in especial

10

the taste for strong drink and tobacco, the immoderate use of which appears to have seriously impaired their constitution. On the whole, says Man, the Mincopies in contact with civilisation have lost their characteristic virtues —their frankness, honesty, love of labour. Unfortunately, this is a remark one must make much too frequently.

RELIGIOUS CHARACTERS.

The Supreme God and Demons.—Man has assured himself of the very real existence of religious ideas and of legends connected therewith, by questioning those natives who were considered by these fellows as most *au courant* with local traditions, addressing himself also to those individuals who had had until then no intercourse with whites. It seems to me that we may accept with confidence the information he has collected. I shall, however, return to this question later.

I have already suggested that the Mincopies believe in a supreme god. Behold the terms in which Mr. Man summarises what they have told him. I translate literally:

1. Although he resembles fire, he is invisible.

2. He was never born, and he is immortal.

3. By him were created the world, all things animate and inanimate, except the powers of evil.

4. During the day he is omniscient, and knows the very thoughts of the heart.

5. He is angry when one commits certain sins. He is full of pity for the unhappy and miserable, and sometimes he deigns to help them.

6. It is he who judges the souls after death and pronounces for each of them its sentence (which sends them to paradise or to a sort of purgatory). The hope of escaping the torments which one endures in this latter place influences the conduct of the islanders.

Behold a truly lofty and spiritual conception! But the childish and crude mind of the savage shows itself very quickly in the ideas which the Mincopies have of the mode of life of their god. Puluga dwells in a great stone mansion in the sky; he eats and drinks; when it rains he descends to earth to gather food; during the dry season he spends most of his time in sleep. The foods which Puluga prefers are certain fruits, roots, and seeds. To touch these during the first half of the rainy season would so enrage the god that another deluge would be the result.

It is from the hand of Puluga that the Mincopies say they have received all that which supports them—mammals, birds, turtles. When one angers him he comes forth from his house, blows, thunders, and hurls blazing faggots. Thus are explained the dreadful tempests accompanied by violent gales, thunder, and lightning. One offends Puluga in very many ways. I have indicated the principal ones above. I will add that to cut up a pig badly, to cook it in an oven, or to roast its flesh are crimes deserving death penalty. Yet Puluga himself never kills the guilty. He points them out to a class of bad spirits called *chol*, and immediately one of these destroys them.

Puluga is not alone in his palace. He lives with a woman of green colour, whom he has created for himself, and who has two names, one of them signifying the "*mother eel*" (*Chanaawlola*). By her he has had a son (*Pijchor*), who lives with his parents and is their prime minister. There are many daughters. They bear the name of *spirits of heaven* (*Morowin*). They are a kind of black angels, who amuse themselves by throwing into bodies of fresh or salt water fishes and crustaceans for human food.

By the side of Puluga, the beneficent and just god, and by the side of these good spirits, the Mincopies have placed many spirits of evil. The most dreaded are *Erem-chawgala*, *Juruwin*, and *Nila*. These are self-created, and have existed from time immemorial. The first is the *demon of the forest*. He has had, by his wife *Chana-badgilola*, many children of both sexes. While the mother and daughters remain at home, *Eremchawyala* and his sons wander through the jungle, ready to pierce with their invisible arrows any one who remains in the darkness without bearing some firebrand, the light of which scares off the spirits.[101] Falling stars, meteors, are so many flaming brands which *Eremchawgala* hurls through the air to discover the unfortunate beings who may be in his neighbourhood. Hence, when they perceive one of these heavenly fires the Mincopies conceal themselves as much as possible, and remain some time silent before resuming their interrupted occupations.

Juruwin is the *demon of the sea*. He also has a numerous family. He possesses several submarine dwellings, and goes from one to the other, carrying in a net the fishes and human beings upon whom he subsists. Every fisherman who is taken with a cramp or experiences some sudden pain believes he has been stricken by Juruwin.

Nila is unmarried. He lives in ant-hills, and although always armed with a knife he rarely attacks human beings. He never kills and devours men, as he subsists upon dirt.

The *chol*, whom we have seen to be the executors of Puluga's vengeance, have a totally different origin. They descend from a common ancestor named *Maiachal*. This being was a man who perished miserably for having stolen a pig killed by one of his fellows. The spirit of the man could not go to Hades, but stopped upon the invisible bridge, to which I shall refer later on. There he lives, with his descendants, who, by Puluga's orders, have joined him under the form of black birds with long tails.

The sun (*Chanabodo*) is a female. The moon (*Maiao-gar*) is her husband. The stars (*Chats*) are their children. This brilliant family lives near the palace of Puluga, but never enters it. The stars sleep during the daytime. The sun and the moon, after having given us light, pass under the earth, and, while sleeping, cast a mild light over the unhappy spirits confined in Hades. The phases of the moon are due, according to the Mincopies, to the habit which this luminary has of covering itself with clouds as they cover themselves with paintings. Partial or total eclipses of the moon are a sign of displeasure on its part; they make, however, little impression. Eclipses of the sun, on the contrary, strike them with profound terror.

The moon and the sun figure as secondary divinities in this mythology. At times they are ministers of Puluga; but they also have their own wishes, which must be respected, under penalty. The supreme god has forbidden the employment, in cooking turtles, of the wood of the tree which gives in its bark a material for textile fibres. The man who disobeys this command will have his throat cut; if the offender is a woman, her breasts are cut off. When the crime has been done in the daytime the sun is the executor of the sentence; if it has taken place at night, the moon must inflict the penalty. Between the first faint dawn and sunrise, one must engage in no noisy occupation; above all, he should avoid twanging the bow-string, for this noise particularly angers the sun, which avenges itself by producing an eclipse, raising a tempest, etc. When the moon is in its third quarter and rises at the setting of the sun, he wishes that one should occupy himself with him alone, and is jealous of all other light. The Mincopies, therefore, then cease

all occupations, halt if they are journeying, and cover
up all fires. When the luminary has risen some degrees
above the horizon they resume their toil and rekindle
their fires.

Mr. Man found no sign of adoration addressed to
trees, to rocks or stones, or to stars, among the Mincopies. Puluga himself, according to our traveller, would
not be the object of any worship. Yet Captain Stokoe,
who also lived among the Mincopies and was much interested in these islanders, declares that they addressed
homage to the sun and the moon.[170]   Lieutenant Saint
John, on his part, believes he has discovered a certain religious character in some of the nocturnal dances, during
which an old man intones the chant alone, quite unlike
what takes place in all the others.[167]

Finally, some precise details, supplied by Mr. Man
himself, tend to invalidate his negations regarding worship. The shaman called to a sick man, whose desperate
condition he recognises, declares that no prayer can pre-
vail upon Puluga to return to him his *spirit*.[83]   One
prays, then, to the supreme god in some circumstances.
Moreover, at the time of a violent tempest the Mincopies burn leaves of the *Mimusops indica*, believing
that their crackling pleases the ear of Puluga and calms
his rage. This practice has really all the characteristics
of a veritable offering.

Nature of Man—The Other Life.—According to the
Mincopies, every man possesses, independent of his body,
two active principles, the spirit (*chawga*) and the soul
(*otyolo*). The spirit is black, the soul is red. From the
former proceeds all good; all bad from the latter. Although both are invisible, they reproduce the form of
the body. When a man is very ill, it is that his spirit
hesitates between this world and the other one. When
one dreams, it is that his soul has quitted his body, while

the sleeper is conscious of what it sees and does. Thus the Mincopies have absolute confidence in the warnings which they believe they receive in dreams. At death, the soul and spirit are separated, but they will be reunited at the resurrection. While awaiting that moment their destiny is very different.

The world is flat. It rests upon an immense palm tree * (barata). This raises itself in the midst of a vast jungle which occupies all the space below man's dwelling place, and which is called chaïtan, a word translated Hades by Mr. Man. It is a very sad abode; for, although visited by the sun and moon, it receives but a feeble light from them, as I have already stated.

When a man dies, his spirit, after haunting for some days the region about his tomb and the camping ground of the tribe, passes into chaïtan. Arrived there, it is what the individual of whom it formed part was at his death, and continues all its earthly occupations. Adults pass their time in hunting the spirits of mammals and birds which Puluga sends them; but the spirits of fishes, turtles, etc., remain in the sea, where they become the prey of Juruwin.

Between the earth and the eastern portion of the sky stretches a bridge made of invisible rushes (pidgarlarchawga), connecting the earth with a place of delights (jereg), which Mr. Man calls paradise. Above it lies jereglarmugu. This is a sort of purgatory, a place of torments which do not continue forever. Like the ancient Scandinavians, and contrary to the ideas most prevalent, Mincopies depict this temporary inferno as ice-cold. This is where Puluga sends the souls of dead who are guilty of certain crimes, particularly those of murderers.

---

* Caryota sobolifera (Man).

If the dead person is a child under six years of age, its soul and spirit do not separate. They betake themselves together to Hades, and are placed under a fig tree (*Ficus laccifera*), the fruits of which serve them as food. Moreover, they are not destined to await the general resurrection. The Mincopies believe that every newborn child has already lived, but only for a few years. Every woman who has lost a little child and becomes pregnant hopes to see live again the little one whom she has mourned; consequently she gives, before it is born, to the little one whom she carries within her the name of the deceased. If she bears a child of the same sex as the earlier one, the identity is considered demonstrated. In the contrary case they say the first child has remained under the fig tree.

A considerable number of legends refer to some vague ideas of metempsychosis. The Mincopies relate that certain of their ancestors have quitted the world under the form of various terrestrial or marine animals. The spirits of those who have not undergone this metamorphosis, although dwelling in Hades, can assist the living. It is one of these who, after the deluge, brought to men the fire which had been extinguished by the inundation, and which he knew how to steal from Puluga. Moreover, all spirits know to a certain extent what takes place in the world formerly inhabited by them, and can be helpful to such as have not forgotten them.

The Mincopies believe in a resurrection. This event will take place as consequence of an earthquake brought about by Puluga's orders. The palm tree which supports the earth will be broken; the earth itself will turn. All living will perish, and change places with their deceased ancestors. These last will secure a new life in all respects like this present one; but sickness and death will have disappeared, and there will be no more marriage. The spirits in Hades sigh for the happy moment which shall deliver them from their monotonous existence, and from time to time attempt to shake the palm tree which supports the earth, thus causing earthquakes.

The First Men.—After having created the world, Puluga made a man, whose name was *Tomo.* He was black, like the modern islanders, but much larger, and bearded. Puluga made him to know the different kinds of fruit trees scattered over the jungle, which then covered only a part of the Middle Island;* he showed him the foods from which he should abstain during the rainy season, and procured fire for him. For this purpose he arranged two kinds of wood in alternate layers, and then called upon the *Sun Mother* to ignite the pile.† The origin of the first woman, *Chana Elewadi,* is told in various forms; all of them, however, suppose the intervention of Puluga. It was he also who taught Tomo the art of making a bow and arrows, of hollowing out a canoe, of hunting and cooking pigs, etc. It was he also who taught Elewadi to weave baskets, to make nets, to paint herself with red ochre (*koibo*) and white clay (*talaog*), etc. One sees that these islanders refer to their god the origin of all arts practised among them.

Become very aged, Tomo was drowned accidentally, and was transformed into a cachalot (*karaducu*), and became the father of all that kind of whale. Elewadi having gone by boat in search of her husband, he overturned boat and crew and drowned the whole party. Elewadi became a species of crab, and her companions were changed into iguanas.

The direct descendants of the first pair are called

---

* The first inhabited locality is called Wotaemi. Mr. Man regards this word as equivalent to garden—Eden. I shall consider this tradition again.

† The composition of the pile, formed of *two kinds* of wood,

Tomola. Become too numerous even during the life of their father, they scattered by couples over all the country after having been provided, by the bounty of Puluga, with all the necessities of life. This dispersion produced diversity of languages. After having created Tomo and Elewadi, Puluga taught them a language which the Andaman tribes say was that now spoken by the inhabitants of the south part of the Middle Island (*Bojigyab*). Thus this one is considered as the mother language. At the time of the separation each group of the Tomola received its own peculiar idiom from God.

The Deluge.—After the death of Tomo and his oldest son men neglected more and more the observance of Puluga's prescriptions. In his anger the god sent a great flood, which covered the whole earth and destroyed all living things.* Two men and two women, who were by chance in a canoe, alone escaped, and were the ancestors of the present islanders.† Puluga created anew for them animals of every species, but he neglected to give them fire. Then it was that one of their deceased friends, touched by their distress, went to seek a brand at the very hearth of God, as I have suggested above. Shortly after, the last interview between Puluga and men took place. The god declared to them that the deluge was a punishment for their disobedience to his commands, and that they would undergo the same punishment again if they fell once more into the same faults. From that time, the

---

makes me believe that the Mincopies formerly knew how to kindle fire by the process practised among so many savage peoples.

* According to one tradition, the anger of Puluga was brought to a head by an assassination committed through treason. In her grief, the mother of the victim openly violated the commands of Puluga, and excited her companions to do the same, uttering a curse which is preserved in the legend.

† The names of the men were *Loralolu* and *Pollola;* those of the women were *Kalola* and *Rimalla.*

Mincopies say, the prescriptions of Puluga have been carefully observed. The *code* of these tribes—if one may use that word—dates back, then, in all probability, to a very remote time.

Up to that time Puluga frequently inhabited the volcanic peak on Barren Island and visited the Andamans under a visible form.* But since then he has retired to heaven, and no one has seen him.

A great number of legends are connected with the beliefs which I have just summarised. Metamorphosis frequently appears as the *finale* of the story. Man enumerates eighteen species of mammals, birds, reptiles, and crustaceans which have descended from transformed Tomola; and he adds that several species of fish have the same origin. No tree or plant figures in this list.

Only three rocks have given rise to legends. All three are situated in the neighbourhood of man's first home. Two of them are said to be marine monsters of unknown species and of gigantic size, who, after having devoured some islanders, remained caught in the mud and were changed into stone. The third is of greater interest. It is a block of sandstone, about nine metres in diameter, whose surface presents many irregular gutterings, apparently due to atmospheric agencies. It is situated on the border of a large but shallow lake. This is the Wotaemi—the Garden of Eden—of the Mincopies, where man first appeared.[101] The islanders believe the depressions excavated in the rock narrate the history of creation and of the exploits of the Tomola. This is a remarkable belief in a population who, as we have seen, have no material means of transmitting its thought. Is there here an un-

---

* Barren Island, distant about thirty leagues from the Andamans, possesses a volcano still semiactive. It is the extreme point reached by the Mincopies around their archipelago, and perhaps it *is* hence that they have taken fire.

conscious recollection of a forgotten art? However that
may be, it is a place respected by all the tribes with whom
Mr. Man communicated.

Miscellaneous Superstitions—Sorcerers.—The Mincopies have no priests, properly so called, but they have some
kinds of sorcerers—or better, shamans—called *okopaïad*,
a word which Mr. Man translates *dreamer*. It is, in fact,
during sleep and in a dream that the *okopaïad* exercises
his power. It is then that he becomes clairvoyant, com-
municates with the powers of good and evil, converses
with spirits, and exercises a mysterious influence over the
property, health, and even life of those about him. Thus
he is much dreaded, and is loaded with presents. No
ceremony or special initiation confers the quality of
okopaïad. A remarkable dream, followed by an unfore-
seen event presenting some relation with it, suffices to
make even a child to be considered as endowed with the
exceptional faculties necessary to penetrate into the supernatural.

Independently of these superstitions, which are more
or less directly connected with their religious beliefs, the
Mincopies have others not so related, whose origin it
would be difficult to explain. I limit myself to mentioning two of these. Meeting with or hearing the song of
certain birds is for these islanders a presage, now good,
now ill. Sneezing is a good augury, and indicates that
one is thought of by an absent friend. One knows that
similar ideas have prevailed and still remain to-day in the
less intelligent classes of the most civilised nations.

General Observations.—The Mincopies are among the
best known savage tribes. Instead of such monsters as
were described before Marco Polo, one has found some
little men, with black skin and woolly hair, but who—
thanks to their relatively regular features, their slight
or lacking prognathism, their lips scarcely thicker than

our own—are much superior to the large majority of Negro races.

As regards intellectual manifestations, we have just
seen that these islanders are now inferior, now superior,
to other populations of the globe who lead a life analogous to theirs. Experience has shown that if intelligence
is as if dormant among them, it is easily awakened, and
appears then nearly equal to that of the European races
themselves. All observations made upon Mincopies who
had not been in contact with whites, and bandits introduced into the Andamans by penal establishments, show
beyond doubt that in the matter of morality these Negritos bear, without disadvantage, comparison with our own
populations.

Finally, to me it is impossible not to regard men who
believe in a supreme divinity, uncreated, omniscient, who
has created all things except maleficent powers, as having
a veritable religion. This exception appears to place
limits to the power of God, but has it not a just cause?
All the *grand religions*, to use Burnouf's expression, have
tried to account for the coexistence of good and evil.
The Mincopies have solved the problem in their way.
Consciously or unconsciously, they seem to have been unable to admit that he whose children they claim to be,
and from whom they declare they receive all earthly
goods, was directly or indirectly the author of their ills.
Was this not also the thought of Zoroaster?

These very comparisons raise a question which has
been often and in many places propounded. Do the lofty
ideas whose existence among the Mincopies Mr. Man has
established really belong to these islanders? Are they
the spontaneous product of their instincts and intelligence? Or have they indeed come from outside? Have
they been brought to the Andamans by some follower of
the great religions of the Orient? Has not Islam in par-

ticular had an influence in shaping this conception of a supreme god and almost pure spirit, which fits in so strangely with the bizarre superstitions which accompany it?

This is precisely the question which Logan asked himself when, *to his great surprise,* he discovered [92] among the Binonas, until then regarded by him as without religion,* what he calls "*a simple and to a certain extent rational theology.*" These Binonas form part of a group of populations which represent in the Malay peninsula the Dravidians of India.† Although in contact with the Malays since the twelfth century, and perhaps from the ninth century, they have preserved their independence, their manners, and their customs in the interior of the peninsula, of which the conquerors really occupy only the coast regions. They live in simple huts, know only a very rudimentary agriculture, live chiefly upon the products of the chase and fishing, or the fruits of the forest. They are plainly, then, in the category of populations which we

---

* On various occasions the Malays had assured Logan that the Binonas had no religious belief, and that their sorcerers (*poyang*) acted for good or ill only through the mediumship of spirits which they controlled.

† When Logan wrote, these tribes were still little known, and the eminent ethnologist was unable to distinguish the different elements whose fusion and mixture had produced the existing condition. Recent materials, especially the photographs brought back by de Saint-Pol Lias and de la Croix, have fully informed us in this respect, as one has seen above. The Binonas, the Udaïs, the Manthras, the Sakaies, all have a Negrito foundation more or less altered by various mixtures. In the southern part of the peninsula the Malay element seems strongly dominant, but even there the intervention of a very different type is marked. The Malay blood could not have given to certain Binonas of Johore an oval face, a well-made chin, and an aquiline nose. These features can only be due to crossing with either Aryan or Allophyllian whites.

call *savages*, whatever may be their moral qualities.* But among these Binouas one believes in a god named *Pirman*, who created the world, and whose will maintains the existence of all things, who is invisible and dwells beyond the skies. Below him are spirits (*jin*), the most powerful of whom is the *spirit of the earth*, *Jin Bumi*. This one plays the *rôle* of a bad angel ; to him are due sickness and death, but all his power comes from Pirman.

By the side of these beliefs, so spiritual, there are found also many kinds of superstitions, which it is needless to enumerate here. In reality, the Binouas have neither priests nor worship ; but their sorcerers—or, better, shamans (*poyang*)—at times play the part of the former, and preside at certain ceremonies which might be called religious. They communicate with the supreme god through a mediator, a secondary divinity, *Jewajswa*, who dwells in heaven, and who alone can approach Pirman. To render him favourable to them, they utter invocations and burn benzoin, the odour of which is agreeable to his nostrils. The *poyang* can cure diseases ; they can also cause death. They owe their supernatural powers to spirits or genii whom they command and from whom they draw inspiration.

In conclusion, to Logan's eyes the whole of the religious beliefs of the Binouas constitutes a very remarkable mixture of theism and Shamanism, very similar to that which exists among the Dyaks of Borneo and the Battas of Sumatra. Among these peoples, one believes also in a supreme god called by the same names, *Diebata*,

---

* In this respect, and in many features of character and customs, the Binouas approach the Mincopies. But, contrary to what we have seen among these last, it appears that war between tribes is unknown among them and the other populations of the same origin.[92]

Juhata, Dewata, in the two islands, while at the same time admitting numerous superstitions connected with Shamanism. The *poyang* of the Binouas and neighbouring tribes, the *blians* of the Dyaks, and the *dato* and *si basso* of the Battas, are at once priests, sorcerers, and curers of disease—that is to say, true shamans.

From these facts and from certain philosophical considerations, Logan concludes that, in Malacca as in the Indian Archipelago, the religion is at bottom only an ancient Shamanism, which probably prevailed throughout eastern Asia before the rise of Buddhism. A theistic idea, borrowed either from Malay Mussulmans or from Hindoos, has placed itself alongside of the primitive beliefs without changing them greatly, especially among the Binouas. Moreover, he considers it very probable that this introduction has come from India. He says: "Not a Mussulman would speak of the single and only God without adding that Mahomet is his prophet."

Such are Logan's conclusions; but, whatever may be the authority of that eminent ethnologist, they do not appear to me to be justified. They have for their source the thought that barbarians or savages like the Dyaks and Binouas cannot rise of themselves to the conception of a creative and all-powerful God. But the facts do not well agree with such a view.

Let us recall, first, that Shamanism, under forms quite varied indeed, still prevails over a great portion of Asia, and even extends into Europe. But in this whole area, among all the nations concerning whom our information is exact, one finds by the side of secondary divinities, or rather spirits more or less deified, a supreme God, creator and preserver of the universe. It is the *Jumbel* of the Laplanders, the *Num* of the Samoyeds, the *Jumman* of the Votiaks, the *Yuma* of the Tcheremis, the *Artoyon*, *Schugotoygon*, or *Tangara* of the Jakouts, etc.[87] All these great divinities are evidently the *single and eternal* God, of whom Mangou spoke to Rubruquis, although he was surrounded by shamans, the chief of whom dwelt close by the great Khan.* Far, then, from being incompatible with a very lofty and spiritual religious conception, Shamanism shows itself associated with this in the countries where it holds the greatest sway. There, as at many other points on the globe, coarse practices and absurd or childish superstitions have too frequently covered up and concealed from Europeans the superior notions existing among these savage populations.

We usually do not possess information concerning the ideas which the sectaries of Shamanism hold regarding their supreme divinity and his attributes, or upon the worship rendered to him. We do, however, know that, while they consecrate to him rude images, the Jakouts declare that their *Tangara* is invisible;[87] we know that the Votiaks, the Tcheremis, etc., celebrate special festivals in honour of their great God, and address to him prayers, which present them to us in a most favourable light. Moreover, it seems to me that the Kalevala gives us sufficient information in this matter. It is true that the most ancient chants of this multiple epic date back only to the tenth century at most;[155] but it appears to me that the revelations which Antero Wipunen made to Waïnamoinen clearly show that the words put in the mouth of a magician, dead centuries before, really teach us the most ancient traditions of the race relative to these difficult questions.† In fine, in the whole geographical area here in question, the religious beliefs appear to me to have a very great analogy with those of the ancient

---

* [43] Rubruquis arrived at Mangou's court at the end of the year 1253.

† The Kalevala.

11

Chinese, who also believed in a *supreme sovereign of heaven* and in subordinate spirits.*

Those who refuse to *savages* the possibility of attaining to the spiritual conceptions which I have just described will perhaps give the honour of these to the compatriots of Confucius, and will attribute them to an influence proceeding from China. But one establishes similar facts upon many other parts of the globe. I limit myself to mentioning a few of these.

In America, among true redskins, we find again coarse Shamanism associated with belief in a *Great Spirit*, only Creator, and directing by his will all the events of this world, just as does *Jumala* of the Kalevala.†

Among the black tribes of California, one of the most savage populations of that country, where sorcerers inspire the profoundest terror, *Chinig-chinig* has created all things; he is invisible and ubiquitous; he sees all, even in the midst of darkness; he is the friend of the good, and punishes the bad.[118]

Among the Natchez, who have neither sorcerers nor conjurers, *Coyocop-chill* has likewise created all things, but he governs the whole world through the intermediary of secondary spirits (*Coyocop-téchou*).[136]

In Polynesia, at Tahiti, *Taaroa* is *toïvi;* he has neither father, mother, nor children. He has a body, but this body is invisible, and the god sheds it as birds shed their feathers. It is this god who has created the world,

---

* The Emperor Chun, 2,255 years before our era, "made sacrifice to the supreme sovereign of heaven *(Chang-ti)*, and the usual ceremonies to the six great spirits, to the mountains, the rivers, and to spirits generally." [135]

† Among others, consult Heckewelder. A spirit truly profound and religious in the Christian acceptation of the word appears remarkably in the prayer which the Lenape warriors addressed to the Great Spirit before departing upon an expedition.

or who has drawn it out of chaos, according to another tradition. But his work once finished, he has given its direction over to inferior divinities.[123, 56] *

It is indeed difficult to explain these facts upon Logan's hypothesis. Nevertheless the Polynesians are only Malay emigrants, and ancient relations between America and the most advanced nations of Asia seem to me to-day beyond question.[166] One might, then, still argue that the former have carried with them to the very ends of Polynesia ideas borrowed by their ancestors from some civilised nation ; that, among the latter, the existence of similar notions is due to a sort of infiltration of ideas coming from the Old World and penetrating even to the most savage tribes of the new continent. But let us betake ourselves to Africa and to the Gulf of Guinea. There we meet again everywhere fetichism with its train of beliefs and practices, in turn ridiculous, puerile, or sanguinary. And yet there also we find again the belief in a supreme God, often unique, and having under his command spirits who execute his will, rather than veritable secondary deities. The great surprise of D'Avezac when Ochi-Fékoué recited to him, in place of a translation of the Lord's Prayer, the prayer which all the Yebons, prostrating themselves, repeat to *Obba-ol-Oroun*, is well known.[10] This *King* or *Master of Heaven* is, according to these Negroes, "an immaterial, invisible, eternal being ; it is his supreme will which has created and which governs all things." D'Avezac has mentioned seven travellers whose narratives contain similar information regarding the religions of the different peoples of the same region. He might have lengthened his list by adding the name of a Negro captain.[175]

---

* I have summarised and discussed the authorities in *Les Polynesiens et leurs migrations.*

Thus in all four quarters of the globe, and among populations of very different race but all belonging to the lowest culture stages of mankind, we establish the co-existence, in one same religious belief, of superstitions the most degraded and of spiritual conceptions the most pure and elevated.* There is, then, nothing strange in the same fact occurring among the Mincopies and the Binoüas.

The latter are a crossed race. Moreover, placed in contact for centuries with the Malays, they might well have borrowed something from their more civilised neighbours. But if this is true, the details given by Logan would tend to prove that they have given the notions so acquired an entirely peculiar form. The Mincopies were placed in conditions very different. Thanks to various circumstances already indicated, they have remained isolated in their little world, and have preserved, especially in the four northern islands, an ethnic purity attested by the uniformity of their external and craniological characteristics. This in itself would go to show that their intellectual, moral, and religious characteristics have remained almost unaltered, or have only changed in accordance with the predispositions of the race and the conditions of existence which had produced these.

In saying this, I do not absolutely deny that the Mincopies have drawn something from outside. They mus-

---

* It would be only too easy to show that the same juxtaposition of dogmas apparently irreconcilable has existed and still exists in the grandest religions and among ourselves. No savage population has believed more firmly in sorcery than the Catholics of the middle ages or the Puritan refugees in America. How many Europeans are still in that condition! The mixture of ideas here discussed, and which appears so strange to an enlightened mind, is, then, really very frequent, perhaps even general, and must, possibly, be accepted as connected most intimately with the nature of man. I have emphasised considerations of this kind in my L'Espêce humaine, and Introduction à l'étude des races humaines.

sacred foreigners whom chance threw into their hands; they killed the companions of Duradawan, but spared him. Similar occurrences might well happen during the centuries preceding the English occupation of the islands. The Andamanese have, perhaps, accepted some notions which have adjusted themselves to their stock of primitive beliefs. Yet, however extensive one may consider such borrowings, it is necessary at least to recognise that these islanders have appropriated them in such a way as to make from all an *ensemble* of beliefs having its own peculiar characteristics.

Thus, long before the arrival of Europeans, the Mincopies, although reported as one of the clearest examples of a people without religion, possessed a whole rudimentary mythology, and, with the Samoyeds, Jakouts, and black Californians, they believed the great fundamental ideas of the proudest religions. They deserve, then, in every way the attention of men who interest themselves in the study of the human races and the manifold problems which this history raises; and we owe many thanks to those English officers, those civil employees, and those physicians who have made us acquainted with it.

CHAPTER V.

NEGRITOS OTHER THAN THE MINCOPIES.

Language.—Luzon : Invasion of the Malays.—Malacca : Mixture of
languages ; camphor language.—Linguistic affinities.—Social
state.—Mincopies ; Aëtas ; culture ; ancient social condition ;
family ; marriage ; inheritance ; adultery.—Industries.—Fire ;
dwellings ; food ; arms ; poisoned arrows.—Religious and moral
characteristics : Superior beings ; spirits ; future life ; chastity ;
modesty ; general character.

Language.—Although dispersed from Andaman to the
Philippines, the Negrito tribes have preserved in a remarkable way all their external and osteological characters. It
is otherwise with their language. This has at times almost
completely disappeared at the touch of superior populations, even when some Negrito groups, still numerous and
enjoying a certain independence, have preserved a relative
purity of blood.

This fact has been recognised at the Philippines from
the beginning of the Spanish occupation. Even in that
island, which owes its name to them, our little blacks
speak the Bisaya—that is to say, a local Malay dialect [139]—
but they mingle with it many foreign words. It seems to
me probable that these last are so much evidence preserved
of the primitive language.

At Luzon it must be even more truly the same. The
evidence given upon that point by de la Fuente has been
fully confirmed by the researches of Dr. Montano, who has
kindly placed his unpublished notes at my disposition with

144

a liberality which I here gladly acknowledge. This author, who speaks Malay fluently, and is familiar with several of its dialects, has discovered in the language of the Aëtas not only grammatical forms but a vocabulary almost exclusively *Tagaloc*. He has verified one by one an hundred and four words collected by Meyer in the dialect of Mariveles; he has noted those which have seemed to him foreign to the Malay languages, and found but seventeen. He even believes it necessary to make reservations regarding some of those.*

Montano has not been able to collect as precise information regarding the language of the Mamanonas or Negritos of Mindanao; but he has seen them make themselves understood by his guides, who spoke a corrupt, or rather simplified, Bisaya. There also, without doubt, the original language has disappeared.

Has it been the same in the Malay peninsula? Montano considers himself unable to answer this question.

---

* Montano counts, moreover, thirteen non-Malay words in the same vocabulary translated into the Negro dialect of Zambales. He has also obtained with difficulty from Aëtas, with whom he found himself in contact, one couplet of a song, which I here reproduce:

Makaalis   ako   ina,
  I leave (oh, my) loved one,

Makpaka baït,   ka,   ina.
  Be very prudent, thou loved one.

Ta! ma papaka sayou, ako   ina,
  Ah! I go very   far,   my loved one,

  Into   ka   man   a   bibing iaumo.
While thou remainest in dwelling thine.

Hanag   bannan   dolipatan   mo.
  Never (thy) village will be forgotten (by) me.

The Negritos of the province of Albay (southeast of Luzon) speak the Bicol fluently. But they are mixed with Malay. The Bisaya, the Tagaloc, the Bicol, the Pampango, etc., are merely dialects of Malay, more or less modified.—*Montano.*

He understood his Manthra * guide readily when he spoke Malay, but could scarcely pick out words here and there when the same individual spoke with his savage compatriots. He believes that the Manthras have at least a peculiar accent, which may be due to several causes.

The Father Pouget, long located at Malacca, who has visited all the tribes of the interior, told Montano that these savages had neither language nor dialect of their own, and that their speech is a mixture of altered Malay and Siamese.

Yet, in his curious work upon the Binouas of Johore,† Logan considers it demonstrated that this tribe, evidently much more mixed with Malay than the Manthras, formerly had its own language, and supports his opinion by many arguments.[93] In the special language, which these indigenes employ when they go into the forest to look for camphor trees ‡ the same author has discovered a certain number of non-Malay words. I have compared some of them with words contained in two vocabularies from Siam and Laos, published by Latham,[86] and could detect no resemblance. A comparison of these same vocabularies with that which M. de la Croix collected among the Sakaies of Perak * led to the same result. On his part, de la Croix

---

* The Manthras are mixed breeds from the neighbourhood of Kessang, province of Malacca, in the peninsula of that name.

† The most southern district of the Malacca peninsula.

‡ This language is called *bássá kápor*—"camphor language." Logan found it in use, and among all the tribes who give themselves up to the gathering of camphor. These tribes believe that they could not discover camphor trees if they used any other language on these expeditions. Montano, who speaks of it in his notes, calls it *bahasa kapour*.

* The province of Perak, two or three degrees north of that of Malacca, is located near the central western part of the peninsula. We have no information regarding the Negrito-Malay tribes that may live farther north.

counts only twelve Malay words out of the ninety composing his vocabulary. The Russian traveller, Miklucho-Maclay, had brought together from among the savage tribes of Johore and of the interior one hundred and seventy, which, when submitted to the judgment of several Malays, had been regarded by them as not of their language.* Finally, de Castelnau, on his part, arrived at analogous conclusions.[26]

From all these facts it seems to me certain that the ancient Negritos of the peninsula of Malacca must have had a language of their own, almost entirely forgotten by one part of their descendants, a little less forgotten perhaps by others, because all have been more or less mixed with the Malays, Siamese, and, it may be, with other ethnologic elements. Is this language related to that of the Mincopies? There is only a theoretical reply, but the relative proximity of the populations permits propounding it. Perhaps Man and Temple will some day tell us how much of truth there is in it.†

Perhaps, too, they will be able to recognise whether the singular affinities claimed by Hyde Clark to exist between the different Mincopy languages and African and American tongues are well founded.[29] Finally, it would be very interesting to learn whether the language of the

---

* [25] The Russian traveller established the identity of language among these tribes, isolated and with no other connection between them, from Johore at the south of the peninsula to Ligor in the south of Siam. This result appears to have struck him with astonishment, but there is nothing surprising in it for one who has occupied himself with the history of the Negritos, considered as a whole.

† I think it would be very interesting in this connection to find out what language is spoken by the Negritos recently discovered in the little archipelago of Tenasserim. Their relative isolation might lead us to hope that the primitive language is here less altered than on the continent.

Puttouas, of the mountains of Amarkantak, which differs from all the Dravidian languages in its neighbourhood,[164] is in any way related to those spoken in the Andaman Islands or in the Malay Peninsula.

Social Condition. — The Mincopies are exclusively hunters and fishermen. Living upon the shores of a sea filled with fishes, close to great forests where boars run at large, and which furnish them besides honey and fruits, they have not felt the necessity of wringing by labour from the soil a supplement to their food supply; and this very luxuriance of food, perhaps, has been of influence in keeping them at the lowest point in the social scale.*

Most travellers who have visited the Philippines have spoken of the Aëtas as never having passed this status, although placed in much less favourable surroundings. Father La Gironière[64] and Meyer[113] are very emphatic on this point, and Giglioli has accepted their statements without hesitation.[60, 59] Rienzi himself, to whom we owe information upon the more happy past of this population, represents them as to-day living exclusively upon wild fruits and the products of the hunt or fishing.[162]

But it is evident that in the Philippines this inferior social condition is the result of the persecution waged against the Negritos by more powerful and vigorous races. No doubt, also, false information, interestedly given by the petty chiefs of Tagal villages to travellers, has led to considering as general a state of affairs perhaps more or less exceptional.† I believe I cannot better reply to such exag-

---

* Francis Day informs us that a very small tribe of Mincopies, camped near the English establishments and receiving daily rations, took besides, in a single year five hundred boars, one hundred and fifty turtles, twenty wild-cats, fifty iguanas and six dugongs.—*Proc. Asiat. Soc. of Bengal.*

† Manuscript note from Montano.

gerations than by quoting almost literally some of the
notes kindly sent me by Montano : *

"The Negritos of the province of Bataan apppear to
fully appreciate the security which the just and enlightened administration of the governor, Don Estanislao
Chaves, gives them. I have visited them in the mountains. . . . The abode of the chief, very comfortable, was
situated upon a hillock surrounded by other eminences.
Several houses were built there, each in a clearing of
some *arpents*, where they raised bananas, rice, sugar-cane,
and, above all, yams. . . . The chief shouted ; immediately cries broke forth in every direction. Soon after the
whole tribe was about me. . . . In the province of Albay,
where conditions must be much as in Bataan, I have seen
a considerable quantity of cacao collected by the Negritos
in the islands of the gulf."

Even among the Mamannas of Mindanao, whose last
survivors are constantly pursued by the fierce Manobos,
the French traveller saw upon the east coast of Lake
Maïnit "a timid tribe, excessively suspicious, but which
had nevertheless built houses, cleared a bit of the forest,
and planted bananas and yams."

Thus all that has been said about the uncontrollable
vagabond instincts of the Aëtas is inexact. If these little
Negroes in some parts of the archipelago lead a wandering life, build no huts, cultivate no land, the fault is that
of their persecutors.

The very rude agriculture of which we have just spoken
is again met with among the mixed-breed Negritos of
India and the Malay Peninsula. Among all, the method
appears to be the same. The Gond, as the Manthra,
commences by destroying the trees, to which he sets fire
when they are half dry. Then he sows or plants in the

---

* These notes have been published now by this traveller in his
Voyages aux Philippines et en Malaisie.

midst of the hollows among the interlacing trunks grain and yams. When the underbrush springs up again he leaves his hut, makes some slight wicker shelters of leafy boughs, and begins again elsewhere. A dog, a few fowls, some pigs, live as they can on these poor clearings. The chase, fishing, roots, and wild fruits seem to furnish the principal resources of these populations.*

Such is the present condition of things. But have not these tribes, to-day half wandering and scattered, known better days and a higher social condition ? One can only reply to this question in a general way.

Excepting the implements of polished stone which I have mentioned, there is nothing about the Mincopics which indicates that they were ever higher than they are to-day. Having, so to speak, in their hands all that is necessary to the satisfaction of the needs of savage life, without relations with foreigners, nothing has come to arouse in them new aspirations ; and their intellectual activity has simply spent itself in multiplying and perfecting the stock of utensils suited to their mode of life. We have seen that in this direction they have given proof of real energy.

On the contrary, in the Philippines it is more than probable that the Aëtas have been more advanced. Rienzi, who has summarised, unfortunately in a very confused way, the traditions relative to these people, represents them as having formerly occupied the whole of Luzon, and as having long resisted the Tagal invasions. They then had a sort of government. A council of chiefs and old men attended to the execution of the laws.†
It is difficult not to suppose that at that time the soil

---

* Unpublished notes of Montano; also his book, *loc. cit.*; also [164], [93].

† Exactly as now exists among the Bhils, half-breed Negritos.—*Rousselet.* [164]

was cultivated at least to the degree described by Montano.

Much more probably is it the same of the more or less crossed tribes of Malacca. Montano tells us that the Manthras still recall the time when their ancestors were masters of the whole country. At that time they say they possessed many writings traced upon tree leaves. This fact supposes in itself a social condition, of which Montano seems to have found a trace in the very name of his guide. This man was called, as his father, his grandfather, and no doubt their ancestors, *Pang-lima-dalan,* a word which our traveller translates " *a lord who administers the palace of a sultan."* [121, 122] This descendant of some great dignitary to-day performs the function of a coolie on the place of a Chinese planter. In the peninsula of Malacca, as in India, the conquest has perhaps destroyed states already considerable and flourishing, but memory of which has gone completely; it has crowded back into the forests and mountains the more or less negroid race which founded them. There this race has fallen into savagery again, just as the Dravidians have done.* It is as if broken and crumbled down into tribes or single families, and the hierarchy of chiefs which Logan has made known among the populations of Bermun is probably all that remains of its ancient social state.†

---

* Among others, the Bhils ; yet these still have permanent dwellings, well constructed and grouped in villages. That which can be considered only hypothetical so long as it concerns tribes of Bermun, appears certain for their brothers the Binonas. Logan [93] tells us that these were governed by kings whose origin was supernatural, and whose descendants still live.

† In his memoir upon the Binouas of Johore, Logan gives some details upon five tribes, to whom all this practically applies. They are the Udaïs or Orang-Pagos, the Jakuns, the Sakaies, the Mintiras or Manthras, and the Besisis. These tribes inhabit the highland of Cunong-Bermun, one of the highest chains of the Malay

Everywhere it appears among the Negritos that the family has resisted this disintegration of the race. The assertions of a Sepoy deserter, too readily accepted by some writers, represented it as somewhat loosely organised at the Andamans. The evidence gathered by Lieutenant Saint-John and Mr. Day had already shown how inexact these first statements were. Those which we owe to Mouat,[125] and, above all, to Man, have finished enlightening us upon this point; and after what I have already said I need not return to the subject.

At the Philippines, even in the unhappy and savage tribe which he visited, Father la Gironière determined some analogous facts. "The Aëtas," said he, "are faithful in marriage, and have but one wife." The young man who has made his choice addresses himself to the parents, who never refuse, but send the girl into the forest, where before day she conceals herself. The young man must find her. If he does not succeed he must renounce all claim to her. One sees that in reality the whole matter is settled by the girl.

The notes and work of Montano confirm and complete those of Father la Gironière. Our traveller makes known also the curious ceremony which sanctions marriage among the Aëtas of Luzon. The two parties climb two flexible trees growing near together, which an old man then makes to bend toward each other. When the head of the man touches that of the girl they are legally married.[122] A great feast and warlike dances complete the festival occasion. Family bonds are very close between these poor

---

Peninsula. Among the Manthras there exist some upper chiefs (*batin*), whose jurisdiction extends over definite regions. Each *batin* has under his orders a *jinang*, a *jukra* or a *jorokra*, and an indefinite number of *panglimas* and of *ulubalangs*. At the death of a *batin* his successor is chosen from among the sons of one of his sisters.— *Logan* [93].

savages. The affection of parents for children is lively, and they, in turn, have for their father and mother equal love and respect. Adultery, theft, or murder are punished with death. But these crimes are extremely rare.

The Aëta does not purchase his wife; he simply gives a small present to his future father-in-law. This one gives his daughter a dowry—some articles which remain her personal property. "Thus," says Montano, "these Negritos know '*biens paraphernaux.*'"

One cannot object to my quoting further the following details from Montano relative to the Negritos of Mindanao:

"Among the poor Mamannas, those former masters of the soil, who have been reported as so much like brutes, I have found the same usages as among the Negritos of Marivelès, the same respect for the aged, the same love for children, the same worship of the dead. In this population, so soon to disappear, custom has the same undisputed power. These customs are no doubt simple, and their performance easy, but still something. It is not necessary to believe that every Mamanna acts as he likes, regardless of every one else. The deceived husband kills his wife, but only if the adultery is clear, in which case the relatives of the guilty woman give their consent to her death. Otherwise he would be considered an assassin, and subject himself to the death penalty, pronounced by the chief of the tribe upon complaint of the relatives of the victim.

"Adultery is, moreover, as all crimes, excessively rare among the Negritos of all these regions. The manners of young girls are very correct; the slightest suspicion on this point would hinder their finding husbands.

"Property is perfectly established, and passes by sale or inheritance. The cleared field is the incontestable property of him who has made it and of his heirs. At the death of a father, if the mother still lives, the property is divided into halves; one goes to the mother, the other to the children in equal shares.

" If the children are already grown, the widow continues to occupy the house of her husband; if the children are little, she takes them with her to the house of her people.

" All differences are settled by the chief of the tribe, but he seldom has to intervene. His decisions are always scrupulously obeyed." [122]

One readily admits that Montano gives us a very different idea of things from his predecessors. It is one more example to be added to the many which show how wrongly one does to depend upon superficial observation of the more backward and savage peoples.

Although more or less mixed with other races, the Negritos of Malacca would no doubt present analogous features of customs if one knew them better. Montano tells us that they never make war; * that parents watch carefully over their young, at need depriving themselves of food for their sakes. Logan tells us that among the Manthras adultery is punished by death, but only—as among the Mamanuas—if proved by evidence. Arrest, pronounced by the chief (*batin*), is executed by the *panglima*. The two guilty ones are laid in a stream, and their heads held under water by a fork. The husband who is convinced of his wife's infidelity, but who cannot prove it, may leave her, on condition of giving her the house and its surrounding fields, a certain quantity of stuffs, some rings, and a little sum of money. The children remain with their mother; she cannot marry again until her divorced husband has taken another wife.

M. de Saint-Pol Lias talked for a long time with To-

---

* Logan had already mentioned this very remarkable fact on the part of savage and hunting tribes. [93]

lilo, chief of a tribe of Sakaies, before Malays who could, if there had been reason for it, have denied his statements. The information, then, is probably correct. In the Sakaies tribes the family is fully organised. The man marries two women, and ordinarily gives the father ten *ringguits* (fifty francs). If he is himself a chief, he gives as much as thirty *ringguits* for a wife. Divorce is allowed, but is very rare. Adultery is considered criminal, but can be atoned for by money payments to the husband—of thirty *ringguits* from each of the two guilty persons. Murder, theft, are unknown in these tribes. Whoever is in need of food asks of the first one met, who never refuses.[108]

Industries.—I have already stated how the different Negrito populations support themselves. I should add that none of those of whom I have spoken are cannibals.* This accusation has rested upon several among them, particularly the Mincopies. But, far from seeking human flesh, the Andamanese regard it as a deadly poison.

All Negritos boil or roast meats; all but the Mincopies know how to make fire, and very probably all employ the same method, by friction of two bits of wood; but even for savages this is a painful and sometimes long labour. Thus the Manthras, for example, who employ two pieces of dry bamboo for the purpose, take much care of their fireplace. This is, in fact, their chief piece of furniture, and consists of a mass of earth enclosed in a frame of

---

* The Negrito-Papuans, mixed with the Papuans of New Guinea and the neighbouring archipelagoes, may have yielded to the influence of example and gone over into anthropophagy, but from lack of precise information it is not possible to decide upon this matter. The confusion which has long existed in reference to these two races, and which some recent travellers more or less maintain, renders any study of either of them alone very difficult. Examination of skulls enables us to refer to one or the other any given population, but it does not enlighten us upon distinctive characteristics in other relations.

12

wood, where one takes care to keep the fire constantly supplied with fuel. Some vessels in coarse clay, for cooking
roots and yams, and some baskets, complete the furniture.
Moreover, a little basket containing lime and betel-nut,
which these savages use in the same way as Malays do, is
almost always present.

In climates cold or temperate the most urgent needs,
after food, are those of lodgment and clothing. It is quite
otherwise in tropical regions. Here clothing is really a
question of luxury; it is often more inconvenient than
useful. It is much the same with lodgment; and, in any
case, the simplest shelter, capable of giving shade in the
daytime, of preventing radiation at night, and of protecting against rain, fully suffices. This is too often forgotten
by travellers, writers who see in extreme simplicity of cos-
tume or habitations a sign of intellectual inferiority and
lack of industry.

The Aëtas are not more clothed than their brothers of
the Andamans. Moreover, those of their tribes who are
constantly pursued by relentless foes do not even build
temporary shelters, and lie down in trees or roll themselves in the warm ashes of a great fire kindled to keep
off the chill of the night. But we have seen that, placed
in more regular conditions of life, they raise huts and can
settle down.

The photographs of de Saint-Pol Lias show us the
Sakaies wearing a simple girdle knotted loosely in front,
with the ends hanging down upon the thighs. Montano
has described the hut of a Manthra family living alone
in the midst of the woods. It is certainly anything but
luxurious; yet it presented this peculiarity—a flooring
two feet above the ground. Most peasant houses *here*
have only bare earth for floor. The poor savage of Malacca has been able to place himself in better hygienic
conditions than the European.

We have seen that among the Mincopies industries of daily application are at times remarkably perfected. Their bows, arrows, canoes, potteries and the like, place them on the level of the most advanced savages, who are far ahead of them in some respects. It is different with the tribes of Aëtas, whom persecution keeps constantly on the move, which is not surprising. Among them the arms for hunting and war are reduced to a short lance, the bow, and a single kind of arrows. But these last are poisoned, and the slightest wound produces, if not death, at least long and terrible sufferings, of which La Gironière has drawn a picture from his own experiences.*

The poison is also used by the Manthras, the Sakaies, and the other tribes of Bermun. But these Negrito mixed breeds, although they are acquainted with the bow and arrows, have replaced them by the *sarbacane*.† One easily recognises in this fact, as in many others, the Malay influence.

The Negrito half-breeds of Malacca know also how to

---

* The Father la Gironière was hurt in the thumb by one of these arrows as the result of digging up an Aëta skeleton, the first brought to Europe, and now in the museum collections. He scarcely noticed the wound, which he thought a scratch made by some spine. After three days of incubation the effect of the poison became noticeable by frightful pains; the entire arm swelled; then the trouble reached the chest. After a month of torture the patient appeared to be near his end; but he resisted. During more than a year, however, he still suffered in his chest. This *ensemble* of symptoms does not at all suggest that which travellers and experimenters tell us of the effect of other known poisons. It would appear that that which the Aëtas employ is of a peculiar nature. But perhaps the treatment pursued by the intrepid traveller may have had some share in the sufferings undergone.

† Montano: Bro de Saint-Pol Lias. The latter has seen a rifled *sarbacane*. Was this an imitation of one of our perfected firearms, or have these savages really independently discovered this method of assuring correctness of aim?

set a dreadful trap for great game, in which they capture
even tigers. They place at the end of a long path, cut
artificially through the underbrush, a strong lance attached to a tree bent and held in place by a snap or catch.
The animal in passing sets the catch free and falls pierced
through.[93]

In India to-day, as in the time of Ctesias, the bow is,
so to speak, the characteristic weapon of the Dravidian
populations. The Gonds alone, it appears, have given it
up, adopting the hatchet and pick.[164]

RELIGIOUS AND MORAL CHARACTERISTICS.

Belief in Superior Beings.—As many other savage
populations, the Negritos, who form the principal subject
of this chapter, have many times been described as absolutely without religion. It is not at all so. Only in un-
derstanding their rudimentary beliefs we must not start
with the ideas which instructed Europeans hold upon
, religious matters, even such as declare themselves un-
believers.

One knows already of this matter in reference to the
Mincopies. One knows how these reputed atheists have
a complete mythology, where exist side by side singularly
spiritual conceptions and childish and bizarre ideas.
When the other Negritos shall have been studied as
thoroughly as the Andamanese, equivalent beliefs may
perhaps be found; but such study has not yet been made.

We are indeed less informed in regard to the Aëtas.
Montano in his notes reports that he found no sign of religion; but, enlightened by a personal experience, he has
guarded himself against concluding that they have no
belief.* La Gironière, while stating that these little Ne-

* Montano had been told that the Bagobos had no religion.
Aided by circumstances, he has found among them a perfectly defi-

groes have no religion, informs us that they adore, at least temporarily, rocks or tree trunks, in which they find a resemblance to some animal. It appears to me probable that the homage is addressed to something superior to these material objects—may be to spirits or genii of the mountains or forests; for Rienzi tells us that these savages believe in bad spirits called *nonos*, and offer them sacrifices.

This belief in spirits and genii reappears among all the tribes of Bermun, and consequently among the Sakaies, the Manthras, etc. Here it has for official representative a body of priests—or, better, of sorcerers—called *poyand* or *pawang*. After having given upon this point details which I cannot reproduce here, Logan summarises his opinion in almost the following terms : " We find in these tribes a pure Shamanism with its accompaniment of charms and talismans. This is a living faith, dating from the remotest times in Asia, which has preserved its original simplicity and vigour, unspoiled by either Buddhism or Mohammedanism."

It is hardly necessary to recall that among the greater part of the Dravidian tribes, among even those which have attained a high degree of civilisation, one recognises a foundation of beliefs analogous to the preceding, underlying the facts borrowed from the various Hindoo sects and from Islam.

Belief in a Future Life.—The Negritos all believe that the spirit survives the body ; that it feels needs analogous to those of the living, and wishes that one should show it attention.* I have previously summarised what Man has

_____

nite religious conception, not at all rudimentary, which he has made known in one of his communications to the Geographical Society.

* The Sakaie questioned by de Saint-Pol Lias stated that he had no idea of superior beings or of another life ; but can this re-

told us regarding the Andamanese. The so precise details which we owe to him have, moreover, confirmed in
general the conclusions which I had drawn in my Étude
sur les Mincopies from the facts already mentioned by
Day.[40]

The Aëtas have a great veneration for the dead. La
Gironière says : " During several years they go to deposit
a little tobacco and betel upon their graves. The bow
and arrows which belonged to the deceased are hung, the
day when he is buried, over his grave, and every night,
according to the belief of his comrades, he comes forth to
go to the chase." [64]

The Negritos of Malacca appear not to have such precise ideas. Logan says that the tribes of Bermun light
a fire for several nights in succession upon the tomb, in
order to prevent the spirit from crying. Montano adds,
that among the Manthras the tomb is placed far from the
houses, " in order that the dead may not hear the crowing
of the cock." But neither of them speak of offerings intended for the spirit of the dead man, although among
the Manthras the tomb is evidently the object of peculiar
cares.

Chastity, Modesty.—Montano has given us information relative to the chastity of young Aëta girls, Man
upon those of young Mincopies. Symes had already recognised this virtue among these latter, and adds a very
significant fact. Two young Mincopy girls, prisoners on
an English vessel, soon became reassured in regard to all
other dangers; but although they were lodged in a room

sult of a short conversation invalidate the circumstantial and precise information given by Logan? Evidently not. It is probable
that Totilo did not care to reply upon a subject touching upon the
most sacred sentiments. Any one who has attempted to draw out a
Basque or Breton peasant upon the superstitions generally received
in his region will readily admit this.

by themselves, they never slept at the same time. They watched alternately over their honour.

Let us add that no one who has so far visited the Andamans has made the slightest allusion to facts or scenes analogous to those which the discoverers of the Pacific archipelagoes so frequently describe. So far as chastity is concerned, the Andaman women appear incontestably superior to the Polynesian women.

Among the accusations usually made against a crowd of savage tribes, one of the most frequent is that of lack of modesty. But one already knows that travellers have often been mistaken in this matter, so far as to have considered as a refinement of immodesty exactly that which in the mind of the natives was only an act of the commonest decency.

We lack precise information upon this point for the greater part of the Negrito populations; but at the Andamans, where the dress is as scanty as possible, we know, thanks to Mr. Man, that this clothing exists, that it has a particular name, and that to show one's self unclad is regarded as indecent by the natives. Although showing itself in other ways than among us, modesty exists no less among these islanders.

Moreover, the history of a Mincopy brought to Europe shows how much these islanders are affected by the sentiments of which we speak. When one wished to photograph John Andaman standing naked, he took off his garments with visible reluctance; he put them on again with evident satisfaction. This man, almost a *savage*, blushed at the thought of being seen naked.

General Character.—From the entirety of the facts here presented, it appears that the Negritos are far from meriting the accusations of which they are too often the object.

The Mincopies, so long looked upon as dreadful cannibals, when seen near by have become a sort of spoiled children, a little capricious, but good in character. Mouat paints this people as gay, laughing, fond of singing and dancing. Far from being intractable and fierce, it has shown itself humane and hospitable as soon as it has ceased to fear.

The English traveller adds : " It is courageous, hardened to toil, adroit, extremely active, and under the influence of civilisation it would become intelligent and industrious." We have seen that Man confirms all these opinions.

Montano tells me, in one of his notes : " Not only are the Negritos *not* fierce, they are truly humane. They care for the sick with much devotion, even when they do not belong to their family."

The same traveller writes : " The Manthra does not lack intelligence, but his thoughtlessness and idleness bar his progress." At the same time he attributes to this people mild manners—as we have already seen. Montano is here entirely in agreement with Logan. There are, however, found among the tribes of Bermun generally a certain inconstancy and a ready susceptibility to emotion. " It is necessary to treat them like children," said he. . This is precisely the expression employed by Saint-John in speaking of the Mincopies. The two populations resemble each other. One sees it in moral as in physical character, and to deny them fundamental ethnic identity is evidently impossible for any one who has at all studied the question.

Conclusion.—There results from this study, it seems to me, one conclusion, evident and easy to formulate. Almost unanimously the populations we have been considering have been regarded as very low in the scale of humanity. In regard to the Mincopies particularly, some *savants*, of great merit otherwise, seem to have believed that here finally one had placed his hand upon the missing link between man and the ape. We have just seen that this is not so; and that where they have lived most outside of movement and mixture—which alone elevate societies—the Negritos show themselves true men in all things and for all things.

CHAPTER VI.

THE NEGRILLOS, OR PYGMIES OF AFRICA.

Ancient travellers; modern discoveries.—Western Negrillos: M'Boulous; Baboukas; Akouas.—Eastern Negrillos: Cincalles; Mazo; Maleas.—Negrillos of the Wellé; Akkas.—Stature; features; colour; proportions.—Tebo and Chairallah.—General observations.—Primitive migrations.—Importance of traditions and of legends.

THE little men of Africa, interviewed by the ancients, and whose very real existence has given rise to so many fables, have been rediscovered only very recently by the moderns.

In 1625 Battel first made known certain facts collected by him in Loango.* At eight days' journey to the east of Cape Negro † is located, according to him, the territory of Mani Kesock, and to the northeast of this "dwells a nation of pygmies who call themselves *Matimbas*, of the height of a boy of twelve years, but of extraordinary bigness. Their food is the flesh of beasts, which they shoot

---

* Andrew Battel. English sailor. made prisoner by the Portuguese in 1589, was taken to the Congo district, where he remained a captive nearly eighteen years. His adventures were published in the collection of Purchas. Walckenaer [18b] has given a detailed synopsis of them, after having shown the evidences of truthfulness in the narrative.

† Not the Cape Negro at 16° 3′ south latitude and 9° 34′ east longitude, on the south of Benguela, but Cape Negro at the western limit of the Bay of Mayomba—perhaps at 3° 30′.

with arrows. They pay Mani Kesock a tribute of elephants' tusks and tails. Although there is no great fierceness in their characters, they do not wish to enter the houses of the Marambas, nor to receive them into their villages. . . . Their women use the bow and arrows with as much skill as the men. They are not afraid to go alone into the woods with no other protection than their poisoned arrows." [185]

Without making known the sources of his information, Dapper [39] gives analogous details about the *Mimos* or *Bakké-Bakkés*, whom he seems to place a little farther south, in the heart of Loango.

Some very recent observations, of which the oldest does not appear to date back beyond 1861, [180, 74] have come to confirm these old statements. The members of a German expedition have rediscovered in Loango, under the name of *Babonkos*, the *Bakké-Bakkés* of Dapper, and have brought back some portraits, and some photographs.* [188, 75] Dr. Touchard has reported the recent disappearance of a Gaboon population, the *Akoas*, [180] of which one small group was yet settled, in 1868, in the woods to the north of the River Nazareth. The Admiral Fleuriot de Langle was able to photograph one of its representatives (Fig. 21). This Akoa was a veritable dwarf. It is the same of the *M'Boulous*, *Chekianis* or *Osiékanis*, visited by Touchard and Marche. [107] Wedged in between the Fans and the Pongoués, they are likely to disappear like their brothers the Akoas.

In grouping together the various information derived from these photographs and descriptions, Hamy has been able to trace a very nearly complete portrait of some of

---

* [188, 75] I borrow from Hamy's work these references, as also the greater part of the following ones relative to the history of the western Negrillos.

these dwarfs of Africa. The Akoa studied by Admiral Fleuriot "appeared about forty years of age, and measured 1ᵐ39 to 1ᵐ40. He was admirably proportioned, He had a very little head, hairs well planted and less woolly than those of Negroes properly so called, a straight nose, the commissure of the lips well marked without displaying anything of that brutal muzzle which some types of African Negroes present." * The photograph justifies these expressions. 'The head is round but relatively strong; its height, as compared with the total height of the figure, would be pretty nearly in the same proportion already reported by Hamy in a Babongo—one sixth.† The face is scarcely a little prognathous. The muscular masses of the thorax and the upper members have outlines at once rounded and firm, but the lower members are thin, the feet are plainly flat soled, and the heels project a little too much.'

Marche attributes to his M'Boulous a dirt-brown colour.‡ The Admiral Fleuriot confines himself to saying that these dwarfs are less dark than their taller neighbours.

One has just seen that the admiral has spoken of the stature of his Akoa only approximately. Marche also limits himself to saying that the M'Boulous do not exceed 1ᵐ60. Dr. Falkenstein has been more precise. The adult Babouko photographed by him was about forty years old, and measured 1ᵐ365.# The mean of these four numbers

---

* Letter from the admiral, quoted by Hamy.

† This proportion is the greatest yet reported in a human race. In this particular the Negrillos outdo the Negritos.

‡ These M'Boulous are generally lean and scrawny, in place of being robust as the Akoas. Marche saw in this the result of the unwholesome environment within which they are confined.

The other was a youth of fifteen years, whose stature was only 1ᵐ025.

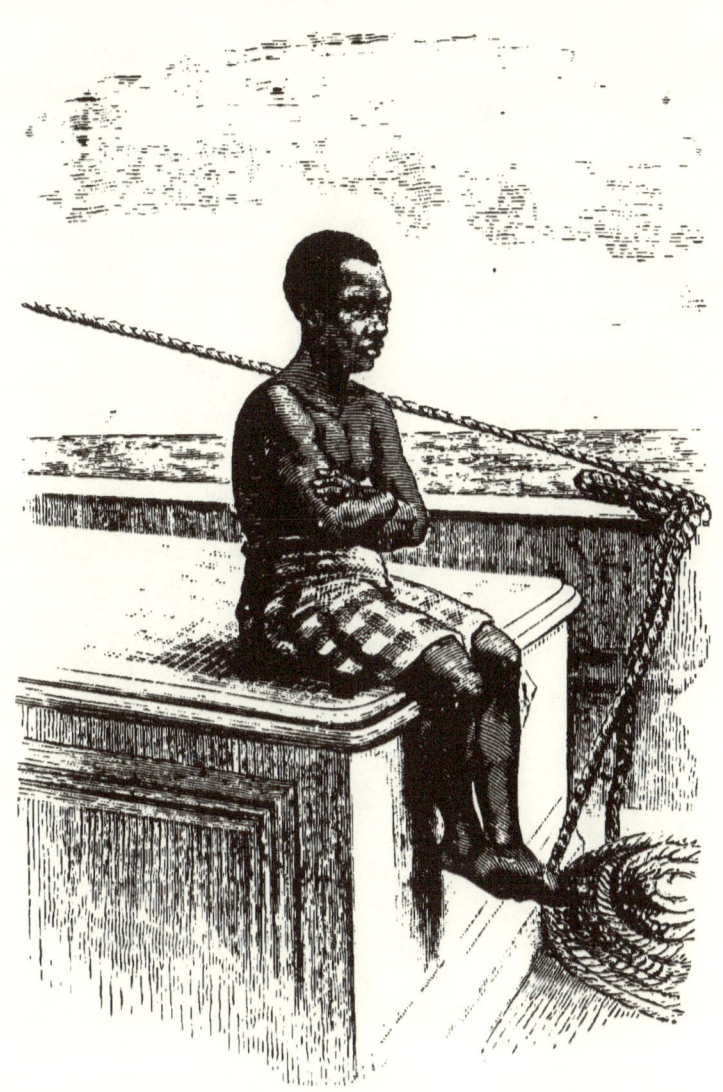

Fig. 21.—Akoa. (After Admiral Fleuriot de Langle.)

at our disposition is 1ᵐ439, but as two of the numbers
were maxima, it is almost certain that this figure is too
large. So far as stature goes, these little western Negroes
are slightly inferior to the Negritos, and approach the
Bushmen, whose mean stature is 1ᵐ370. But we shall see
that there are other Negrillos whose stature descends
even lower.

Moreover, the Negrillos differ from the Bushmen in an
anatomical character of even greater importance. The
latter are clearly dolichocephalic or subdolichocephalic.*
On the contrary, the Akoas, the Bongos, etc., are brachycephalic, or at least subbrachycephalic.† The measures
taken on the skulls brought back by de Langle, Marche,
etc., have placed this fact beyond question ; moreover, it
is apparent from a simple inspection of the photographs
(Figs. 21, 25).

Hamy has not contented himself with recognising and
characterising the Negrillo type among the tribes, remained
more or less pure, in the Gaboon, lower Ogowé, and Loango regions. He has pursued it further, and shown that
this type has played a very real and important ethnologic
rôle in the formation of several populations of those countries and neighbouring districts ; populations all of which
are related, moreover, to the Negro type properly so called.
Making use of information of every kind, he has shown
that crossing between dolichocephalic and brachycephalic
Negroes could alone account for the mixture of characters,
and especially for the morphological differences of the
head established from individual to individual among the
various tribes of the basins of the Ogowé, of Fernand Vaz.‡

---

* Index, 77·45.   † Ibid., 83·23.

‡ I ought to recall here, among other studies, that made by Hamy
of the craniometric results obtained by Owen upon a collection of
skulls brought back from this region by Du Chaillu. The learned
Englishman presented the measurements themselves. From them

On their return from the perilous voyage which was crowned by the discovery of the Alima and of the Licoma, Brazza and Ballay collected in an island of the upper Ogowé four skulls and one complete skeleton—to-day in the anthropological gallery of the museum. But, of these five skulls, two have a mean horizontal index of 82·24, and are therefore almost truly brachycephalic;[73] the other three are dolichocephalic. The former are the heads of Negrillos, the latter of Negroes.

Let us add that observations gathered by Marche among the N'Javis, the Apindjis, the Okotas, and the Akoas show that among these populations with relatively round heads the stature is, moreover, notably reduced.[*] Among the N'Javais it does not reach 1ᵐ60. Among the Akoas the mean stature of men is 1ᵐ50 to 1ᵐ52, that of women from 1ᵐ40 to 1ᵐ43.[107] At the same time the colour pales, the forms are elegant—above all, among the women, whose figure, a little plump, is very agreeable. Evidently the Negro type proper is here modified in places by a distinct ethnological element, and we may consider all this region as having formerly been, as even now being in a

---

our countryman calculated the indices, and showed that, among ninety-three skulls in the collection, forty-nine only were dolichocephalic or subdolichocephalic, thirty-three were mesaticephalic, eleven subbrachycephalic, two brachycephalic. The intervention of an ethnic element pertaining to this last type appears very clearly from this discussion, which has been for Hamy the beginning of all his works upon the subject.[73]

* Hamy connects the Obongos met with by Du Chaillu near Niembouai in the land of the Ashangos (1° 58′ 54″ south latitude and 11° 56′ 38″ east longitude). But the dirty-yellow color, and, above all, the hair growing in little tufts tightly coiled, have led to connecting these dwarfs with the Bushmen. Yet the traveller did not observe, in any of the women seen, either steatopygia or tablier. Some uncertainties, then, are possible relative to the ethnic affinities of the Obongos which cranial measurements alone can remove.[97]

degree, a centre of Negrillo population. I shall later return to this distinction to be made between the past and the present.

I believe that the Tenda Maié, country of small area included within a bend of the Rio Grande, should be considered as another centre of the same nature, but located more to the north and west. Behold what Mollien said of it, who visited these countries in 1818 : " There is little uniformity in the general character of the physiognomy of these ; but the inhabitants of the village of Faran are remarkable for the littleness of their stature, the slightness of their limbs, and the gentleness of their voice. They are truly the pygmies of Africa." *[119] In spite of the incompleteness of this brief notice, it is easy to see that the Tenda Maié supports a mixed population, of which the Negrillos are an element.

Although the Tenda Maié is very distant from the spot where the Nasamones of Herodotus were taken prisoners, it is difficult not to connect the little men of whom the Greek historian speaks with the pygmies of Mollien. The upper basins of the Rio Grande and the Niger cannot be very distant from each other, and it is easy to admit that they formerly supported the same races of men.

The Gaboon, the Ogowé, the Loango, are very distant from the Tenda Maié, and between the two extreme points one has as yet reported no Negrillos. I am disposed, however, to admit that these different populations of little stature are related. We know that the whole Guinean region has been the theatre of successive invasions, which have led to the seacoast conquerors coming from the interior. The direction in which these swarming tribes marched, their murderous habits, of which the Dahomans still give to-day an example only too well

---

* The village of Faran is situated at about 14° 15′ west longitude and 10° + north latitude.

13

known, easily explain how a relatively feeble race might
—*must* necessarily—have disappeared over a considerable
area. We have just seen this disappearance taking place
in our days, under our eyes, among some of these tribes.
It is doubtless one of the last scenes of a drama whose
earlier acts go far back into the past.

I believe we may, from the entirety of the facts, conclude that the Negrillos of the Rio Grande and those of
the Gulf of Guinea district are near relatives, and that
both are related to the little men reported to Herodotus
by the pilgrims of Cyrene.

Almost directly east of the Gaboon pygmy group, in
Central Africa, there probably exists a great Negrillo centre of population, of which the ancients could hardly
have known. The information gathered by Stanley from
Ahmed, son of Djoumah, seems to me too precise not
to have a basis of truth.[177] This ivory dealer had seen
the little men of whom he spoke; he had fought with
them; he admitted that he had been beaten by them;
and his accounts agree with all the other information
gathered by the great American traveller. From all evidence it appears that towards the centre of the region
comprised in the great bend of the Livingstone there
dwells a numerous population of dwarfs called *Vouatouas*,
spread over a great area, and perfectly independent.* On
his journey to Ikonndon (2° 53′ south latitude) Stanley
captured an individual belonging to this tribe or a neighbouring one. This Vouatona was 1ᵐ41; he had a large
head, a face surrounded with an uneven growth of beard,
and a light chocolate colour. Like the little Negroes of

* Upon Stanley's great map this region is placed at about 3°
south latitude, and at 19° east longitude. The trader adds that the
Vouatouas are also called *Vouakouaangas*, *Vauakoumas*, and *Voua-
koumous*.

Battel, these Vouatouas are hunters of the elephant and users of poisoned arrows.

Dr. Wolff, in betaking himself to Loullengo, king or chief of the Bahoubas, met with a population which is no doubt related to Stanley's Vouatouas. These *Batouas*, as he calls them, are evidently of the same colour—a yellowish brown, lighter than that of the Negroes of greater stature. Yet the traveller asserts that they have no beard. These Batouas, moreover, would be the smallest race known if the information given by Dr. Wolff is exact. None of them, according to him, surpass 1ᵐ40, and the mean stature would be 1ᵐ30. The Batouas are numerous in the region, but they do not for that mix with the rest of the population. They live by themselves in villages scattered over the Bahouba territory.[68] In spite of the meagreness of our information relative to the Negrillos of Central Africa, the *ensemble* of their physical and social characters plainly connects them with those of whom we have already spoken. We are now about to find entirely similar features among their brothers, the descendants of the pygmies of Homer and of Pomponius Mela.

The tradition relative to these latter has never been lost. It has been preserved particularly among the Arabian geographers, who have placed a *River of the Pygmies* to the south of Abyssinia. Leon d'Avanchers thinks he has identified this river with a stream which rises in the Auko Mountains, a little north of the equator. It is in this region and under the thirty-second degree of east longitude that the eminent missionary placed his *Wa-Berikimos*,[9] called also Cincallès, which is equivalent to *What a marvel!* The eminent missionary himself saw in the kingdom of Gera several of these "dwarfs, beings deformed, short, big-headed, at most four feet in height" (1ᵐ30 *circa*).[8]

The information collected by d'Abaddie from Amace,

ambassador of the King of Kullo, and from a woman, native of Kaffa (near 6° north latitude and 34° east longitude), confirm the preceding fact. The *Malas* or *Maze-Maleas* were a little over 1ᵐ50 in height; they are black, and rarely reddish (*taym*).* The information kindly supplied to me by d'Abbadie appears to locate these small Negroes a little farther to the north. But this very fact would suggest that here, as in western Africa, they are dispersed over a more or less extended area, and that their tribes bear different names. Everything suggests, then, that there exists south of the country of the Gallas a centre of Negrillo population, and I believe I am not rash in connecting these eastern tribes with the pygmies of Pomponius Mela, just as I have identified with the little men of Herodotus the dwarfs of Senegambia.

As modern travellers have advanced farther and farther up the Nile, they have gathered new testimonies relative to populations of very little stature. The existence of true pygmies thus became more and more probable, so much so that in the *Instructions*, drawn up by a committee of the Academy of Sciences, for the expedition projected by d'Escayrac de Lauture[88, 89] it was deemed necessary to call especial attention to the subject. But, one knows it, the Europeans met no little men in ascending the Nile to its sources. Speke alone saw at the court of Kamrasi a deformed dwarf, whose portrait he gives us. But this design and the details accompanying it show that Kymenia, far from belonging to a pygmy race, did not even know of the existence of these little blacks.[176]

It is Schweinfurth who has had the honour of demonstrating what truth the myth of Homer concealed, and of justifying the words of Aristotle. But to do so he was obliged to quit the Nile Valley, to gain the valley of the

---

* Manuscript communication from M. d'Abbadie; also ¹.

Wellé, to pass through the country of the Niam-Niams, and to penetrate to that of the Monbuttos, whom he first visited. It was at the court of Munza that he discovered the dwarf race still called in the country by the name of *Akkas* which Mariette has read by the si le of a portrait of a dwarf upon a monument of the ancient Egyptian empire.

From information given to the eminent traveller by Adimokoû, chief of the little colony supported by Munza near his royal residence, it appears that the country of the *Akkas* or *Tikki-Tikkis*, is situated at about 3° north latitude and 25° east longitude.* This country is probably great. Tolerated by the surrounding populations and protected by their powerful neighbours, the Akkas appear to occupy a continuous area and number nine distinct tribes, each with its own chief or king.†[172] At the time of Schweinfurth's visit these tribes had submitted, at least in part, to Moûmmeri, one of Munza's vassals, who had come to render homage to his sovereign at the head of a veritable regiment of these little Negroes, so that the European traveller had at once under his eyes several hundred of these dwarf warriors.[172]

In exchange for one of his dogs Schweinfurth obtained

---

* Munza employed the word *Akka* to designate these little blacks; Moûmmeri, their ruler, called them *Tikki-Tikkis*.

† This journey is one of the most remarkable among those which have so rapidly increased our knowledge of the interior of Africa. It lasted from July, 1868, until the first part of November, 1871. The greater part of it was in countries absolutely unexplored previously by Europeans. The explorer had gathered rich collections of every kind, numerous observations, notes, drawings, maps. Almost all these scientific treasures perished in a fire. One can appreciate the profound grief of a *savant* compelled to recount his journey almost entirely from his memory. His work is, none the less, the most precious for a knowledge of regions until then entirely unknown.

from Munza one of these Akkas, whose portrait he has
given.* He intended bringing him back with him to
Europe, but the poor Nsévoué died of dysentery at Berber,
to the south of Khartoum. Perhaps his skeleton, found
by some traveller, will figure some day in one of our mu-
seums, and will furnish to science the anatomical facts
which now are lacking to it.

In fact, the information which we have regarding the
Akkas has all been collected upon living individuals, and
but few of them. The measurements and notes taken by
Schweinfurth perished in the fatal fire which devoured
the fruit of three years of travels and studies, and it was
very difficult to make up this loss even in part. However,
Marno had the good fortune in his travels to meet with
two female Akka slaves, a young girl and an adult.[100, 74, 73]
Another adult female, Saïda, sent to Italy by Gessi Pacha,
has been hastily studied by Giglioli.[62] Chaillé-Long Bey
also saw a woman who came from the country of the
Niam-Niams in company with a sister of Munza.[99, 100] I
reproduce her picture here (Fig. 22). Vossion, vice-consul of France at Khartoum, has briefly described a male
adult in an unpublished letter, which he has permitted me
to consult. But although these pieces of evidence confirm
and supplement each other in some points, they would
have left much to be desired if a most fortunate circum-
stance had not supplied European anthropologists the op-
portunity of studying for themselves the curious human
race of whom we speak.

---

* Since Munza has learned the value of the Akkas as an object
of curiosity, he has given some of them from time to time to the
great merchants of ivory who visit him each year. Thus an individual of this race reached Khartoum, sent as a present to the Governor of Soudan by Emin Bey (Dr. Schnitzer). This is the one
briefly described by Mr. Vossion, vice-consul of France, in a letter
from which I present an extract farther along.

FIG. 22.—AKKA WOMAN PLACED BESIDE A MAN OF AVERAGE HEIGHT.
(After Chaillé-Long-Bey.)

A traveller more courageous than wise, Miani, had followed in Schweinfurth's footsteps, and had arrived among the Monbuttos. Less fortunate than his predecessor, he succumbed to the fatigues of the journey and died, bequeathing to the Society of Italian Geography two young Akkas whom he had got in exchange for a dog and a calf. After some vicissitudes, Tebo and Chairallah were received by a man of science and of heart — Count Miniscalchi Erizzo—who had them brought up under his own eyes.* [57] They could thus be followed and studied at leisure, while their photographs, liberally distributed by the Geographical Society, went to arouse everywhere the observations of anthropologists (Figs. 23, 24, 25).

This mass of data has had for first result the dissipation of certain doubts which had been expressed upon the subject of the reality of Schweinfurth's discovery. Some persons regarded the first individuals measured by travellers as chil-

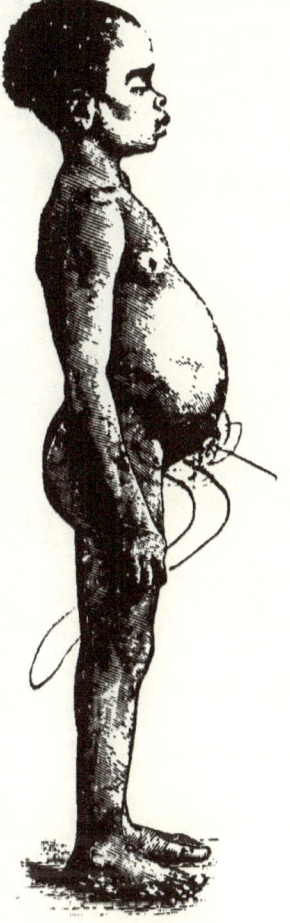

FIG. 23. — TEBO, SIDE VIEW. (After photograph of Count Miniscalchi.)

* Already, on their arrival at Cairo, Tebo and Chairallah had been examined by Colucci Pacha, Régny Bev, Dr. Gaillardot, and by Messrs. Schweinfurth, Owen, Cornalia, and Panceri, whom chance had brought together in the capital of Egypt. Their observations have appeared in the Bulletins de l'Institut Egyptien in 1873 and 1874. These little Negroes have also given occasion for many publications. [132, 133, 153, 19, 106, 32, 187, 62, 63]

dren, and wished to consider Tebo and Chairallah children destined to grow larger.* The precise observations

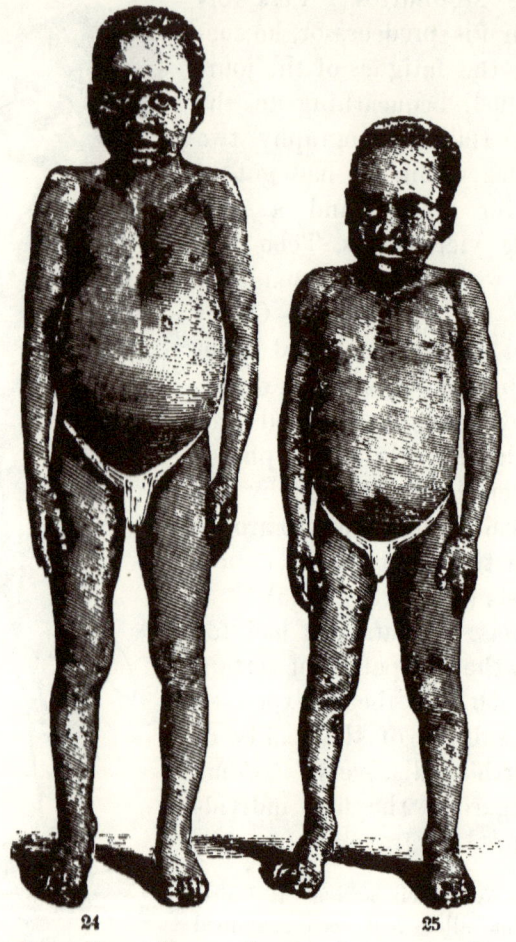

FIG. 24.—TEBO, FRONT VIEW.   FIG. 25.—CHAIRALLAH, FRONT VIEW.
(After photographs of Count Miniscalchi.)

of Marno, those of Giglioli and Chaillé-Long, upon three
women, those of Vossion upon a man, have replied to the

* Panizza;[133] also the Anthropological Society of Madrid.

first hypothesis; and the growing old of at least one of the Akkas of Miani, without his passing, without even reaching, the maximum stature suggested by Schweinfurth, has refuted the second.[*]

The Russian traveller measured six men; none, he said, exceeded 1ᵐ50. Vossion's man, aged thirty-two, was only 1ᵐ31. Tebo, the older of Miani's Akkas, had taken on the characteristics of manhood, and appears to have stopped growing at the height of 1ᵐ42, very nearly the mean of the three numbers. The woman of twenty to twenty-five years old, measured by Marno, was 1ᵐ36; that of Chaillé-Long, 1ᵐ216 at most; Saïda, 1ᵐ34; giving a mean of 1ᵐ305. The mean of the two sexes would be 1ᵐ356. These numbers place the Akkas in the matter of stature below the Mincopies, or even below the Bushmen. But the number of measures taken upon African pygmies is yet much too small for us to regard the result as satisfactory. This reservation is so much the more justifiable as no traveller has yet found an Akka presenting a stature so short as that of the Bushman woman, measured by Barrow, of 1ᵐ14, or that individual of the same race

---

[*] Some doubt has arisen upon the purity of blood of the Akkas of Miani, and Hamy has made formal reservations on the subject. These reservations, perhaps, have some foundation in the case of Chairallah. On the one hand, his cephalic index is very low (77·52); on the other hand, in their beautiful work upon the Akkas, Mantegazza and Zannetti, founding the prediction upon the presumed ages of the two subjects and upon the laws of growth, stated that Tebo would cease growing at a lower stature than Chairallah. The result has confirmed this prediction. Chairallah, still growing, was already 1ᵐ41; Tebo, with all the characteristics of an adult, and whose growth appeared to have ceased, had stopped at 1ᵐ42 (Giglioli). Moreover the latter had a very high cephalic index (80·23). Even then, if one should have some doubts about Chairallah, and believe that he had perhaps some little blood from the Negro race, it would not be the same regarding Tebo.

to which Dr. Weisbach attributes 1ᵐ only. Yet the observations of Dr. Wolff, which I have above recalled, appeared to confirm the general conclusion resulting from these measures. One might indeed say that these African Negrillos, evidently all of the same stock, were in reality the smallest human race.

Schweinfurth attributed to the Akkas a very large head and a large and almost spherical skull. This last detail is certainly exaggerated. The highest index accurately made is that resulting from the measurements of Marno; it is only 82·85—equal to about 80·85 upon the dry skull. The mean for three young subjects is 78·03, or more than 76 on the dry skull.* We are far from the true dolichocephaly of the Negroes, and find again the figures which we found to characterise the Negrillos.

The colour of the Akkas, according to Schweinfurth, recalls the colour of coffee slightly roasted. The observations upon Tebo and Chairallah confirm this opinion; but Count Miniscalchi has noticed that this colour is deeper in summer, paler in winter. The hair is almost the same colour, lighter in Chairallah than in Tebo. In both it is distinctly woolly and tufted. The beard, which has appeared in Tebo upon the chin and the upper lip, is of the same character.

Schweinfurth has represented Nsévoué as very prognathous with an aquiline nose in profile, but the end of which is as if immersed in the thickness of the upper lip. In him the chin protrudes. On the contrary, it is very retreating in Bômbi, whose nose is also more detached. The photograph of Tebo is in these two points more like the latter than the former type. The lips are, more-

---

* Hamy, taking into consideration the slight development of the temporal muscles in young subjects, diminishes the index obtained from measurements made upon the living by one unit only, in order to secure that of the dry skull. He would call this, then, at least 77.

over, not so thick as in Negroes, and are even described as thin by Vossion and Schweinfurth.

All the descriptions agree in attributing to the Akkas, men and women, an extreme abdominal development, which causes the adults to resemble the children of Arabs and Negroes. In the photographs of Tebo and Chairallah this feature is most pronounced. Panizza, making an anatomical examination of the causes of this development, attributed it to the unusual size of the left lobe of the liver and the spleen, as well as to the large amount of fat accumulated in the mesentery.

This exaggeration of the contents of the abdomen entailed anatomical consequences which have also attracted the attention of all observers. The chest, relatively narrow and flattened above, is dilated below in order to contain this enormous paunch. On the other hand, this projection of the abdomen demands, for maintenance of the equilibrium, that the lower portion of the spinal column should also project forward. Hence results among the Akkas the remarkable hollowing which has led to comparing the curve of the spinal column to an S.*

---

* This conformation has given rise to a singular misunderstanding, which has led to many discussions. In a communication made to the Egyptian Institute (December 5, 1873) Schweinfurth compared the curvature of the spinal column to a C. The eminent traveller was apparently speaking only of its lower portion, and meant that the concavity of the C should face backward. But under the influence of preconceived ideas, and in the hope of finding in the Akkas that link between man and the apes for which search has so long been made, some adventurous spirits thought that the whole column was in discussion, that the concavity of the C turned forward, and that consequently the Akkas resembled in this respect anthropomorphic apes. Before having seen the photographs I combated, at the Society of Anthropology and elsewhere, this idea as incompatible with the mode of locomotion in man and with the agility which all evidence attributed to the Akkas. Broca,

But it is evident that the abnormal development of the abdomen is not, among the Akkas, a true race characteristic, and that it is largely due to their manner of life, to the quality of the food, perhaps also to the general conditions of their habitat. This fact results from some observations of Count Miniscalchi, who has seen, after some weeks of regular and wholesome diet, "the extreme development of the abdomen disappear and the vertebral column resume its normal state." The same change was wrought in Saïda.

In order to terminate this physical sketch of the Akkas, it remains to speak of the limbs. The upper are long, and terminate in hands of great delicacy (Schweinfurth).* The lower limbs are short relatively to the trunk, and curve in somewhat. The feet also are bent in the same direction, rather more than those of other Africans.

The Akka women seem to greatly resemble their husbands. Giglioli speaks of Saïda as having a thick figure, short neck, arms neither slim nor long, hands rather large than small. The colour of this Akka was like that of Chairallah, very like that of a mulatto. The hair, of a sooty black, formed little balls less clearly isolated than his; prognathism very pronounced. This description agrees very well with the pictures of Chaillé-Long. This last authority adds that in his *Tikki-Tikki* the breasts hung down markedly, although she asserted that she had had no children. He says, too, that she had very little hands and feet (Fig. 22).

The physiological characteristics of the Akkas are those of most savage races. Their senses are very acute,

---

as well as Mantegazza and Zannetti, later developed the same arguments in support of an opinion common to us all, and which all the facts now acquired justify.

* The photographs of Tebo and Chairallah and the cast taken upon Tebo do not justify these praises.

and Schweinfurth on several occasions insists upon their extraordinary agility. According to the Monbuttos, these little Negroes leap about in the high herbage like grasshoppers. Nsévoué partly preserved this little habit during his stay with Schweinfurth, and could never carry a plate without spilling more or less of its contents.

The Akkas are very courageous. "They are men, and men who know how to fight," said Moûmmeri, in speaking of those who accompanied him. They are great elephant hunters; they assault them with very short bows, and with lances hardly longer than themselves.* Long Bey confirms all these details, and adds that the women are as warlike as the men—which recalls in every particular the facts given by Battel.[99, 100]

Schweinfurth gives a very sad picture of the character and intelligence of Nsévoué. He represents him as loving to see men and animals suffer, as being unable to learn Arabic or any of the dialects of the country. Count Miniscalchi, on the other hand, found in Tebo and Chairallah affectionate pupils, appreciative, and disposed to learn. Both, but especially Tebo, had a real fondness for music. Two years after their arrival in Europe these two Akkas could read and write. Their father by adoption placed under the eyes of his colleagues, in 1879, two letters written and composed by them without any aid, a facsimile of which was inserted in the transactions of the congress. They had not, on that account, forgotten their own language. Miniscalchi has been able to gather from them several hundred words, and to prepare with their help a grammar of their tongue, which he considers the same as the idioms of the Niam-Niams.†

---

* See the portrait of Bômbi. Schweinfurth does not say that the arrows are poisoned.

† Miniscalchi used with them the Arabic language, which they spoke fluently.

What have these Akkas become under the influence of European climate and of an education applied for the first time to representatives of this ancient race, always savage, and found two or three degrees south of the equator? One understands how much interest attaches to this question, and we owe much to Giglioli for having replied to it in detail.*

Tebo has always perfectly stood the usually cold winters of Verona. Chairallah has had fevers, had much coughing, and suffered with rheumatism during his first two or three years. Both are now entirely acclimated. It is the same with Saïda.

Tebo has been modelled, and his bust is in the museum. In comparing it with his photograph taken in 1874 it is seen that he has lost his childish air. His forehead is less full, without, however, being as retreating as Nsévoué. In this respect he is more like Bômbi. His prognathism is somewhat more marked. His other features are little modified.†

The general character of the two Akkas has remained sensitive, impulsive, and recalls that of our children. They love to play; their movements are quick; when they walk they naturally go at quickstep.‡

Tebo is more affectionate, more faithful to his duties;

---

* [63] This memoir was written in 1880, consequently five years later than Count Miniscalchi's.

† Giglioli thinks he can recognise with the eye some slight elongation of the head. An examination of the bust and the measurements, necessarily only approximate, which I have taken upon the plaster, do not give me such an impression.

‡ All the preceding might also apply to Saïda, yet she has not been dealt with as her fellow-countrymen. She has remained a servant, without learning either to read or write. She speaks Italian fluently, and a little German, which is the language of her mistress. She is at times capricious, and she loves to play with children (Giglioli).

his conduct has always been excellent. Chairallah, more intelligent, has shown at times some instincts of hatred and revenge. Yet they have never had quarrels with their young companions, and they love each other tenderly.

Both have been baptised, and show a certain amount of devotion in religious exercises, yet their spiritual director does not regard their convictions as very deep.

Both of them have forgotten their mother tongue, and have almost forgotten Arabic. They speak Italian perfectly, but had at first much difficulty in pronouncing words where two z's occur—*bellazza, carezza.*

Both experience very strongly the sentiment of emulation. In class they have shown themselves superior to their European schoolfellows of ten or twelve years old. The grades which their teacher placed before Giglioli prove that they have stood remarkably well in the tests they have passed through in composition, arithmetic, grammatical analysis, and in dictation.*

The Countess Miniscalchi gave music lessons to Tebo. Giglioli has heard him play upon the piano, with some sentiment and much exactness, two quite difficult passages.†

One sees, in spite of their little stature, their long arms, their pot-bellies, and their short legs, that the Akkas are indeed really men; and those who have thought to find in them half apes should by this time be fully disabused.

---

* Chairallah had obtained ten (perfect mark) for dictation and penmanship; Tebo, ten for dictation. The other grades are eight and nine in all subjects except arithmetic, where Chairallah falls to seven and Tebo to six. One finds here again the general fact that savages are inferior in the direction of scientific aptitudes.

† Unfortunately the education of Tebo and Chairallah has been interrupted. Both to-day perform service in the Miniscalchi family (Giglioli).

14

The totality of facts just presented leads me to general considerations, which I shall state briefly. And, first, in going from Senegambia and the Gaboon towards the country of the Gallas and Monbuttos, we have established the existence of several human groups which are characterised by little stature, by a head relatively large and round, by a colour less dark than that of the Negroes proper, by instincts and manners almost similar. With Hamy, we would recognise in these groups so many representatives of a special race—the race of Negrillos—who in Africa correspond to the Negritos of Asia and Melanesia.

It is evident that the ancients have had concerning these Negrillos—as concerning the Negritos—some more or less precise knowledge, and that they have made from them their African pygmies; but they have placed them in three geographical localities where they do not to-day exist; one must go farther from Europe in order to find them. Moreover, these pygmies appear to us as forming centres of population isolated and widely separated. Finally, at one of these centres at least, we witness the decadence of the race and its fusion with neighbouring populations of greater size and strength.

All these facts recall too strongly what we have seen has taken place, and is now taking place, among the Negritos for us not to refer it to the same causes. Everything unites to make us believe that the Negrillos were formerly more numerous; that they formed populations denser and more continuous; that they have been crowded back, separated, divided, by superior races. Their history, if we could only know it, would certainly present resemblances to that of their Eastern brothers.

But we have seen that in the Orient everything suggests that the Negritos have preceded, on the soil where we find them, the races which have oppressed, dispersed, and almost annihilated them. As to the Negrillos, analogous facts lead to a similar conclusion. We are thus led to admit as very probable that the little brachy-cephalic Negroes have occupied at least a large part of Africa prior to the Negroes properly so called, who are characterised by a greater stature and by dolichocephaly. These last are the Papuans of Africa, as the Negrillos are its Negritos.

These comparisons do not result from a superficial examination of the African and Indo-Melanesian blacks; they are justified by a detailed study of their skulls. This study places in evidence extremely striking resemblances between the two great anthropological formations which represent the Negro type at the two extremities of our continent.* [157]

Whence can come this close relationship between populations separated by such vast spaces and by so many and such diverse races? Are these resemblances and agreements due to a community of origin? These questions, and many others, had been formulated even before the discovery of the Negrillos, which causes their still more imperious presentation. There have been many replies.

Logan has sustained with much wisdom, and in examining the question from various points of view, the idea that the Negroes, originating in Africa, have penetrated into Asia and into Melanesia by a slow infiltration taking place over the sea. He makes them play an important rôle among the populations of Madagascar.[94, 96] Flower is disposed to admit that the little black race, developed in the southern part of India, has spread east and west, peopling Melanesia and Africa. It is from it that have come the Negroes of large stature.[51] Allen also derives the African Negroes from Asia, and seeks to show that they have left some traces of their passage upon several points in the in-

---

* De Quatrefages and Hamy.

termediate countries.[3] Prof. Seeley claims that the Negro
race formerly occupied a belt of land stretching from
Africa to Melanesia, which is now submerged.[3]

The authors whom I have just cited have considered
only the origin of the black races. I have shown long
since in my courses, and suggested in one of my books,
that one cannot separate the history of these races from that
of their yellow and white sisters.* I have returned to a detailed study of the subject in another work.[156] Behold, in
a few words, the solution which I believe I have given to
the general problem. Mankind originated in Tertiary
times, somewhere in northern Asia. Migrations began at
that period ; and without doubt from that moment the
species commenced to differentiate itself on account of
the differing conditions of existence which its tribes en-
countered. The Glacial period caused a great migration,
radiating out in every direction ; yet either then, or earlier, the various populations grouped themselves about, or
in the interior of, the central highland of Asia. There
the three fundamental, physical, and linguistic types of
mankind arose. All are yet represented in this region.
No other point on the globe shows anything similar, and
this fact justifies, I believe, the conclusions I have drawn.

The black type appeared in the south of Asia, between
the highland and the sea. Its representatives, pressed between the yellow peoples on the north and the whites on
the west, could not, like their brothers, extend over vast
continental areas. Very early they had to seek by sea a new
country—above all, when invasions, which the existence
of mixed races clearly proves, came to dispute with them
the possession of a domain relatively narrow. To escape
the invaders, there was no resource but flight by sea ; and,
in consequence of difference in habitat, they migrated,

---

* The Human Species.

some east, others west.   Thus they were the first to people the eastern archipelagoes and the islands of the Bay
of Bengal.   They arrived in Africa by crossing the Strait
of Bab-el-Mandeb and the Gulf of Aden.   Everywhere,
moreover, the Negritos and the Negrillos preceded the
Papuans and the true Negroes.   This fact is proved by
the geographical distribution of these different races, as I
have shown on various occasions.

The study of the little Negro races will suggest one
last thought.

In speaking of their pygmies the ancients have mingled
very true facts with exaggerations and fables.   Modern
science, sometimes misled by its rigidity, has long considered only that which was impossible in the tradition relative to the little men of Asia or of Africa, and has therefore rejected the whole at once.   We have just seen where-
in it was wrong, and from that even we may draw a lesson.

When we are dealing with traditions or legends of
people less learned than ourselves, and above all with
those of savage peoples, however strange or bizarre they
may appear to us, it is well to study them carefully.   A
good number of these legends enclose interesting and very
real facts, concealed by superstitions, misunderstandings,
habits of language, errors of interpretation.   The task of
the man of science should be like that of the miner who
separates gold from the rock.   Very often he may, with a
little study and wise criticism, bring out some important
truth from this mass of errors.

CHAPTER VII.

RELIGIOUS BELIEFS OF THE HOTTENTOTS AND THE BUSHMEN.

Hottentots and Bushmen.—Hottentots: physical characters.—Rôle of the woman.—Poetry.—Language.—Place of origin of the race.—Age of stone at the Cape.—Religious beliefs of the Bushmen; dualism; superstitions.—Religious beliefs of the Hottentots; old information on the subject.—Good gods.—Tsûi-goa, supreme god.—The strife against Gaunab.—Profound faith of the Hottentots in Tsûi-goa—Absence of religious edifices and of idols.—Great religious festivals; hymn to Tsûi-goa.—A martyr of Tsûi-goa.—Heitsi-eibib.—His tombs.—His births.—His strife against the lion and against Gama-gorib.—One of his deaths, followed by resurrection.—Khâb (the moon).—The legend of the hare.—Nanub (the storm-cloud); Gnrub (the thunder); Nabas (the lightning).—Hymn and chanted dialogues.—Khunuseti (the Pleiades).—Bad gods.—Gaunab, the great god of evil.—The Mantis Gaunab.—The vassals of Gaunab.—Refutation of an hypothesis of Mr. Hahn.—Gurikhoïsib, the first man.—His combat with the lion.—The future life.—Spirits of the dead, bad and good.—Spirits of ancestors.—Worship: priests; sorcerers.—Various superstitions.—Mythological theory of Mr. Hahn.

WHEN the Dutch, under the leadership of van Riebeek, founded Cape Colony, in 1652, the southern end of Africa was occupied by two populations very similar in some respects, but distinguished nevertheless by certain physical characters and of very dissimilar modes of life. The first, the more important, and whom the Europeans already knew, inhabited only the coast and the fertile plains. It was of somewhat tall stature, attaining a mean of 1ᵐ663. The features of the face were anything but beautiful (Fig. 26). To a skull narrow and elongated from in front backward, to the characteristic hair of the Negro, this type joined a yellow-brown colour, more or

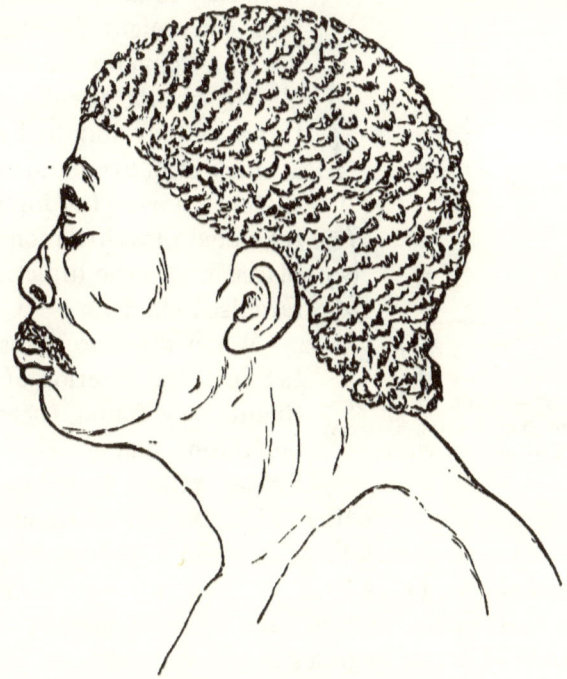

FIG. 26.—BUST OF SWOON, HOTTENTOT. (From a bust modelled upon the living subject. Collection of the Museum.)

less dark and often ruddy—so much so that even to-day these natives call themselves *red men* (Fig. 27).* These Africans were essentially herders, possessing numerous herds of cattle, of sheep, and of goats, knowing how to

---

* *Ava Khoib.* "This word," Hahn says, "is synonymous with *Khoï-Khoï.* The Hottentots call the Europeans *Uri Khoin* (white men), and the Bantus *Nu Khoien* (black men)." [67]

work iron and copper, and acquainted with the art of pottery. At the time of Kolbe they formed sixteen distinct nations, each designated by a special name, but divided into petty tribes.* They dwelt in temporary villages, the huts of which were easy to take down and transport, convenient for the mode of life of a nomadic, pastoral people. These *krauls* usually contained three to four hundred souls, and at times even five hundred. Some customs, having the force of laws, regulated these little communities, placed under the direction of hierarchised chiefs.

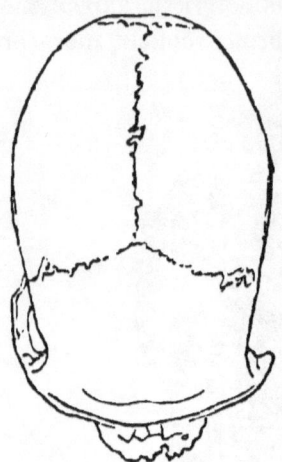

FIG. 27.—SKULL OF HOTTENTOT FROM CAPE COLONY. (Museum collection.)

When the Europeans penetrated into the interior of the continent they found there another population, characterised by a still lighter yellow tint, but quite as homely as the preceding (Figs. 28, 29). Although having hair of the same sort, these men had a skull relatively broader and shorter (Figs. 30, 31); but their most striking feature was their little stature. As we have already stated, the stature of these pygmies of the Cape descends to a mean of 1ᵐ37 among the men and 1ᵐ22 among the women. They are, however, vigorous and remarkably agile. These little men live exclusively by hunting; they scarcely erect the simplest temporary shelters, and their industry is limited to the making of a bow, arrows, and a coarse pottery.

---

* 80 Walckenaer admits seventeen nations. But he does not recognise that "the Bushies" are only hordes of dispersed Hottentots who have adopted the mode of life of the Bushmen. Perhaps, too, he meant these latter themselves, who were not then distinguished from the Hottentots.

Always wandering in little bands of from fifteen to fifty persons, and having no bond of union, these typical savages, driven back into the most frightful deserts, were incessantly warring with all the other inhabitants of the country, who hunted them and killed them like wild beasts.

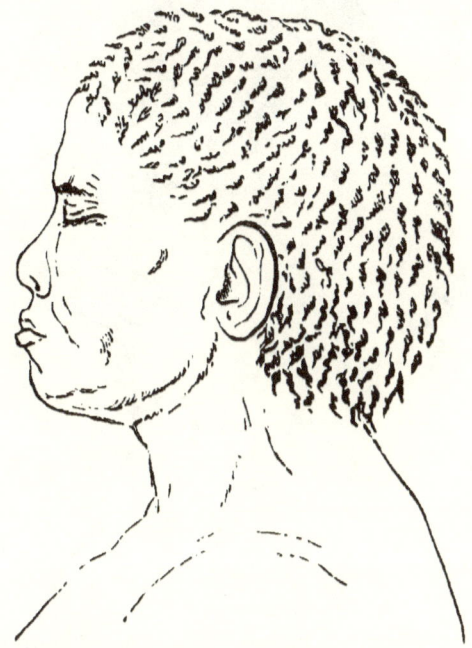

Fig. 28.—Bust of Yunka, Bushman. (From a mould made upon the living. Collection of the Museum.)

These last are those who are habitually called Bushmen, Bosjesmans, Boschismans. Those of whom I spoke first are the Hottentots. These names are purely European in origin. The first are easily understood; no one has discovered the etymology of the second. Until very recently no one knew what the Bushmen called themselves, and even Hahn says nothing in this matter. But Arbousset and Daumas have discovered that they call

themselves among themselves 'Khuaï.[6] The Hottentots
call them Sûn,* an expression which may be translated by
aborigines, and style themselves *Khoï-Khoï*, literally *men-
men* or THE men.†

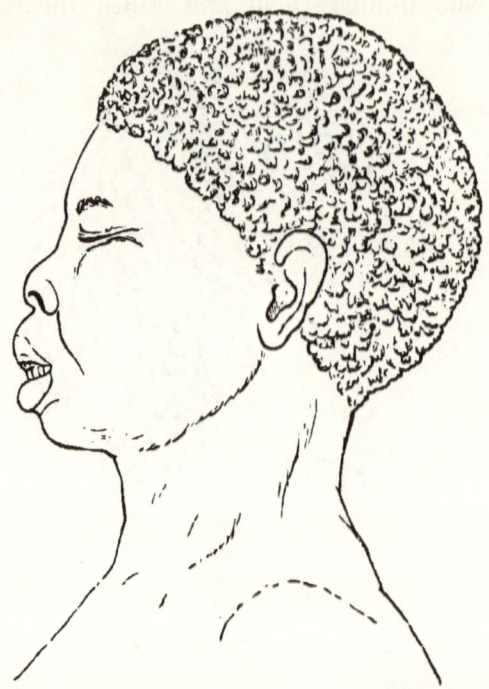

FIG. 29.—BUST OF SOARTJE BARTMANN, CALLED THE HOTTENTOT VENUS.
(From a mould taken after death. Collection of the Museum.)

---

* In the singular, Sâb (Hahn).[67] The official documents of the
Cape call them Sonqua. One also finds them called by the names
Batuas, Baroas, Bushies, Bosmanneken, Housouanas. . . . It is necessary not to confound with the Sûn those Khoï-Khoï whom persecution has driven back into the deserts, where they lead the same life as
the true Bushmen. This is an error into which Levaillant and other
authors have fallen. It may be that we can thus explain the con-
tradiction in the narrative of Captain F. Alexander and the reflections that Hahn makes upon it.

† [67] Various authors or travellers have written *Choï-Choin*, *Koe-
Kaeb*, *Quaiqua*, *Quaqua*, etc.

From this very fact one might draw the conclusion that the Bushmen have at first occupied the whole region, that the Khoï-Khoï are conquerors. All the studies made to the present time support such a conclusion; they even permit us to go further. Already some travellers and anthropologists have regarded the Bushmen as representing the local pure race, and the Hottentots as being the result of a crossing of this race with various Negro populations. The detailed examination of skulls has fully confirmed this result, which may be considered a definite acquisition to science.[157]

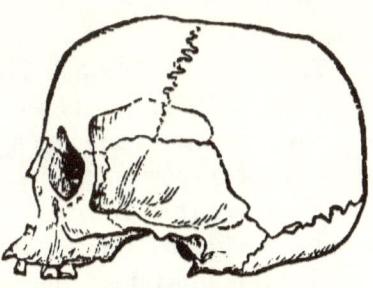

FIG. 30.—SKULL OF BUSHMAN. (Collection of the Museum.)

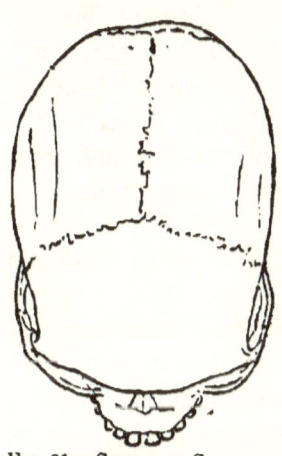

FIG. 31.—SKULL OF SOARTJE BARTMANN, BUSHMAN WOMAN. (Collection of the Museum.)

The Sàn and the Khoï-Khoï are far from being to-day what they were at the time of the discovery. Here, as in so many parts of the globe, the so-called civilised and Christian European has accomplished the dreadful work with which he seems to be charged. Over a vast region he has substituted himself for the local races, after having exterminated them. He has shown himself as cruel, as cravenly fierce, as any band of savage heathen. Of the sixteen nations of Hottentots enumerated by Kolbe, the greater part have disappeared. The survivors are more or less modified by contact with the whites and as the result of the influence of the missionaries, yet some tribes have preserved intact the manners and beliefs of their ancestors. To save from oblivion these remnants of the past of one of the most curious human races is evidently to render a service to anthropology.*

This is the work which Mr. Hahn seems to have undertaken. His authority seems to me incontestable. He has lived for nine years among the Khoï-Khoï, and knows their language perfectly; he is interested in them, but not to the degree that sympathy gets the better of his judgment; he guards himself against the sources of error, which he enumerates; generally he first simply presents the facts, reserving their discussion until afterwards. If he has gone further than his predecessors in the examination of the question specially considered in his book, I can see no reason for doubting the new facts which he teaches us.

Hahn devotes his first chapter to making the Sân and the Khoï-Khoï known to us, but this chapter is very short. The author only aims to give a summary idea of the degree of industry attained by the different tribes of the Khoï-Khoï, and of the good qualities he has met with in them. This double purpose is sufficiently attained.

The Hottentots were apparently a valiant population, who made much of military courage, and had instituted a sort of order of chivalry to honour individuals who distinguished themselves by military exploits. Their customs were pure and their impulses honest. Unfortunately all their good qualities were connected with an extreme filthiness. The Khoï-Khoï were perhaps the dirtiest

---

* In colour the Khoï-Khoï, and above all the Sân, are connected with the yellow type; by their hair both are essentially Negroes. Among the Sân the horizontal cephalic index is almost exactly the same as that of the south Chinese (Sân, 77·45; Chinese, 77·22). Among the Khoï-Khoï the index is lower.

people on the globe. Kolbe and many other travellers have given details on this subject, which it is useless for us to repeat here.

Without insisting upon the manners and customs of this curious people, I ought to mention what Hahn tells us of the condition of the women. All travellers have made them out a kind of slaves, charged with the heaviest burdens of labour, and badly treated by their husbands, whose task was confined to hunting and caring for the animals. It is, in fact, so outside; but indoors, Hahn tells us, the positions are reversed. Here the woman (*taras*) reigns supreme mistress. She controls and owns everything, and the husband cannot, without her permission, take a bit of meat or a drop of milk. If he thinks to infringe the law, the neighbours punish him by taking away a certain number of sheep and cows, which go to increase the personal property of the wife. More: at the death of a chief whose son is under age it often happens that his wife inherits his power and becomes *gau-tas*, "*queen of the tribe.*" Some of these women chiefs have left honoured names in the native traditions.

The oldest daughter has also great privileges. She alone milks the cows, and it is to her that one applies for a little milk, as is shown in the short song, of which Hahn gives text and translation: "My lioness, art thou afraid that I will bewitch thee? Thou hast milked the cow with thy gentle hand. Embrace me. Turn me out some milk, my lioness, daughter of a powerful man."

I find another custom mentioned by Mr. Hahn which I have not seen described elsewhere. Children take the names of their parents, but by a sort of exchange, the girls bearing that of their father, the boys that of their mother, the last syllable showing the sex. The son of a woman named Arises is named Ariseb; the daughter of her husband, Xam-hab, takes the name of Xam-has.

The religious chants and profane songs of the Hottentots are generally accompanied by dances, and sometimes by pantomimes. Further on I will give some examples of the former. The latter are often satirical. An unpopular chief is often sung by the girls, who compare him with the ravenous hyena and the cowardly jackal. An unequal marriage, or the slightest incident, may become material for couplets. Behold an example of them:

The poor young Kharis is much frightened ;
She suffers with colics,
And rolls herself on the ground like a hyena which has eaten poison.
The town runs to assist at the scene.
Everyone is terrified !
But they become calm, and one says,
    "Oh, that is nothing !"

Hahn discusses the question of language at some length. I limit myself to mentioning an interesting fact. The Sân and the Khoï-Khoï occupy almost the same area, yet the last have a common language, the dialects of which resemble each other so closely that the most widely separated tribes understand each other at once. On the contrary, the Sân languages differ from Khoï-Khoï as much as the English from the Sanscrit, and have no relationship among themselves. Yet these Sân languages and the Khoï-Khoï spring from the same stock, as is shown by their common possession of the series of *clicks*. The vocabularies themselves have preserved numerous resemblances. Linguistic facts agree, then, with the results drawn from the examination of the physical characteristics, and lead us to admit again the fundamental unity of that human race which has originally populated the Cape regions. As to the diversity of languages spoken by the Sân, it is easily explained by the disintegration and isolation of their tribes.

We may also remark that the Sân can count only to two, or at most to three. A single tribe forms an excep-

tion to this rule ; it counts to twenty. Hahn thinks it
has received its numerals from some other tribe. The
Khoï-Khoï, however, all have a complete decimal system
of numeration. Hahn gives them the credit of this invention, which he ascribes to the necessity of counting
their cattle when they gave up their hunting for a pastoral life. It is much more probable that their domestic
animals and the means of knowing their number came
to them equally from the Negro tribes whose blood flows
in their veins.

On different occasions Hahn makes allusion to the
separation of the Khoï-Khoï into two branches, to a great
migration having for its point of departure the tomb of
their ancestor *Gurikhoïsib;* but he does not define himself in the matter. He speaks of their first home, but
nowhere does he locate it. Without doubt he has explained these matters in some publication which I do not
know. In any case there can exist no doubt either as to
the fact of the migration or its general direction. Livingstone, in summarising the information gathered by himself
and that scattered through the writings of other travellers,
expressed himself thus regarding the Hottentots : " The
race of cattle which they raise come probably from the
north-northeast, a part of the continent from which the
natives all make the first emigrations of their ancestors
start." * It is in that direction, in the mountains of
Abyssinia, that Negroes are yet found whose language
presents certain analogies to those of the Hottentots.
The importance of these analogies may be exaggerated, but

---

* [91] The sheep of the Cape, like those of Senegal, are covered
with stiff hair, and not with wool. This fact also seems to indicate
that the race came from the hottest parts of Africa. Our European sheep have perfectly preserved at the Cape their fleece
of wool, which they owe to their domestication in the temperate
regions.

they are none the less very real.* It is also to the north-
northeast of the Cape that was located the Land of Punt
of the old Egyptians; and whoever has seen the queen of
that country figured by Mariette in the paintings of the
Exposition of 1867, will admit the extreme resemblance
between her and the Hottentot Venus whose cast is at
the Museum. These facts, added to some others, into the
details of which I cannot here enter, teach us, at least
approximately, at once regarding the ancient habitat of
one of the elements of the race, the origin of its industries, and the extent of the migrations which it must have
accomplished in order to reach the Cape regions. Perhaps
tradition had preserved some remembrance of those great
journeys among the *nations* which flourished before the
coming of the Europeans; but one readily understands how
the extermination of some, the dispersion of others, must
have caused the historical legends to be forgotten.[67]

Yet one may certainly affirm that none of these legends
dates back to the time when the first ancestors of the
Khoï-Khoï came to take possession of extreme South Africa, no more than our most distant memories mention
the time when man in our land dwelt side by side with
the elephants and rhinoceroses. Like the rest of the world,
the Cape districts have their ages of stone, of which the
most ancient was contemporaneous with our Palæolithic
epoch. The discoveries of some English investigators[170, 49]
prove it, and the beautiful work of Mr. Gooch, who, after

---

* The celebrated missionary Robert Moffat relates that, having
one day given a Syrian an idea of the Hottentot languages, this one
told him that he had seen in the market at Cairo some slaves much
lighter in colour than the Negroes, who spoke such a language.[117]
These could certainly not be Hottentots from the Cape. Alfred
Maury[112] had admitted the existence of clicks among some Abyssinian tribes, but after a conversation with Schweinfurth he was
much less certain, although still holding that clicks occur among
some Kaffir and Nubian peoples.

having described and figured the geological structure and
the physical geography, summarises in the following terms
the result of his researches upon this important point :
" All these terraces, all these levels, yield instruments of
stone in their Quaternary deposits." * Thus from that
epoch man was at the Cape as well as on the plateaus of
Brazil and in the pampas of Buenos Ayres.

The religious beliefs are much better preserved. It is
to these that Mr. Hahn's book is specially devoted. In
treating of this subject, in showing that there is among
the Khoï-Khoï anything more than a rude Shamanism,
the author has to fear lest persons shall attribute the relatively high conceptions which he makes known to an infiltration of Christian doctrines. He has foreseen the
objection. He declares that, to avoid such an interpretation, he has omitted every legend or myth which could
be subject to it, even though he has felt sure of its purely
indigenous character.

Truly, one can only approve of such scruples ; but may
Mr. Hahn not have carried them too far ? No one was
more capable than he of discriminating between what was
original and what was added on later. The result of this
labour would have enabled the reader to form a more complete idea of the sum total of beliefs to which this people
had attained, and would perhaps have justified some conclusions on the subject, to which I shall later have to make
some reservations.

---

* 65 The author divides the age of stone of South Africa into five
periods. The first alone belongs to Quaternary times, and corresponds to our Palæolithic : the four others are contained within the
Recent Epoch of the geologist. These four periods are characterised
at once by the nature of the rock employed and by the progressive
development of industries. In the discussion to which the above
cited memoirs have given rise one has several times remarked the
great resemblance existing between certain objects collected at the
Cape and others which have been found in Europe and in India.

15

It is difficult to see how the populations here considered can have been represented, even in these days, as without religion and materialistic. Long have I, in my courses and elsewhere, shown how little foundation such statements have,* and how very much all the testimony collected upon points the most remote, by travellers the most different, confirm the general statement made by Livingstone[91] : "However degraded these peoples may be, there is no need of telling them of the existence of God or of a future life. These two truths are universally admitted in Africa. All the phenomena which the natives cannot explain by an ordinary cause are attributed to the divinity. . . . If we speak to them of a dead man, they reply, 'He is gone to God.'"

Mr. Hahn, wishing, no doubt, to keep strictly to the special fact which he aimed to make clear, speaks only of the Khoï-Khoï or Hottentots proper, and considers the beliefs of the Sân or Bushman only very incidentally. Since he contrasted the two branches of the South African race in social and industrial matters, it is singular that he did not show how they resemble or diverge from each other in reference to the matters specially treated in this work. Perhaps he has not himself collected the necessary materials. We must not forget that the Bushmen are most difficult to study. For a long time travellers only knew them by hearsay; meetings have been rare, interviews have been short, and usually disturbed by mutual distrust. In such circumstances it is very difficult to inform one's self regarding the beliefs which refer to what is most sacred in the human heart, and of which the savage speaks only with the greatest reluctance. What we can state of ourselves will illustrate the matter. It is not in tarrying at an inn that a Parisian would obtain from a Brittany peasant the slightest detail regarding *korigans* or the

---

* The Human Species.

laveuses de nuit. Three months of residence and intimate relations with a Basque family with whom I lodged
was necessary before I could obtain some incomplete notions regarding superstitions which still exist at the gates
of Bayonne.

Yet, as the Europeans have gone in greater numbers
and farther into these lands, the Bushmen have become
better and better known. At the end of his first journey (1812) Campbell knew that these natives had a confused idea of a great Being to whom they attribute all
that which is beyond human power. But, in spite of
his friendly relations with Makoun, Bushman chief of
Malalarin, he could find out nothing about the future
life. He was more fortunate on his second voyage.[185]
He learned that the Bushmen believe in a sort of resurrection, and place a spear by the side of the dead, that
they may hunt and defend themselves. Having found
Makoun again, he learned from him with difficulty some
details concerning a male god named *Goha*, who lives
above them, and concerning a female god named *K'o*,
who lives below. The name of the former singularly
recalls that of the great god of the Khoï-Khoï, and I shall
later speak again of this point. They also told Campbell
of a kind of spirits or nymphs who come at times to
mingle in the dances of the natives.

Later, Arbousset and Daumas, favoured by circumstances, obtained some more precise details regarding
the religious ideas of the Bushmen who live in the Blue
Mountains. These savages say that there is in heaven
a *kaang*, or chief, to whom they give the title of *K'ue-
Akengteng*, "*the master of all things.*" This kaang
makes to live and to die; he gives or withholds rain and
game. One prays to him at times of famine and before
going to war, while executing the dance of the *mokoma*
during an entire night, "In the words of the natives,

'he cannot be seen with the eyes, but one knows him with the heart,'" says Arbousset.[6] These Bushmen also believe in another life, and have a proverb : "Death is but a slumber."

If the Sân have a good god, they have also a bad one (*Ganna*).[67] Thus even among the savages—unquestionably the lowest among mankind—we find again this conception of the two principles which under one form or another recurs in all religions. We shall see further on that it is the same among the Khoï-Khoï, and that the spirits of good and of evil recognised among the two sister races are identical.

These same Bushmen also venerate certain antelopes, among them the blesbok (*Antilope pygarga*), and adore a species of caterpillar, which they call *n'go*. This creature constructs for itself from straws, etc., a little tube, much like the case of a caddis-fly larva, from which it only extends its head and the first pair of legs, in order to seek food and to move from place to place. When the Bushmen go hunting they try to find one of these caterpillars and address it a veritable prayer, that it may guide their arrows to the prey, which shall nourish them.*

Thus we see united in these Bushmen the grossest fetichism and some notions, vague, no doubt, but touching upon the most lofty conceptions. Yet Arbousset says these tribes have far less superstition than the blacks. Their very precarious mode of life and their social disintegration have no doubt dwarfed among them the development of mythological conceptions. From the same

---

* Arbousset [6]: *'Kaang ta, ha a ntanga ē ? 'Kaang ta, 'gnou a kna a sē gē. Itanga 'kogou 'koba hou ; i'konté, i kagè, itanga, i'kogou 'koba hou ; 'kaang ta, 'gnou a kna a sē gē.* "Lord, do you not love me? Lord, a male gnu bring me. I love to fill my stomach. My older son, my older daughter, love to fill their stomachs. Lord, lead a male gnu under my arrows."

causes there has not been able to form itself among these wandering populations anything like a class of men specially charged with presiding over religious manifestations. Nowhere have I found mention among the Bushmen of any one who directs the dance of the *mokoma*, who plays any *rôle* in the preliminaries of marriage, etc. It seems that among them pure fetichism has placed itself side by side with those fundamental instinctive beliefs common to all the other South African tribes.

It is different with the Hottentots. Among them travellers have always found, and still do find, those *surri*, who play alternately the part of master of ceremonies and priest—those doctors,* those *makers of rain*, whom so many voyagers have described, and whom Livingston has made to speak so strangely[91]—that is to say, that here superstitions are definite and numerous. At the same time the principal events of life are celebrated by festivals and ceremonies having, at least in a degree, a religious character. I shall refer for the details—often revolting—to the travellers who have collected them, and principally to Kolbe.

One knows that the facts given by Kolbe have been declared untrustworthy by a certain number of those who have followed him, and have bitterly assailed him even when they have done naught but to quote him. Walckenaer has already warmly protested against these attacks, and has shown their origin. Among others, he has well shown how our celebrated astronomer La Caille was led into error by the employees of the Cape Company, which Kolbe had made too well known.[80] This rehabilitation of the old German voyager is fully confirmed by the testimony of Mr. Hahn. Every traveller well acquainted

---

* [80] Kolbe distinguishes the priest (*surri*) from the doctor, and ascribes to this latter a superior rank in the clan.

with the manners and customs of the Bergdamaras * could
endorse the greater part of the book of Kolbe upon the
Hottentots. One may, then, with confidence consult these
data collected before Europeans had been able to disperse
or transform the local populations.

But I have already stated that these coarse superstitions are not all of the religion of the Hottentots. Even
the first travellers who explored their territory have been
able to see this. These have recognised their belief in
a *great chief*, called by them the supreme regulator
(*Khourrou*), the Lord (*Khub*),[183] and also a *devil* (*Dan-
goh* or *Damoh*); they have mentioned homage rendered
to the moon. Kolbe confirmed by new observations and
fuller details all that his predecessors had said. He made
known the ceremonies performed at the different phases
of the moon, the general sense of the prayers addressed to
that luminary, and saw, in the *ensemble* of the practices,
all the characteristics of a true worship. At about the
same period George Smith reported the festivals celebrated in honour of the Pleiades; he summarised in a few
words the prayer which the Khoï-Khoï chanted in chorus
to the supreme god, and which I shall reproduce further on.

These citations suffice to put the general fact beyond
doubt. Before any theological notion, derived from Europe could have modified the conceptions of the Khoï-
Khoï, these peoples admitted the existence of superior
beings able to influence their destinies for good or ill;
they addressed prayers and homages to them; they had
a religion and a worship. But we had no details regarding these good or bad beings, concerning their number or
their hierarchy; we knew nothing of their legendary his-

---

* Tribe of Negro origin, located in the country of the Grand
Namaquas, whose customs and language it has adopted, and which
it preserves better than the Khoï-Khoï themselves (Hahn).

tŏry. It would have been strange, however, if the Hottentots had *not* possessed a mythology, at least rudimentary, for traces of one have been found even among the Australians. Mr. Hahn has filled up this gap. He makes known the names of the gods of the Khoï-Khoï; he teaches us regarding their relationship and their adventures; then he tries to trace back to the beginning of these fables. Let us see, then, what he teaches us on the subject.

*Tsūi-goa.**—The supreme god of the Hottentots is *Tsūni-goam, Tsūi-goa, Tsūi-goab*, whose name is found more or less altered or modified in the narratives of various travellers. One legend collected by Hahn recounts that this god was differently named formerly. It described him as having been a great chief, from whom were descended all the Khoï-Khoï tribes. He declared war against another chief called *Gaunab*.† This one had at first the advantage in several conflicts; but at each new combat his adversary felt his strength increase, while he (Gaunab) felt his own decrease. Finally Gaunab was conquered and killed, but in his death agony he struck his enemy in the knee. From that time the conqueror took the name of *Tsūi-goa*, "the wounded knee."

In this legend the god assumes certain human characteristics, but at the same time he is represented as capable of accomplishing marvellous things. According to the old man who informed Mr. Hahn, Tsūi-goa foresaw the future; he died and rose again a number of times; he has reappeared a number of times among his children, and his coming has been celebrated with festivals and dances. He it is who has given men abundance of sheep and of cattle; it is he who collects the clouds and sends

---

* This is the title Mr. Hahn usually employs.

† One will see further on that this Gaunab is nothing else than the bad god.

rain ; it is he who renders the cows and the ewes fertile.
All good things come from him. He lives in a beautiful
heaven, all red ; his enemy, Gaunab, dwells in a dark
heaven, all black.

It is easy to see that this narrative reproduces, in a
form and with details inspired by the mode of life of the
Khoï-Khoï, that idea of the strife between the spirit of
good and the spirit of evil which has given birth to so
many mythological stories. We shall see later that Gaunab is in fact the name which these peoples give to a bad
divinity. Yet the superior *rôle* played by Tsûi-goa in the
belief of these people is not very plainly marked. But
informations more precise will complete our enlighten-
ment on this point. Those which Kolbe collected, either
himself or from other writers, show us that the Hottentots
believed in a supreme being, *Gounia-Tiquoïa*, "God of all
the gods,".regarded by them as creator of the world and
living things, and as governing all things.[67]

One finds this belief again in the words of Harisimab,
present chief of the pagan tribe of the Habobes, and sworn
enemy of the missionaries. Interrogated by our author
regarding the origin of his people, he replied : "All things,
the Habobes also, have been made by Tsûi-goa in this
country ; and the Lord (*Khub*) * has made us and given
us the country ; he gives us rain and makes the grass
grow." This agreement between the words of the old
traveller and the Haboba chief should settle all doubts.
Tsûi-goa was, and is still, among the unconverted Khoï-
Khoï, the creator of all things, the dispenser of things the
most precious to pastoral tribes. Much other evidence
comes to the support of this conclusion.

It is nevertheless unfortunate that Hahn has not insisted more strongly upon this point, especially in so far

---

* This word was also used with the same meaning at the time of
Valentyn.[67]

as it relates to the creation of man. It is incidentally, and in a note that he calls Tsûi-goa the creator of the Khoï-Khoï, and makes known the tradition of the Koranas. According to the old men of that tribe, Tsûi-goa, after having made a man and a woman, *Kanisma* (" the ostrich feather") and *Hau-na-maos* ("yellow copper"), gave them cows, whose milk they should drink, a jackal's tail to dry the sweat from their brow, a stick for a *kiri*, a quiver, arrows, a bow, and a shield. It is from Tsûi-goa that they expect all that good fortune which is to come to them. Moreover, Hahn calls the Khoï-Khoï Adam, *Eixalkhana-biseb*, or *Gurikhoïsib*, and identifies the latter with the god *Heitsi-eibib*, of whom I shall speak later. Perhaps the tradition is silent on this point; perhaps here also the author is influenced by a theory which I shall later discuss.

However that may be, the Hottentots speak and act as if they saw in Tsûi-goa a beneficent father, all-powerful and omniscient. The sentiments which this belief inspires singularly resemble those which the firmest Christians gain from their convictions. Hahn does not say so in just those words; he does better—he proves it by examples. The interjection *Tsûi-goatse!* (*Thou, O Tsûi-goa!*) is equivalent to our "Great God!" Stricken by some misfortune which he deems unmerited, the Hottentot cries, "O Tsûi-goa, what have I done to be so severely punished?" Unjustly accused, and unable to prove his innocence, he calls on his god, "O Tsûi-goa, thou alone knowest that I am not guilty!" Exposed to some grave danger, he counts upon the help of Tsûi-goa, and, escaping from it, he gives him the credit of his deliverance. So much Hahn has been able to establish for himself. He traversed the Kalahari Desert in a wagon. The heat was frightful; in consequence of an unexpected delay the supply of water was exhausted, and they were very far from the nearest spring.

The night came; they were lost. The caravan was threatened with death by thirst, and the traveller, filled with rage, began to vent it on the guide, who was a hardened pagan Haboba. " What have you done? To-morrow we shall be eaten by jackals and vultures! Who will help us in this danger?" he cried. The Hottentot coolly replied, " Tsûi-goa will come to our help."—" What foolishness! You and your Tsûi-goa are two stupid fools."—" Certainly, master, he will help us." In the morning they found water, and when each had refreshed himself the guide said to Mr. Hahn : " My dear master, yesterday you were on the point of killing me, but the Lord prevented you ; and now are you convinced that the Lord has come to our help?"

What would the most fervent missionary have thought and felt?

The Khoï-Khoï raise neither temples nor shrines, either for Tsûi-goa or others of their divinities. They simply have some sacred places, which they never pass without depositing some little offering and accompanying it with invocations. I shall return later to this subject. But they have great religious festivals, accompanied by dances and chants, connected almost always with some celestial phenomenon. The first annual rising of the Pleiades, among others, is sacredly celebrated. As soon as the constellation, impatiently looked for, appears, all the mothers ascend an elevated place, carrying their babies in their arms, and teach them to extend their little arms towards the friendly stars. The population then gathers for the dance, singing a hymn in honour of Tsûi-goa.[171]

Mr. Hahn here reproduces the narratives of George Schmidt, who, sent out by the Moravians in 1736, first attempted to introduce Christianity among the Hottentots.[117] The invocation which the old missionary heard, but of which he gives only a brief *résumé*, was really then a product of the native inspiration, with no possible admixture of ideas borrowed elsewhere. But we *know* it to-day. Hahn has been present at the sacred dance (*gei*) which celebrates the return of the Pleiades. He has recovered the chant which accompanies it; he has found that it is everywhere the same among the different tribes scattered over the various points of the area still occupied by the Khoï-Khoï. He has given the text and translation:

Tsûi-goatse !
Thou, O Tsûi-goa !
Abo itse !
Thou father of the fathers !
Sida itse !
Thou, our father !
Nanuba avire !
Let stream the thunder-cloud !
En χuna ûire !
Let please live (our) flocks !
Eda sida ûire !
Let us (also) live, please !
Kabuta gum goroö !
I am so weak indeed !
Gâs χao !
From thirst !
As χao !
From hunger !
Ta χurina amre !
That I may eat field fruits !
Stats gum χave sida itsao ?
Art thou, then, not our father ?
Abo itsao !
The father of the fathers !
Tsûi-goatse !
Thou, Tsûi-goa !
Eda sida gangantsire !
That we may praise thee !
Eda sida khava khaitsire !
That we may give thee in return !

Abo itse !
Thou, father of fathers !
Sida Khutse !
Thou, our Lord !
Tsûi-goatse !
Thou, O Tsûi-goa !

The Hottentots do not confine themselves to the great public festivals. They have their domestic, or rather individual, worship. In the morning, at the first streaks of dawn, they leave their huts and go to kneel down behind some bush. There, with face towards the east, they address their prayer to Tsûi-goa, the father of the fathers.

It is needless to emphasise the character of these practices and songs or the nature of the sentiments which they attest. Whoever will consider these data will quite understand the calm confidence of the guide of Mr. Hahn. One can see also the source of the peculiar difficulties which Protestant missionaries, the only ones who have laboured in this part of the pagan world, meet with in the work of converting the Hottentots. The missionary finds here no material symbol ; he cannot overturn temples or idols to demonstrate thus the helplessness of gods of stone or wood ; he has to contend against ideas. But missionary and subject have the same fundamental notion in common—that of a supreme being, creator, and kind father of his creatures, whom one should honour and to whom one should pray. The Hottentot can then reply to the missionary that he brings nothing new, and one cannot be surprised that Tsûi-goa has had his martyrs. Hahn cites one example. A celebrated chief in the colony, Xanib, surrounded by enemies and ordered to embrace Christianity if he would save his life, replied : "Never ! My Tsûi-goa is as good as your Christ." He at once received the mortal blow.

We shall see later that Mr. Hahn identifies Tsûi-goa with some other divinities. It is the consequence of criticism based upon a theory which I must make known. The Khoï-Khoï do not appear themselves to have thought of such a fusion, judging by what our author himself says. Their supreme god seems to have his own independent existence. It is to be regretted that our author is not more explicit in this respect, and says nothing of the ideas which these people hold as to the nature of the *father of fathers.* The *anthropolatry* of which one finds traces in the legend cited above, and in some others, attains at times to conceptions remarkably spiritual. In Polynesia, Taaroa, the Indonesian chief who discovered the Tonga Islands, was regarded at first as a secondary deity; * then as a god of the first class; † then, finally, was declared *toïvi,* having neither father, mother, nor descendants, but having created all that exists.‡

Has something similar taken place in the Cape district? Perhaps Mr. Hahn could have told us. But he always attributes to Tsûi-goa neither father, mother, wife nor son, and he never relates any story with reference to him such as he tells abundantly in the history of the other gods. Tsûi-goa seems, then, to inhabit his red heaven alone, far beyond the moon, according to Kolbe [80]; beyond the blue sky, as told by Hahn in another account. His worshippers believe no less that he hears their prayers and watches over them. They have, then, singularly purified their conception, in so far as our first cited legend has

---

* At Tonga, which he fished up out of the sea, they showed Mariner the rock upon which the fish-hook of Taaroa caught. The fish-hook itself was long preserved in the family of the Tui-Tonga, regarded as lineal descendants of the god. [108]

† At New Zealand Taaroa is one of the six first gods, son of Rangi and of Papa—Heaven and Earth (Grey). [66]

‡ It is at Tahiti that Taaroa becomes the supreme god. [123, 56]

been the point of departure for the beliefs found among
these tribes by Kolbe and Hahn.

Heitsi-eibib.—The Hottentots recognise another good
god, concerning whom the earlier travellers gathered some
incomplete information, but whom Hahn makes much
better known. All the great Namaqua tribes call him
Heitsi-eibib; the Koras give him the name of *Garubeb.*

All the Namaqua questioned by our author gave him
identical information. Heitsi-eibib is their great-grand-
father. He was a very powerful and rich chief, who possessed cows and sheep in abundance. He conquered and
exterminated all enemies who attacked his people. He
was very prudent and wise. He dwelt in a land to the
east. Behold why the door of the hut of these people
faces east, why the pole of the waggon at rest is pointed
east, why the tombs open in that direction and the faces
of the buried dead are turned thither.

Until this point the story confines itself within the
limits of reason; but it soon goes beyond them. Heitsi-
eibib foresaw the future; he could assume all forms. Like
Tsûi-goa—in fact, more frequently than he—he has died
and come to life again. At the end of each of these lives,
he has been buried, and his tombs are scattered over all the
lands formerly inhabited by the Hottentots. These are
heaps of stones, a kind of cairns, of no great size. That
described by Lichtenstein was only from twenty to thirty
metres in circumference. They are usually situated in
narrow defiles hemmed in by two mountains. Every Hottentot who passes near these tombs deposits there, as an
offering, a piece of his garment, flowers, a branch of a tree
or bush, a stone which increases by so much the size of
the monument, or even a zebra dropping. Sometimes
also honey or mead is brought thither. The Namaqua
say that Heitsi-eibib walks at night in desert places,
and that he is only satisfied when, upon his return, he

finds that some one has shown him homage. He protects those who honour him, procures for them good journeys, preserves them from all danger, gives them good advice, teaches them how to kill lynxes and other wild animals. When they are hunting, the Namaqua habitually repeat the following prayer under their breath:

> O Heitsi-eibib!
> Thou, our grandfather,
> Grant me happiness!
> Give me game,
> Make me find honey and roots,
> That I may bless thee again!
> Art thou not our grandfather,
> O Heitsi-eibib?

Heitsi-eibib seems to have been reborn—several times, perhaps. A virgin who sucked the sweet juice from a grass stalk (*hobeya*) bore a son, who rapidly grew to robust manhood. It was the grandfather, who returned among his children. Another tradition is more singular. A cow which was cropping a certain sort of grass gave birth to a calf, which quickly grew to be a great bull. The men of the tribe pursued it to kill it, but all of a sudden it disappeared, and in its place they saw a man busy *making a tub*. It was the god who had taken on the human form.

Legends abound in the history of Heitsi-eibib. I shall cite but a few, and these in abridged form.

The god lived on friendly terms with the lion, who at that time had wings and dwelt in the trees. But the animal having profited by its advantage to surprise and devour the cattle of the tribe of Heitsi-eibib, this one lay in ambush for him and cut off his wings. From that time dates the unceasing enmity between the descendants of the two old-time friends.

Heitsi-eibib is also seen in combats with beings whose

nature is not defined and who contend by magical means. Here is an example: *Gama-gorib*, the lion, and he, lived in the same country. One day Heitsi-eibib, separated from his companions, sent after them; but he waited in vain, and a roaring informed him that they could not come at his call. He then set himself to find them; and without making himself known, as was his custom among the Khoï-Khoï, he traversed the kraal of Gama-gorib. This one sent him an invitation by the hare to come and see him and to have a trial of strength with him.* But he had a deep cavern, into which he hurled everyone who came near his dwelling, and left them to die. Heitsi-eibib could not escape the common lot. He was defeated, and hurled into the abyss. But he spoke to it, saying, " Cavern of my ancestors, raise your floor and lift me up so that I can leap out." The cavern obeyed, and the battle began again. Heitsi-eibib was again thrown to the earth and then hurled into the cavern, whence he escaped a second time in the same way. For the third time he came to blows with Gama-gorib. This one was at the end of his powers, and his adversary killed him with a blow dealt behind the ear. Then Heitsi-eibib, addressing the cavern anew, said, " Cavern of my ancestors, raise your floor a little that my children can come out." And the cavern raised its floor, and all the children of Heitsi-eibib came forth. Then the god cursed the hare: " From this day I curse thee! Thou shalt carry no more messages; thou shalt eat no more by day; thou shalt eat at night only;

---

* The duel proper exists among the Hottentots. He who believes himself insulted challenges his adversary by offering him a handful of earth. If the challenge is accepted the offender seizes the hand and the dust falls to the ground. If it is not accepted, the challenger throws the dust in his enemy's face. The duel may take place by kicking, with clubs, or with the spear and shield.

and only then shall one hear thy voice." The rabbit, thus cursed, fled, and still runs.

Heitsi-eibib is married. His first wife, or rather his wife of first rank, is Urisis or Soris, the sun; he has by her a son, Urisib, "the day." But he had also a second wife,* whose name the legend does not give. These two wives have their part to play in the events accompanying one of the deaths and one of the resurrections of the god.

I reproduce this passage from the book, suppressing some repetitions:

Heitsi-eibib, at this time very aged, travelled with his family. Arrived in a valley where there grew a vine full of ripe grapes, they ate of them, and were immediately in great pain.† The old man called his wife Urisib and said to her: "I feel that I cannot live long. When I am dead cover me with stones. Observe what I order. Do not eat the grapes of this valley, for if you do I shall give you my sickness, and you shall die as I do."

Thus he died, and was covered with stones, as he commanded. The wife and son departed. While they were busying themselves with their new camp they heard some one who had eaten grapes singing:

> I, father of Urisib,
> Father of that poor boy,
> I, who ate raisins and died,
> I am a very lively dead man.

The young wife recognised that the noise came from the direction where Heitsi-eibib had been buried, and said

---

* The Khoï-Khoï have often a first wife (ga-iris, "the older wife," "the great wife") and a second wife (a-ri-s, "the young wife") (Hahn).

† Mr. Hahn has himself experienced the bad results of the Cape grapes. He was taken with dysentery after eating some of them. He adds that the natives, not knowing how to treat the attacks, often die from them.

to Urisib, "Go and look." The son went to the tomb, found the footprints of his father there, and returned. Then the young wife said to him : " It is he, and he alone. Do as I command. Look out for the wind ; creep along, keeping to leeward of him. Surprise him on the path to the tomb ; and when you have seized him do not let him go." So it was done. Heitsi-eibib, having seen them : leaped from the tree to the earth and tried to escape them, but he was caught near the tomb. Then he said to them : " Let me go ! I am a man who has been dead, and I will poison you." But the young wife cried out, " Hold the rogue well ! " So they led him home, and from that day he was healthy and well.

Many other legends relate to Heitsi-eibib. They strongly resemble the preceding, and are always more or less similar to our nursery tales. I find nothing in the history of this god which recalls the lofty ideas which exist—at least in the germ—in what the Khoï-Khoï say of Tsûi-goa. Such anyway is the impression resulting from the texts. Yet in one very short passage, which I shall consider later, Mr. Hahn, in assimilating these two gods with one another, asserts that they are invoked in the same way and that one gives them the same titles. But then why not have placed alongside of these puerile fables, of which I have given examples, either some fragments of a hymn where Heitsi-eibib is called *the father of fathers*, or some tradition which represents him also as living beyond the blue sky? If these hymns and traditions exist, why not have made them known? This is one of the places where one feels only too strongly the lack of sufficient information, which I have already mentioned.

Khâm, Khami, Khâb (*the Moon*).—This defect is more noticeable, and even more regrettable, in regard to *Khâb* (the moon). The name signifies *he who returns*, and well expresses the dominant thought which the ap-

parent transformations of this luminary have raised
among the Hottentots. The importance attached by
them to its different phases early attracted the attention
of travellers, and led them to suspect the existence of religious ideas. Kolbe has well shown that it is the object
of a veritable worship. At the new and full moon the
natives sacrifice animals and offer flesh and milk. These
offerings are accompanied by dances, prostrations, and
chants in which they salute the return of Khâb. They
ask him for good weather, pasturage for their herds and
flocks, and much milk. Kolbe has informed us, moreover, that the moon was regarded as an inferior *Gounia*,
representing the superior god (god of gods, *Gounia-
Tiquoïa*), as the visible image of an invisible deity.
When the moon disappeared they regarded him as dead;
his return was considered a resurrection. Eclipses inspire
great terror. Hahn has seen a whole population at such
a time utter groans and cries of grief.

Unfortunately, our author speaks of Khâb only incidentally, so to say, and in order to identify him with
Tsûi-goa and Heitsi-eibib. It appears probable that he
accepts Kolbe's views as true, and that things are now as
in the days of the old traveller. Witnesses are not lacking on this point, but it would have been none the less
interesting to have had Hahn's ideas. Above all, it would
have been important to have known those religious chants
which are sung throughout entire nights, and to have
judged how far they support or oppose the identifications
proposed by Hahn.

The Namaqua, who have preserved many traditions
forgotten in the regions nearest the Europeans, preserve
a curious story which Hahn quotes from another traveller
and which he regards as authentic. They relate that the
moon wished one day to send a message to men. The
hare offered to carry it. " Go, tell men that they shall

rise again, just as I die and rise again," said he. But the hare attempted to deceive men, and said to them, " You shall die, as I myself die." To punish him, the moon cursed him.* Behold why, among the Namaqua, men must abstain from eating the flesh of the hare, evidently regarded an impure creature.†

Nanub (*the Storm-Cloud*); *Gurub* (*the Thunder*); *Nabas* (*the Lightning*).—In a country where rain is generally accompanied by terrific tempests it is not surprising that electrical phenomena have strongly impressed the native imagination. The Hottentots have distinguished and personified the cloud which bears the bolt, the thunder, and the lightning. They make of them a family. The storm-cloud is the father; he is named Nanub, Nanum, or Nanu—that is to say, the pourer, the filterer. One prays to him, saying: " O Nanub! Lord, make rain now ! "

As the result of certain general ideas, which I shall mention later, Hahn identifies the storm-cloud *Nanub* and the thunder *Gurub* (the thatcher) with Tsûi-goa. But it plainly results from his own facts that the Hottentots clearly distinguish these three gods from one another. We have seen above that they pray Tsûi-goa *to permit Nanub to make the rain to fall.* They also incontestably make of Gurub a distinct person, a male, of whom Nabas (the lightning) is the sister. In fact, when they see a great storm rising, and when the air trembles with the roaring thunder, they gather together for one of those sacred dances—*gei*—of which I have already spoken, and sing

---

*Captain James Alexander, who collected this story, had the complete confidence of the Namaqua. An aged Namaqua said to Mr. Hahn, " That man has the odour of a red man," wishing thereby to show how much this traveller had known how to fraternise with these natives (Hahn).

† [67] A very similar legend exists in the Fijis.

the following hymn, given by Hahn. I retain the actual
name of the god in my translation. Hahn replaces it by
titles:

Curub di Geis.

THE HYMN OF THE THUNDER.

Nanum oatse!
Son of Nanum !
Gari Khoi Gurutse!
Thou brave, loud-speaking Guru !
Oùse gobare!
Talk softly, please !
Havië t'am n-a-Tamilô,
For I have no guilt.
Ubatere!
Leave me alone ! (Forgive me !)
Oûtago χnige,
For I am become quite weak (quite stunned, perplexed).
Gurutse,
Thou, O Guru,
Nanum oatse!
Son of Nanum!

Moreover, Hahn has been present at a dance and has
collected a song, which shows exactly what the lightning
is in the Hottentot mythology. A member of the tribe
has been struck by lightning. The inhabitants of the
kraal blame her for it in chorus, and she, represented by
a single person, replies in solo:

Nabas di Geis.

THE DANCE SONG OF THE LIGHTNING.

CHORUS.

Aibe nuris Nanuse!
Thou, daughter of Nanub, daughter-in-law of Aib ! *
Ti gâda go gamse!
Thou who hast killed my brother !
Gaïses gum ûb na goeö!
Therefore thou liest now so nicely in a hole !

---

* The rainbow.

SOLO.

Gaise to go sa gâba a gam.
(Yes), indeed, I have killed thy brother so well.

CHORUS.

Gaises gum âb na goeö!   ·
[*Well*] *therefore thou liest (now) in a hole!*
Gorob Khemi go usense!
Thou who hast painted thy body red like Goro!
Som auba naba tam asse!
Thou who dost not drop the " menses"!
Eiχalkhanabiseb aose!
Thou wife of the copper-bodied man!

One sees by this song that Nabas is not only daughter
of the thundering cloud (Nannb), but also that she has
a husband. The imagination of the natives has made
of the lightning a female deity, and has given her as wife
to the Khoï-Khoï Adam, who figures here as the son of
the rainbow, and whose name, according to Hahn, means
the *man with a copper body.*

Other Mythological Personages.—Another divinity of
the Khoï-Khoï, and perhaps of the Sân, is *Toosib,* " the
old man of the waters." He is described as a great red
man, with white hair. Before drinking at certain rivers
one must throw in some little offering, saying: " O grandfather, son of a Bushman, give me food! Give me flesh
of rhinoceros, of antelope, of zebra, and all that I desire!"
Failure to perform these rites is to expose one's self to
the anger of the god. The guide of Captain Alexander,*
under the impulse of ardent thirst, forgot to comply with
these prescriptions. Taken with an attack of dysentery,

---

* Captain Alexander speaks of his guide as being a Bushman.
Hahn tells us that he belonged to a tribe of poor Namaqua who are
at times so called because they have no cattle and live almost like
the Sân.

he did not fail to regard the disease as a punishment in-
flicted by Toosib.

Hahn has plainly not sought to make known all the
personages who figure in the mythology of the Hottentots. There are some whom he simply mentions by
name, such are *Tsavirub* or *Aib* (the rainbow), *Amab*,
Oas, etc. He gives a little more detail in reference to
myths connected with astronomy.

The Khoï-Khoï appear to have distinguished a great
number of constellations and to have given names to several stars. Naturally fable have drawn upon this field so
well adapted to stimulate the imagination. The stars are
for them the eyes or spirits of the dead. From this belief they have constructed a characteristic curse: "Thou
who art happy, may misfortune fall upon thee from the
star of my grandfather!"

The Pleiades (*Khanuseti*) are the stars of rain; their
return announces the opening of the rainy season, which
plays so important a part in the life of these pastoral people. Thus are explained the festivals which greet their
appearance. In some myths they are represented as children of Tsûi-goa. They have for their husband Aldebaran
(*Aob*), or rather the constellation of which that star is
the most noticeable, and which includes a part of our
Hyades and of Orion. Unfortunately, misunderstanding
has crept into this household. The Pleiades one day said
to their husband: "Go, kill us those three zebras; but if
you fail of them, do not dare to return to the house."
Aob took his bow and arrow; he shot, and missed his aim.
As the lion was watching and guarding the zebras on the
other side, he could not regain his arrow. Fearing the
wrath of his wives, he seated himself, where he still remains, suffering from hunger and thirst. It is almost
unnecessary to remark that the arrow, the zebras, and the
lion are so many other stars or constellations.

Gaunab or Gauna.—The divinities of whom I have
so far spoken are all beneficent. It is otherwise with
Gaunab, Gaunam, or Gauna. He is the *supreme bad being*,
as Tsúi-goa is the *supreme good being*. It is he who
causes all ills; it is he who makes beasts perish, who gives
men up to fierce beasts, who makes their best-laid plans
go awry, and sends them all sorts of diseases; his name
signifies *the destroyer, he who exterminates*. One saw
above how he fought with Tsúi-goa and was beaten. A
missionary has collected another version of this legend of
the strife between the powers of good and evil; but it is
needless to reproduce it here. It presents the same anthropomorphic character, and ends also with the defeat of
Gaunab.

In these different combats Gaunab is reported as killed
by his adversary, but evidently one admits that he returns to life, since he *inhabits a black heaven*, as we have
seen. Moreover, the worship which the Khoï-Khoï rendered him at the time of Kolbe, and which still exists,
leaves no doubt in the matter. Hahn has been able to
satisfy himself of the fact. One prays to him and offers
him sacrifice to avert harm. It is a pity that the author
has not here gone into some details, and has not made
known the terms of the invocations made to the spirit of
evil. It would be of interest to compare them with the
hymns chanted in honour of Tsúi-goa.

It is probably with this worship of Gaunab that one
must connect the homage accorded by the Hottentots to a
species of *mantis*.* Kolbe gave most exact details upon
this point. He saw the natives show a profound respect

---

* This species has not yet received a scientific name, so an eminent entomologist tells me; it is rare at the Cape, but common in
the Isles of France and Bourbon. It is well known that among
ourselves, in the South, the "praying mantis" (*Mantis religiosa*) is
also the object of various popular superstitions.

for this orthopterous insect whenever they came upon one; he saw sacrifices made in its honour when it appeared inside a kraal, and he concluded that the Hottentots considered it a beneficent divinity.* On the other hand, the astronomer La Caille believed that it was, in their eyes, a creature of ill omen. But Hahn has several times been able to show that all the details given by Kolbe are yet, to-day, perfectly accurate. At the same time he has learned with surprise that this insect, greeted with such joyous demonstrations, and which it is absolutely prohibited to kill, bears among the Khoï-Khoï the name of the bad principle, *Gaunab*. These apparent contradictions are easily explained, if we admit that the mantis is to the minds of this people a sort of incarnation of God. Fear only will account for the manifestations which greet its coming; but perhaps they also imagine that its presence is proof of the momentary appeasing of the spirit of evil.†

However that may be, the Khoï-Khoï believe that Gaunab shows himself at times—now under the form of a little humpbacked man, now under that of a deformed monster covered with hair and clad in white.

One has seen that the rainbow (*Tsavirub* or *Aïb*) is the father-in-law of the lightning. An aged Namaqua gave Hahn another version relative to this phenomenon. According to him, the rainbow is a fire kindled by Gaunab, into which the god precipitates and causes to perish those who have allowed themselves to be deceived by him. The individuals who are supposed to have died in this way are

---

* La Vaillant has denied the accuracy of the facts reported by Kolbe; but this traveller, who has known how to see many things well, was little suited to the study of the religions of savage peoples, and has absolutely not understood that of the Hottentots.

† The details given by Kolbe [80] upon the veritable despair which seized some Hottentots on seeing a little child about to kill one of these sacred insects appears to me to justify this interpretation.

called *Gauna-ô-Khoïn* (the dead people of Gaunab), *Sau-bo Khoïn* (the people of the shadow), etc. The old men, who were formerly allowed to die of hunger in a closed hut, either because they could no longer take care of themselves or because they were suspected of witchcraft, took their place among these subjects of Gaunab.

If one will recall what I said above about the Bush-men, he will see that we find again among the Khoï-Khoï, under names identical, or nearly so, the two divinities of good and evil recognised by the San. This is one more evidence of the very close relationship of the two peoples. Hahn, speaking here only of Gaunab, sees in that fact a proof that the worship of the bad god is older than the division of the race. He goes yet further, and believes that Gaunab alone was worshipped in those remote times, and that the existence of Tsûi-goa was admitted later. Then he extends this idea into a generalisation. According to him, man saw at first in Nature only infernal powers The notion of a beneficent being would be the product of a more advanced intellectual culture.

I cannot accept this theory; it is too much in con-tradiction with facts established among a crowd of savage peoples. Even among the lowest Australians one has found the dualistic belief which is concealed within all religions. Schweinfurth is, I think, the only traveller who, after serious investigation, admits the existence of one people who know only bad spirits.* But, admitting that this single exception really exists, it would be far from favouring the ideas of Hahn. In fact, the Bongos of whom Schweinfurth speaks are by no means at the bottom of the scale of civilisation; they are much above

---

* 172 Burchell had said something analogous of the Bachapins, a fragment of the Bechuanas. But Livingstone and Gazalis have shown that he was led into error and knew only a part of the re-ligious beliefs of these Kaffir tribes.

not only the Bushmen but also the Hottentots. It is not
a people beginning, but, on the contrary, a people who are
advancing. They have passed the two lower stages of culture. They are essentially agriculturists. When they clear
a piece of woodland for agricultural purposes they carefully leave the fruit trees. They plant in furrows, and they
reset the young plants. They are skilful metallurgists,
and their high smelting furnace is at once very ingenious
and very sensible. Their outfit is truly very rudimentary,
but they use it so well that several of their products would
bear comparison with those of English workmen. They
work wood as well as iron, construct huts well supported
by tree trunks, and they adorn tombs with carved figures
representing the dead. They are indeed, then, far from
that state of intellectual infancy during which, according
to Hahn, man already adored a devil, but had not arrived at
the notion of a god. If it is true that they do not now
know a god, it is probably because, affected by an idea
found among several African tribes, they have at last forgotten him.*

Gama-gorib.—Gama-gorib, Hahn says, is almost the
same as Gaunab. But, to judge from the legends, he is
very distinct, and seems to occupy the second place in the
army of evil. He is the adversary of Heitsi-eibib, as Gaunab is of Tsúi-goa. I have given the story of one of the
conflicts, and it is needless to enter into further details,
which, moreover, would teach us nothing new.

To these upper demons are attached a crowd of spectres and bad spirits greatly feared by the Hottentots.

The First Man.—I have already said that Hahn gave

---

* Some Negro populations of West Africa, although admitting
the existence of a good god, say it is useless to offer sacrifices to him,
since he always does good, and keep homage for the bad gods whom
they have to swerve from their bad intentions. The long holding
of such a notion might lead to the loss of the idea of a good god.

to the being whom he calls the Khoï-Khoï Adam the
name of Eiχalkhanabiseb, which means *the man whose
body has the lustre of copper.* The same person is also
called *Gurikhoïsib*, " the primitive man." The legend is
inconsistent, for this first man has a mother, whose name
the author does not give, and lives in a kraal where there
are maidens.

However that may be, one very detailed legend shows
us Gurikhoïsib living in the midst of the animals. One
day he took a notion to play. The leopard, ape, hyena,
serpents, etc., were present at the party. The man lost
all his copper bracelets. Then he began to quarrel
with the lion, and they defied one another. Gurikhoïsib
went home, poisoned his arrows, sharpened his spears;
his mother anointed him with melted butter mixed with
a sweet buchu,* and encouraged him by improvising a
song in his honour (*gare*). The fight took place near a
pond where our author had been taken by his guide.†
The lion, attacked by the dogs and hindered by arrows
and darts, fled, and was discovered by his mother, who
heard his last sigh and buried him, while Gurikhoïsib
was received with a song of triumph. From that time the
descendants of the lion have tried to avenge their ancestors, and the Khoï-Khoï wage merciless war against them.

It is, moreover, easy to understand that Gurikhoïsib
has taken a place in the native mythology; he is regarded
as a sort of demigod, who protects the people against
harmful beings, and, above all, against the lions.

Future Life.—From some details occurring in what
precedes I think one will have already concluded that

---

* Perfumed powder obtained by pulverising a species of spiræa.

† The pond of Khubirsaos, about 23° 29′ south latitude and 16°
28′ east longitude. Hahn was much impressed by the interest and
exactness with which his guide told him all the movements and
actions of the combat.

the Hottentots believe in another life. It is a fact which Kolbe had already placed beyond doubt, although it has been denied by some of his predecessors as well as by some of those who have come after him. The personal observations of Hahn have upon this point fully confirmed those of the old traveller.*

I have mentioned what the Hottentots say of the stars, and one might conclude from that that they place the dwelling of those who are gone in the sky; but I have nowhere found an explicit statement to that effect. On the other hand, many facts show that they regard the spirits of the dead as haunting, at least for a time, the neighbourhood of their tombs. At the death of one of its members, whatever the age or sex, the whole kraal moves, taking pains to leave the hut of the deceased intact, together with all its contents—furniture, arms, and garments. To carry away the least thing would be to expose themselves to be followed by the spirit of the dead.[80]

One has already seen that certain spirits are, so to say, vassals of Gaunab, the god of evil. To this category belong also spirits of all individuals who have not been properly buried and whose bodies have been eaten by hyenas or vultures. As consequence of this idea, criminals, victims of vendetta, slaves killed by their master, enemies killed in combat, are given up to birds of prey and beasts, in order that, after they have been devoured,

---

* Perhaps some missionaries most deserve reproach for these misunderstandings, and among them Moffat [117] in particular. It is difficult not to be surprised and pained in reading what he has written upon the subject of the claimed atheism of the Hottentots. One would say that he was afraid to find among these pagans anything that resembled religious ideas. A faith too exclusive has evidently misled "the Nestor of living missionaries." To him "man is without conscience until the will of God has been declared to him." Evidently, when a man holds such views he is poorly prepared to understand the questions here considered.

they may become so many *Gauna-ora-Khoïn.* Some of
these spectres, called by the special name of *bausan,*
wander during the darkest nights, and even enter kraals,
terrifying the inhabitants.   .

The spirits just mentioned are maleficent. Those of
persons who were always distinguished by wisdom and by
virtues, and who have been regularly buried, are, for the
Hottentots, so many good genii. Woods, mountains,
prairies rivers, are consecrated to such, called by Kolbe
heroes, or saints. Every person passing in the neighbourhood of such places stops to meditate upon the virtues of
the dead man and to implore his protection. One believes
in the power of their intervention, and if he escapes some
great danger it is to them that he should ascribe the
credit. Kolbe one day met a Hottentot who was dancing and singing by himself, with devoutness, in a desert
place. Questioned by the traveller, he replied that, over-
taken there by a profound slumber, he had passed a re-
freshing night and had waked up only twenty feet away
from a great lion, who let him go unharmed. He said
the saint of the valley only could have protected him
against the fierce beast.

In each family the ancestors are considered almost as
household gods. One makes prayers to them and offers
them gifts. But in order to be heard it is necessary to go
to perform the ceremonies at the grave itself. Hahn tells
a characteristic anecdote in this connection. In one of
his journeys he met beyond the frontier of the Kalihari
Desert a party of Namaqua, under the lead of a great
woman of the country (Geiksois), whom he knew because
he had enjoyed her bountiful hospitality. He asked her
jocosely if she had come hunting in these barren deserts.
"My friend," she replied, "do not joke. I am in great
distress. The drought and the Bushmen have destroyed
many of my goats and cattle. I go to my father's grave;

I go to weep and to pray there. He will hear my voice, he will see my tears, will give success to my husband, who is hunting ostriches, so that we can buy again some female goats and cows, that our little ones may live."

"But your father is dead," replied the traveller; "how will he be able to hear you?"

"Yes, he is dead," she replied, "but he only sleeps. We Khoï-Khoï always, if we are in trouble, go and pray to the graves of our grandparents and ancestors. It is an old custom of ours."

I call the reader's whole attention to this paragraph. It confirms with additional details all that Kolbe had already said upon the belief of the Hottentots in the survival of *a something* from man after the earthly death, of the influence which *that something* may exercise over the destiny of the living, and of a sort of worship rendered to it. If one remembers that the Khoï-Khoï address prayers not only to their recently deceased parents but even to Heitsi-eibib, the first ancestor of the race, it must be seen that they believe in the immortality of that *something*.

Controlled by certain conceptions of natures various and even opposite, which I have often had to combat, one perhaps will claim that we have here only the result of contact of the natives with Europeans. But it is impossible to explain matters at the Cape in this way. The worship, or, if one prefers it, the honourification, of saints, and faith in the power of their mediation is an essentially Catholic belief, rejected by all Protestant sects. But the Cape and its dependencies have been colonised only by Protestants—by Hollanders, French who fled at the revocation of the edict of Nantes, English. This fact explains why these countries have been evangelised only by Protestants. The first missionary who attempted the conversion of the Hottentots was a Moravian, George Schmidt, who

came to the Cape in 1736,* consequently several years
after the voyage of Kolbe.† The beliefs here discussed
then belong properly to the Khoï-Khoï.

The Hottentots, moreover, have no clear idea either as
to the nature of spirits or of their mode of existence.
Kolbe discovered nothing among them which corresponded
to heaven or hell. He concluded that they have no notion of reward or punishment connected with good or bad
actions. Hahn is silent in this matter. Perhaps this is
one of the points upon which he has not cared to tell all
he knows. A people who consider the stars as the eyes of
some dead persons, but at the same time make of *others*
the people of Gaunab, have certainly at least a somewhat
confused idea of the rewards which await the good and
the bad.

Worship, Priests, Sorcerers.—I have already said that
the Khoï-Khoï have no sort of figures intended to represent their deities, and that they construct no building
consecrated to worship. One cannot give that name
either to the *cairns* regarded as tombs of Heitsi-eibib, or
to those which cover the bodies of some saints, and which
grow slowly in consequence of the accumulation of stones
or branches of trees which are deposited there as offerings. One cannot even regard as chapels those temporary
booths of green boughs and flowers under which men
alone eat flesh of cattle offered in sacrifice. Yet they
have sacred places which they never pass without praying.
These are, as I have stated, certain rocks, hills, rivers, etc.
The homage, moreover, is not addressed to the material

---

* Some Danish missionaries sent to the Indies by the King of
Denmark, Frederick IV—Plutschau, Zeegenbal, Boving—were at
the Cape at the same time as Kolbe; but they only touched there.
Hahn and Moffat agree in giving to George Schmidt the title of
first missionary to the Hottentots. [67, 117]

† 1705 to 1713.

object, whatever it may be, but to the god or spirit believed to reside therein. I do not anywhere find that
these places are the object of pilgrimage, or that numbers
of people betake themselves there to hold religious ceremonies in common. These, rather, take place within the
kraal. It is there, in the round public place enclosed by
the huts, that one celebrates the return of the Pleiades
and of the new moon, or that, with eyes fixed upon the
Pleiades, they invoke Tsûi-goa.

Among the Hottentots there exists nothing resembling
a sacerdotal caste. Each kraal has its priest (*surri*), whose
position is sufficiently modest. To begin with, he is elected, which seems to exclude all idea of a special character
resulting from his relations to the divinity. In the next
place, in the local hierarchy he holds only a fourth rank,
after the civil chief, the military chief, and the doctor.
He plays an important part in the ceremonies which accompany marriage and the passage of boys into manhood,
perhaps also in funerary rites. But he is not even mentioned in connection with the great religious ceremonies
addressed either to the good or the bad principle. He
makes no public prayer; he gives no instruction to the
people in religious matters. He is, then, as Kolbe says,
a *master of ceremonies* rather than a *priest*, in the acceptance we give that word.

By the side of the *surri*, whose functions connect him
more or less with the worship of the good gods, are found
sorcerers, among whom Hahn places *the makers of rain*.
These receive their power from Gaunab, who teaches to
whom he pleases the diabolical art of enchantment and
bewitchment. We have no information upon the nature
of the relations which can be established between the evil
genius and men. There is no mention either of compact
or of oath, yet the sorcerers are, in a sense, ministers of
Gaunab. The Hottentots extremely fear their incanta-

17

tions, and attribute to them almost all the misfortunes
which strike their persons or their cattle; they have re-
course to a vast number of amulets and practices to protect themselves against them.

Various Superstitions.—One may consider the ideas
so far discussed as really belonging to the *religion proper*
of the Hottentots. There are others which are veritable
superstitions.* There are a number of ideas without apparent relation to the mythology of these people, but
which are none the less accepted as articles of faith, and
give rise to special practices which one cannot neglect
without danger. Hahn devotes a long chapter to these;
I will limit myself to quoting a few of them.

Fire appears to play an important *rôle* from this point
of view. At the birth of a child one must fire a little
faggot without employing either stove or metal, but by the
friction of two pieces of wood; this must be kept burning
until the umbilical cord drops, and must not be used
for any domestic purpose. If these prescriptions are not
rigidly observed the child will die. When a Hottentot
goes forth to the hunt his wife lights a special fire, and
should do naught but attend to it until he returns. Should
it go out, the husband will bring back no game. At certain epochs one makes sheep pass through a fire fed with
green wood and giving much smoke. I have nowhere
seen a statement that the Hottentots submit themselves
to this ceremony, of which traces are found even in
France, especially in Brittany.[158]

Certain animals, particularly elephants and serpents,
can recognise guilty persons, and go into the midst of a

---

* I have long insisted, both in my courses and in my books,
upon the distinction that should be made between *religion* and *superstitions.* I consider it as important to make this clearly in the
case of the lowest savages as in the case of the most civilised peoples; but this is too often forgotten.[143, 156]

crowd to kill them without attacking any of their companions. The tribe of the Amaqua one day surprised
the Damara, and made a great carnage and carried away
much booty. One of the aggressors made himself conspicuous by his extreme cruelty. on returning home he
was attacked in his hut by a black lion, who tore him to
pieces. The Amaqua are still convinced that this lion
was really a Damara, who had taken this form to avenge
his tribe.

Hahn has gone to much trouble to find among the
Namaqua some trace of serpent worship, but with no
success. This creature figures largely, however, in the
superstitions of the Cape, as everywhere else in the world.
Here, as elsewhere, there exist *charmers* who fearlessly
handle the most dangerous species; one of them procured
for our author all that he wished of them. The sorcerers,
of course, enjoy this privilege in the greatest degree. The
Hottentots say they only need to hiss to make all the serpents of the neighbourhood run to them. Near every
spring there dwells a serpent; if he departs or is killed
the fountain dries up. Serpents are very fond of milk;
they suck cows, and even women. Analogous superstitions
exist among ourselves. A particular species (*huitsibis*)
lives between the horns of the cana.* Finally, the natives believe in the existence of serpents with human
virile organs, who seek women during their slumber
(*ganin-qub*). Hahn passed the night in a kraal where
the whole population were under arms and greatly excited
because a young girl believed she had seen one of these
strange incubi.

Mythological Theory of Hahn.—Hahn is not content
only to make known the religious beliefs of the Hottentots; he has desired to explain them, and has thus

---

* *Antilope oreas,* Pallas: *Oreas canna,* Gray.

been led to a theory which rests mainly upon linguistic considerations. He seeks in etymology a rational interpretation of the names of the divinities of whom he has spoken, and believes he can thus follow back mythological conceptions to their origin.

Our author, naturally, first occupies himself with Tsúi-goa. He recalls the fact, according to the legend, that the two words mean the *sick* or *wounded knee*. But he thinks it strange that the infinite being should be called by a name which makes him only a simple person playing a part in a common tale, and he proposes a very different explanation. The root *tsu*, says he, signifies literally *sick, wounded;* but a recent wound is the colour of blood—it is red. T'sú, by extension, then, has the same meaning. On the other hand, the verb *goa* means "*to walk, to approach.*" *Goab, goam,* is "*he who walks, he who approaches.*" The first meaning can be very well applied to the knee ; the second can be used in speaking of the day, which is on the point of appearing. The words *Tsúi-goab, Tsúi-goam,* ought, then, to be translated by "*he who comes red.*" He is, says Hahn, the red morning, the rosy dawn, the aurora.

The same line of thought conducts our author to identify with the night the god whom we have seen to be the foe of Tsúi-goa. From the root *o*, "*to die,*" come the words for "*to sleep, death, slumber,*" etc. The night kills, so to say, all the men whom it puts to slumber. The male being who personifies it well merits, then, the name of *Gaunam*—that is, "*the destroyer.*"

Hahn considers it as demonstrated that, in their origin, the words *Tsúi-goa* and *Gauna* have been employed only to express the succession of day and night. But the primitive meaning is lost ; the religious sentiment and mythology apply themselves to the task, and the legend is born. Every evening man dies and the night envelops him ; he relives at the break of day ; he turns his eyes towards the east, and sees the sky tinted with red ; he concludes from that that a battle has taken place and that blood has flowed. Thus has arisen the history of the struggle between Gaunab, the inhabitant of the dark sky, and Tsui-goa, who gains his victory at the price of a wounded knee.

After having shown Tsui-goa to be only the personification of the dawn, Hahn, by the employment of the same method, and thanks to comparisons which seem to me at times to be very forced, identifies with him the greater part of the divinities of whom I have spoken. According to him, Khab, Heitsi-eibib, Gurub, Nanub, etc., are all *the Infinite One, the lord of life and light.* He hardly makes one exception upon the subject of Gurikhoïsib, the first man. He seems to regard him as a distinct personage, admitting that here the worship of ancestors has been fused with that of the supreme being. It is to be observed that in this astronomical myth, as Hahn understands it, the sun *Urisis* plays only a subordinate *rôle*, becoming the wife of the moon, *Khab*, assimilated to Heitsi-eibib.

In fact, one sees that Mr. Hahn belongs to that school of mythologists which counts so many eminent adepts in Europe, and in France itself. As Max Müller,[128] as Alfred Maury,[111] he seeks in the literal meaning of the names of divinities the interpretation of the myths; he traces back all the personages of the Hottentot pantheon to a small number of personified natural phenomena. According to him, the Khoï-Khoï, in their religious development have followed the same road as the Aryan peoples, and he thinks that if they had not been stopped by the imperfection of their language they would have invented as beautiful a mythology as that of the Iranians or the Greeks. Such as it is, he says, this mythology has had for point of departure the belief in a supreme being whom all the Khoï-Khoï, long before their separation invoked under the name of Tsûi-goab, and who has played among them exactly the same *rôle* as Dyaus among the ancestors of our own race.

Thus Hahn applies Hindoo theories to the mythology of the Khoï-Khoï. I am not competent to follow him in this field; but the masters in linguistics whom I have consulted have unanimously replied that the Hottentot languages are not sufficiently known in their history and their development for it to be possible as yet to pursue such a method. I can only endorse this judgment.

Hahn summarises in the following terms the general impression which his long studies upon the beliefs of the Hottentots have given him: " If the word *religion* corresponds to a faith in a *heavenly father*, who is near his children in their sufferings; if it expresses a belief in an *all-powerful master*, who sends the rains and good weather; if it includes the idea of a *father of lights*, from whom cometh every good thing; if this father is at the same time a *rewarder*, who sees all things and who punishes the wrong and rewards the right; if religion translates the longings of the heart after the *invisible*, with the hope of seeing it face to face, in a better world; if it implies at once the feeling of human feebleness and the acceptance of a divine government, we ought not to hesitate about placing the Khoï-Khoï on our own level."

I cannot here consider the many questions which these conclusions raise, and confine myself to making a single remark. Either our author exaggerates the loftiness of the religious beliefs of the Koi-Koi, or he has not given us all the data necessary for appreciating them. Without doubt many of the facts—the so clear declaration of Arisimab, the hymn to Tsûi-goa, the conduct of the Haboba guide, etc.—plainly show the belief of the Hottentots in a god, creator and all-powerful, who watches over men as over his children; and the brave Xanib, in preferring death to apostasy, has shown that they can die for him if need be. Without doubt, also, the worship of ancestors, dating back to Heitsi-eibib, shows a belief in a future life which almost, if not quite, reaches immortality. But in the facts given by Hahn I see nothing that warrants attributing to the Khoï-Khoï that high longing towards an intimate communion with the supreme God, nothing that suggests even a little definitely a reward kept for the good, a punishment awaiting the wicked. In this regard, far from being equal to the Aryans, they are below many peoples who have remained at a much lower social stage than they have attained. In particular, the Mincopies have made for their supreme god a far more spiritual conception, and have arrived at far more definite and just conceptions regarding the future destiny of man than the Hottentots. But perhaps Hahn has written his opinions after taking into consideration that material which he has judged best not to give us.

In spite of these gaps Hahn's book possesses the greatest interest. He makes us acquainted with a whole new, rudimentary mythology, which brings together, as those of so many other savage peoples do, very elevated ideas and the most childish fables. Moreover, this mythology belongs to one of the oldest, perhaps *the* oldest, of African races. For this reason it has a double interest. The author has added an important chapter to the history of those *little religions*, too often neglected, and a knowledge of which throws so sure a light upon some of the problems which the study of their *great sisters* propounds to the mythologists.*

---

* Émile Burnouf recognises as *great religions* only Christianity, Judaism, Mohammedanism, Brahmanism, Buddhism.[23] They are

the most important in the numbers of their adherents. Out of 1,392,500,000 souls in the population of the globe, these five religions, according to Hubner, include 1,136,500,000. But the same author estimates that the number of different religions in the world is nearly 1,000. The little religions are certainly in the majority. To neglect them in the study of comparative mythology would be like a naturalist who, to gain an idea of the organisation of animals, studied only the vertebrates.

APPENDIX A.

LIST OF BOOKS, ARTICLES AND AUTHORS REFERRED TO
IN THE TEXT.

(The small numbers in the text correspond to the numbers in this list.)

1. *d'Abbadie.* Bul. Société de Géographie, third series, vol. ii.
2. *d'Albertis.* New Guinea: What I did and what I saw.
3. *Allen, F. A.* The Original Range of the Papuan and Negrito Races, Jour. Anth. Inst., vol. viii.
4. *Anderson.* The Semang and Sakai Tribes of the Malay Peninsula, Jour. Indian Archipelago, vol. iv.
5. *Anthropological Society of Paris.* Bulletin, third series, vol. iii.
6. *Arbousset et Daumas.* Voyage d'exploration au Nord-est de la colonie du Cap de Bonne-Espérance, entrepris en 1836.
7. *Aristotle.* History of Animals.
8. *Avanchers, Léon des.* Lettre à M. d'Abbadie, Bul. de la Soc. de Géograph., fifth series, vol. xii.
9. *Avanchers, Léon des.* Esquisses géographiques des pays Oromo ou Galla, dits pays Somali, et de la côte orientale d'Afrique, Bul. de la Soc. de Géograph., fourth series, t. xvii.
10. *Avezac.* Notice sur les pays et le peuple des Yebous en Afrique, Mems. de la Soc. d'Ethnol., vol. ii.
11. *Baker, Samuel W.* Discovery of the Albert Nyanza, New Explorations of the Sources of the Nile.
12. *Banier.* Mémoires de l'Académie des inscriptions et belles-lettres, 1729, vol. v.
13. *Barrow.* Vol. xvii of Walckenaer.
14. *Beccari.* Appunti etnografici sui Papua. Cosmos. 1877.
15. *Blair.* Selection of Records of Government of India, No. xxv, The Andaman Islands. Appendix ii.
16. *Bourgeois.* Congrès international d'anthrop. et d'archéologie préhist., 1868.
17. *Brander.* Proc. Roy. Soc. of Edinburgh, 1878-'79.

18. *Broca.* Rapport sur les caractères physiques des Mincopies, Bul. de la Soc. d'Anthrop., 1861.
19. *Broca.* Les Akkas, race pygmée de l'Afrique Centrale, Rev. d'Anthrop., 1874.
20. *Brooke, Capel.* Voyage en Suède, en Norvège, en Finmark et au Cap Nord.
21. *Brooke, Capel.* Trans. of the Ethnological Society, vol. v.
22. *Buffon.* Complete works.
23. *Burnouf.* Revue des Deux Mondes, 1864.
24. *Busk.* Description of Two Andamanese Skulls, Trans. Ethnol. Soc., new series, 1866.
25. *Campbell.* The Ethnology of India, Journal of the Asiat. Soc. of Bengal, vol. xxv, part ii.
26. *Castelnau.* Revue de Philologie, 1876.
27. *Du Chaillu.* L'Afrique Sauvage.
28. *Choris.* Voyage pittoresque autour du Monde, book vii.
29. *Clark, Hyde.* Notes on the Languages of the Andamans, Jour. Anth. Inst., vol. iv.
30. *Colebrook.* On the Andaman Islands, Asiatic Researches, vol. iv.
31. *Comrie.* Anthropological Notes on New Guinea, Jour. Anth. Inst., vol. vi.
32. *Cornalia.* Lettre sur les Akkas de Miani, Archivio por l'Antrop., etc., 1874.
33. *Crawfurd.* History of the Indian Archipelago.
34. *Crawfurd.* On the Malayan and Polynesian Languages and Races, Journal of the Ethnol. Soc. of London, vol. i, 1848.
35. *Ctesias.* History of India.
36. *Cunningham.* Cited by Logan, Jour. Indian Archipelago, vol. vii.
37. *Cuvier.* Le Règne animal.
38. *Dalton.* Descriptive Ethnology of Bengal.
39. *Dapper.* Description de la basse Éthiopie.
40. *Day.* Observations on the Andamanese, Proc. Asiat. Soc. of Bengal, 1870.
41. *Distant.* Jour. Anth. Inst., vol. viii.
42. *Dobson.* Jour. Anth. Inst., vol. iv.
43. *Dubeux and Valmont.* La Tartarie.
44. *Dumeril and Bibron.* Histoire naturelle des Reptiles, vol. iii.
45. *Earl.* The Papuans.
46. Bulletin de l'Institut *Égyptien.* 1873-'74.

47. *Ellis.* Report of Researches into the Language of the South Andaman Island, from the papers of E. H. Man, appendix to Man's book.
48. *Elphinston.* Aboriginal Inhabitants of the Soil.
49 *Feilden.* Notes on Stone Implements from South Africa, Jour. Anth. Inst., vol. viii.
50. *Fichte.* On Certain Aborigines of the Andaman Islands, Trans. Ethnol. Soc., new series, vol. v.
51. *Flower.* On the Osteology and Affinities of the Natives of the Andaman Islands, Jour. Anth. Inst., vol. ix.
52. *Flower.* Stature of the Andamanese (making known Brander's work), Jour. Anth. Inst., vol. x.
53. *Flower.* Additional Observations on the Osteology of the Natives of the Andaman Islands, Jour. Anth. Inst., vol. xiv.
54. *Fryer.* A Few Words concerning the Wild People inhabiting the Forests of the Cochin State, Jour. of the Royal Asiat. Soc. of Great Britain and Ireland, second series, vol. iii.
55. *Fychle.* Trans. of the Ethnological Society, vol. v. Cf. No. 50.
56. *Gaussin.* Traditions religieuses de la Polynesie, Tour du Monde.
57. Congrès international des Sciences *Géographiques,* vol i.
58. La Gazette *Géographique,* 1887.
59. *Giglioli.* Viaggio intorno al globo della pirocorvetta Italiana Magenta.
60. *Giglioli.* Studi sulla razza negrita, Archivio por l'Antrop. e la Etnol., vol. v.
61. *Giglioli.* Nuove notizie sui popoli negroidi dell'Asia e specialmente sui Negriti, Archivio por l'Antrop., etc., vol. ix.
62. *Giglioli.* Gli Akka viventi in Italia, Archivio por l'Antrop., etc., vol. x.
63. *Giglioli.* Alteriori notizie intorno ai Negriti ; gli Akka viventi en Italia, Archivio por l'Athrop., etc., vol. x.
64. *la Gironière.* Vingt années aux Philippines, 1853.
65. *Gooch.* The Stone Age in South Africa, Jour. Anth. Inst., vol. xi.
66. *Grey.* Polynesian Mythology.
67. *Hahn.* Tsûi-goam, the Supreme Being of the Koi-Koi, 1881.
68. *Hamy.* La Nature, 1876, February 12th.
69. *Hamy.* Documents pour servir à l'anthropologie de l'île de Timor, Nouvelles Archives du Mus. d'histoire naturelle de Paris, vol. x.

70. *Hamy.* Rapport sur l'anthropologie du Cambodge, Bul. de la Soc. d'Anth. de Paris, vol. vi.

71. *Hamy.* Sur les races sauvages de la péninsule malaise et en particulier sur les Jakuns, Bul. de la Soc. d'Anth. de Paris, second series, vol. ix.

72. *Hamy.* Les Négritos à Bornéo, Bul. de la Soc. d'Anth. de Paris, second series, vol. xi.

73. *Hamy* Note sur l'existence de Nègres brachycéphales sur la côte occidentale d'Afrique, Bul. de la Soc. d'Anth., second series, vol. vii.

74. *Hamy.* Essai de co-ordination des matériaux récemment recueilles sur l'anthropologie des Négrilles ou Pygmées de l'Afrique équatoriale, Bul. de la Soc. d'Anth., 1879.

75. *Hartmann.* Die Negritier.

76. *Heber.* Travels in India, cited by Pritchard.

77. *Hodgson.* Jour. Asiat. Soc. of Bengal, vol. xxv.

78. *Huxley, T. H.* On Two widely Contrasted Forms of the Human Cranium, Jour. of Anat. and Physiol., vol. i.

79. Journal of Anthropological *Institute,* vol. xi.

80. *Kolbe.* Description du Cap de Bonne Espérance, in Walckenaer.

81. *Lafonde.* Jour. de l'Institut historique.

82. *Laglaïse.* La Papouasie ou Nouvelle Guinée occidentale, cited in this work by Meyners d'Estrey.

83. *Lane-Fox.* On Mr. Man's Collection of Andamanese and Nicobarese Objects, Jour. Anth. Inst., vol. vii.

84. *de Langle, Fleuriot.* Croisières à la côte d'Afrique, 1868.

85. *Latham.* Descriptive Ethnology, vol. ii.

86. *Latham.* Elements of Comparative Philology.

87. *Latham.* The Native Races of the Russian Empire.

88. *de Lauture.* Bul. de la Soc. de Géographie, fourth series, vol. xii.

89. *de Lauture.* Comptes rendus de l'Academie des Sciences, 1856.

90. *Lawes, W. G.* Ethnological Notes on the Motu, Koitapu, and Koiari, tribes of New Guinea, Jour. Anth. Inst., vol. viii.

91. *Livingstone.* Explorations in South Africa.

92. *Logan.* The Orang Binua of Johore, Jour. of the Indian Archipelago, vol. i.

93. *Logan.* The Binua of Johore.

94. *Logan.* The Ethnology of the Indian Archipelago, Jour. of the Indian Archipelago, vol. iv.

95. *Logan.* Ethnology of Eastern Asia and the Indo-Pacific Islands, Jour. Indian Arch., vol. iv.

96. *Logan.* Ethnology of the Indo-Pacific Islands, Jour. Indian Arch., vol. vii.

97. *Logan.* Physical Characteristics of the Mintira, Jour. Indian Arch., vol. i.

98. Dialects of the *Melanesian* Tribes of the Malay Peninsula, Jour. of the Straits Branch of the Royal Asiat. Soc.

99. *Chaillé Long Bey,* Central Africa.

100. *Chaillé Long Bey.* Voyage au Lac Victoria Nyanza et au pays des Niams-Niams, Bul. de la Soc. de Géog., sixth series, vol. x.

101. *Man.* On the Aboriginal Inhabitants of the Andaman Islands, Jour. Anth. Inst., vol. vii, and in reprinted form.

102. *Man.* Jour. Anth. Inst., vol. xi.

103. *Mantegazza.* Studi antropologici ed etnografici sulla Nuova Guinea, Archivio por l'Antrop., etc., vol. vii, 1877.

104. *Mantegazza.* Bul. de la Soc. d'Anth. de Paris, third series, vol. iii, 1880.

105. *Mantegazza.* Nuovi studi craniologici sulla Nuova Guinea, Archivio por l'Antrop., etc., vol. xi, 1881.

106. *Mantegazza and Zannetti.* I due Akka del Miani, Archivio por l'Antrop., etc., 1874.

107. *Marche.* Trois voyages dans l'Afrique occidentale.

108. *Mariner.* An Account of the Natives of Tonga Island.

109. *Marno.* Mittheilungen der Anthrop. Gesel. in Wien, Bd. v.

110. *Masson.* Narrative of Various Journeys in Beluchistan, Afghanistan, and the Penjab, cited in L'Univers.

111. *Maury.* Histoire de la religion de la Grèce antique, 1859.

112. *Maury.* La Terre et l'Homme, fifth edition.

113. *Meyer.* Die Philippinen und ihre Bewohner.

114. *Meyer.* Ueber hundert fünf und dreissig Papua Schädel von Neu Guinea und der Insel Mysore, Mittheil. aus dem Kais. zool. Mus. zu Dresden, Bd. i, 1875.

115. *Meyer.* Anthropologische Mittheilungen über die Papuas von Neu Guinea, mit der anth. Gesel. in Wien, Bd. iv, 1874.

116. *Micluko-Maclay.* Ethnologische Excursionen in der Malayischen Halbinsel. Archivio por l'antropologia e la etnolog., vol. ix.

117. *Moffat.* Twenty-three Years in South Africa.

118. de *Mofras.* Exploration du Territoire de l'Orégon, des Californies et de la mer Vermeille, 1844.

119. *Mollien.* Voyage dans l'intérieur de l'Afrique, aux sources du Senégal et de la Senégambie.

120. *Montano.* Revue d'Ethnographie, vol. i. (See No. 121.)

121. *Montano.* Quelques jours chez les indigènes de la Province de Malacca, Revue d'Ethnog., vol. i.

122. *Montano.* Voyages aux Philippines et en Malaisie.

123. *Morenhout.* Voyage aux Îles du Grand Ocean (in Tour du Monde).

124. *Mouat.* A Narrative of an Expedition to the Andaman Islands in 1857.

125. *Mouat.* Adventures and Researches among the Andaman Islands, 1863.

126. *Mouat.* Selection of the Records of the Government of India, No. xxv, the Andaman Islands.

127. *Mouat.* A Few Notes on Some Skulls of the Hill Tribes of India, Trans. Ethnol. Soc., vol. vi.

128. *Müller, Max.* Essays upon Comparative Mythology.

129. Bulletin de la Société *Normande* de Géographie, 1886.

130. *Owen.* On the Osteology and Dentition of the Aborigines of the Andaman Islands, Trans. Ethnol. Soc., new series, vol. ii.

131. *Owen.* On the Psychical and Physical Characters of the Mincopies or Natives of the Andaman Islands, Brit. Assoc. Rept., 1861.

132. *Owen.* Examen des deux Nègres pygmées de la tribes de Akkas ramenes par Miani du fleuve Gabon., Bul. de la Soc. d'Anth., 1874, with remarks by Broca, Hamy, and De Quatrefages.

133. *Panizza.* Sur les Akkas, Bul. de la Soc. d'Anth.. 1874.

134. *Pavie.* Les heros pieux, les Pandavas, Revue des Deux Mondes, 1857.

135. *Pauthier.* La Chine.

136. *le Page du Pratz.* Histoire de la Louisiane, 1758.

137. *Pickering.* The Races of Men, edition of 1851.

138. *Pliny.* Histoire naturelle.

139. *Pritchard.* Researches into the Physical History of Mankind.

140. *Pruner Bey.* Bul. de la Soc. d'Anth., 1866.

141. *de Quatrefages.* Bul. de la Soc. d'Anth., vol. i, 1860.

142. *de Quatrefages.* Cours d'Anthrop. du Museum; Nègres asiatiques et melanésiens, Gazette medicale de Paris, 1862.

143. *de Quatrefages.* Rapports sur les progrès de l'Anthropologie, 1867.

144. *de Quatrefages.* Jour. des Savants, 1879.

145. *de Quatrefages.* Bul. de la Soc. d'Anth., 1881.

146. *de Quatrefages.* Rapport sur le concours du prix Godard, Bul. de la Soc. d'Anth., second series, vol. iv.

147. *de Quatrefages.* Bul. de la Soc. d'acclimatation.

148. *de Quatrefages.* Études sur les Mincopies et sur le race négrito en général, Revue d'Anthrop., vol. i.

149. *de Quatrefages.* Note sur un Négrito de l'Inde centrale, Bul. de la Soc. d'Anth., second series, vol. vii.

150. *de Quatrefages.* Nouvelles Études sur la distribution géographique des Négritos et sur leur identification avec les Pygmées asiatiques de Ctésias et de Pline.

151. *de Quatrefages.* Thenay et les Îles Andaman, matériaux pour l'hist. nat. et prim. de l'homme, third series, vol. ii.

152. *de Quatrefages.* Tableau des races de l'Inde centrale, Revue d'Anthrop., vol. i.

153. *de Quatrefages.* Observations sur les races naines Africaines à propos des Akkas, Bul. de la Soc. d'Anth., 1874; also Comptes rendus de l'Academie des sciences, 1874.

154. *de Quatrefages.* Les Polynésiens et leurs migrations.

155. *de Quatrefages.* Hommes fossiles et hommes sauvages.

156. *de Quatrefages.* Introduction à l'étude des races humaines, 1887.

157. *de Quatrefages and Hamy.* Crania ethnica.

158. *Quellien.* Revue d'Ethnographie, vol. iv.

159. *Quetelet.* Anthropometrie.

160. *Raffles and Crawfurd.* Description of Java.

161. *Relation* des voyages faits par les Arabes et les Persans dans l'Inde et la Chine dans le IX⁰ siècle de l'ère chretienne, 1849.

162. *Rienzi.* Oceanie.

163. *Rousselet.* Essai d'une carte ethnologique de l'Inde centrale.

164. *Rousselet.* Tableau des races d'Inde centrale, Revue d'Anthrop., vol. ii.

165. *Rousselet.* Note sur un Hô autochtone des forêts de l'Inde centrale, Revue d'Anth., vol. i; also Bul. de la Soc. d'Anth., second series, vol. vii.

166. *Saint-Denis.* Mémoire sur le pays connu des anciens Chinois sous le nom de Fou Sang, Comptes rendus des seances de l'Academie des inscriptions et belles-lettres, 1876.

167. *Saint-John.* Notes on the Andaman Islands (arranged by Sir Edw. Belcher), Trans. of the Ethnol. Soc., new series, vol. v.

168. *de Saint-Pol Lias.* Sur le rivière Pluss, intérieur de le presqu'île malaise, La Nouvelle Revue, 1882.

169. *Samuells.* Jour. Asiat. Soc. of Bengal, vol. vii.

170. *Sanderson.* Notes in connection with stone implements from Natal, Jour. Anth. Inst., vol. viii.

171. *Schmidt, George.* Cited by Hahn.

172. *Schweinfurth.* In the Heart of Africa.

173. *Semper.* Die Philippinen und ihre Bewohner.

174. *Smith, Hamilton.* The Natural History of the Human Species.

175. *Snelgrave.* Relation de quelques parties de la Guinée in Walckenaer, vol. viii.

176. *Speke.* Source of the Nile.

177. *Stanley.* Through the Dark Continent.

178. *Stoliczka.* Note on the Kjoekkenmoeddings of the Andaman Islands, Proc. Asiat. Soc. of Bengal, 1870.

179. *Symes.* Relation de l'ambassade anglaise envoyée en 1795, dans la royaume d'Ava.

180. *Touchard.* Notice sur le Gabon, Revue maritime et coloniale, vol. iii.

181. Leschenault de *la Tour.* Relation abrégée d'un voyage aux Indes orientales, Mems. du Mus. d'hist. nat., vol. xi.

182. *Traill.* Statistical Sketch of Kamaon, Asiatic Researches, vol. xvi.

183. *Valentyn.* Cited by Hahn.

184. Bibliotheque universelle des *Voyages,* vol. xxi.

185. *Walckenaer.* Histoire générale des voyages.

186. *Wallace* (cited by Lane-Fox). Jour. Anth. Inst., vol. vii.

187. *Zannetti.* Gli Akka del Miani, Archivio por l'Antrop., etc., 1874.

188. *Zeitschrift für Ethnologie,* 1874.

APPENDIX B.

VARIOUS articles relative to the little races discussed in this book have appeared recently. References to the more important are given below. These are mainly taken from Prof. Mason's bibliographic lists :

Bartels, M. Beitrag zur Volksmedicin der Kaffern und Hottentotten, Verhandl. d. Berl. anthrop. Gesellsch., Berl., 1893, vol. xxv, 133-135.

Bertin, G. The Bushmen and their Language, Jour. Royal Asiat. Soc., vol. xviii, 51-81.

le Clerc, Max. Les pygmées à Madagascar, Revue d'ethnog., Paris, vol. vi, 323-335.

Deniker, J. Les Hottentots au Jardin d'acclimatation, Revue d'anthrop., Paris, third series, vol. iv, 1-27.

F., J. Chimpanzees and Dwarf in Central Africa, Nature, London, vol. xlii, 296.

Flower, W. H. Description of Two Skeletons of Akkas, a Pygmy Race from Central Africa, Jour. Anth. Inst., London, vol. xviii, 3-19, 73-91.

Flower, W. H. The Pygmy Races of Men, Proc. Royal Inst. Great Britain, London, vol. xii, 266-283.

Gillet de Grandmont. Le stéatopygie des Hottentots du Jardin d'acclimatation, Revue d'anth., Paris, third series, vol. iv, 194-199.

Haliburton, R. G. The Dwarfs of the Atlas Mountains, London (David Nutt), 41 pp., 8vo.

Laborde, M. Étude expérimentale sur les poisons de flèche des Négritos (Sakayes) de la presqu'île malaise, Bul. Soc. d'anth., Paris, vol. xi, 194-196.

Lombroso, C. Ueber ein neues Mutterschaftsorgan und über das

Becken des Hottentottenweibes, Wien. med. Wochenschr., xliii, 741, 786.

Ploix, C. Les Hottentots, ou Khoï-Khoï et leur religion, Revue d'anth., 1887, 570–589 ; 1888, 270–289.

Schils, G. Le race jaune de l'Afrique Australe, Le Museon, Louvain, vol. vi, 224–231 ; 339–349.

Schlichter, Henry. The Pygmy Tribes of Africa, Scot. Geog. Mag., Edinburgh, vol. viii, 289–301.

Sievers. Die Zwergvölker in Afrika, Verhandl. der Oberhess., Gesellsch. f. Nat. u. Heilk., Giessen, vol. xxviii, 114–117.

Stanley, Henry M. In Darkest Africa, 2 vols ; see indices for scattered references to pygmies.

Stanley, Henry M. Les Pygmées de l'Afrique Centrale (extract), Nature, Paris, vol. xviii, part ii, 67–69.

Topinard, P. La stéatopygie des Hottentots du Jardin d'acclimatation, Revue d'anth., Paris, third series, vol. iv, 194–199 ; 249–252.

Topinard, P. Présentation de quatre Boshimans vivants, Archiv für Anth., Braunschweig, vol. xviii, 287.

Werner, A. The African Pygmies, Pop. Sci. Monthly, New York, vol. xxxvii, 658–671.

STANLEY has not contributed so much to our real knowledge of African pygmies as might have been expected. He gives some measurements, taken upon five individuals, which are here reproduced for comparison :

*Measurements taken by Dr. Emin on Some Akkas in Stanley's Company.**

NAME.	Tokbali. 20 years.	Girl, 15 years.	Woman, 35 years.	Boy, 15 years.
Height standing	1ᵐ360	1ᵐ240	1ᵐ365	1ᵐ280
Height to shoulder	1ᵐ116	1ᵐ021	1ᵐ110	1ᵐ090
Height to navel	0ᵐ835	0ᵐ725	0ᵐ785	0ᵐ970
Arm length, shoulder to finger tip	0ᵐ707	0ᵐ571	0ᵐ580	0ᵐ540
Breadth between shoulders	0ᵐ320	0ᵐ304	0ᵐ295	0ᵐ260
Circumference below nipples	0ᵐ710	0ᵐ660	0ᵐ710	0ᵐ640
Circumference under armpits	0ᵐ720	0ᵐ660	0ᵐ710	0ᵐ630
Length of head	0ᵐ200	0ᵐ176	0ᵐ180	0ᵐ175
Breadth of head	0ᵐ147	0ᵐ150	0ᵐ145	0ᵐ140
Breadth of nose	0ᵐ060	0ᵐ060+	0ᵐ065	0ᵐ065
Circumference of skull	0ᵐ530	0ᵐ535	0ᵐ510	0ᵐ510
Length of foot	0ᵐ220+	0ᵐ190	0ᵐ212	0ᵐ160

Bodies covered with stiffish grey, short hair.

Measurement was also made upon a pygmy about twenty-one years old captured at Avatiko (see In Darkest Africa, vol. ii, p. 40). The figures recorded by Mr. Bonny are : Height, 4 feet; head circumference, 20¼ inches;

---

* In Darkest Africa, vol. ii, p. 164, note.

from chin to top of head, 24¼ inches; circumference of chest, 25½ inches; of abdomen, 27¾ inches; of hips, 22½ inches; of wrist, 4¼ inches; of muscle of left arm, 7½ inches; of ankle, 7 inches; of calf of leg, 7¾ inches; length of index finger, 2 inches; of right hand, 4 inches; of foot, 6¼ inches; of leg, 22 inches; of back, 18½ inches; of arm to tip of finger, 19¾ inches.

INDEX.

THE END.

POPULAR ASTRONOMY: A General Description of the Heavens. By CAMILLE FLAMMARION. Translated from the French by J. ELLARD GORE, F. R. A. S. With 3 Plates and 288 Illustrations. 8vo. Cloth, $4.50.

" M. Camille Flammarion is the most popular scientific writer in France. Of the present work no fewer than one hundred thousand copies were sold in a few years. It was considered of such merit that the Montyon Prize of the French Academy was awarded to it. The subject is treated in a very popular style, and the work is at the same time interesting and reliable. It should be found very useful by those who wish to acquire a good general knowledge of astronomy without going too deeply into the science."—*From Translator's Preface.*

WOMAN'S SHARE IN PRIMITIVE CULTURE. By OTIS TUFTON MASON, A. M., Curator of the Department of Ethnology in the United States National Museum. With numerous Illustrations. 12mo. Cloth, $1.75.

This is the first volume in the ANTHROPOLOGICAL SERIES, edited by Prof. Frederick Starr, of the University of Chicago. The series is undertaken in the hope that anthropology—the science of man—may become betterknown to intelligent readers. While the books are intended to be of general interest, they will in every case be written by authorities who will not sacrifice scientific accuracy to popularity. In the present volume is traced the interesting period when with fire-making began the first division of labor—a division of labor based upon sex—the man going to the field or forest for game, while the woman at the fireside became the burden-bearer, basket-maker, weaver, potter, agriculturist, and domesticator of animals.

THE FARMER'S BOY. By CLIFTON JOHNSON, author of " The Country School in New England," etc. With 64 Illustrations by the author. 8vo. Cloth, $2.50.

The memories of the farm which are cherished by so many dwellers in cities are preserved in this delightful volume in tangible form. Mr. Johnson follows the work and play of farm life through the seasons, illustrating its quaint and picturesque features, and presenting a volume which has, among other merits, that of a truthful history of life.

SONGS OF THE SOIL. By FRANK L. STANTON. With a Preface by JOEL CHANDLER HARRIS. 16mo. Cloth, gilt top, uncut, $1.50.

" Here is one with the dew of morning in his hair, who looks on life and the promise thereof and finds the prospect joyous. Whereupon he lifts up his voice and speaks to the heart; and lo! here is Love, with nimble feet and sparkling eyes ; and here is Hope, fresh risen from his sleep ; and here is Life made beautiful again."—JOEL CHANDLER HARRIS.

New York: D. APPLETON & CO., 72 Fifth Avenue.

D. APPLETON & CO.'S PUBLICATIONS.

IDLE DAYS IN PATAGONIA. By W. H. HUD-
SON, C. M. Z. S., author of "The Naturalist in La Plata," etc.
With 27 Illustrations. 8vo. Cloth, $4.00.

"Of all modern books of travel it is certainly one of the most original, and many,
we are sure, will also find it one of the most interesting and suggestive."—*New York
Tribune.*

"Mr. Hudson's remarks on color and expression of eyes in man and animals are reserved for a second chapter, 'Concerning Eyes.' He is eloquent upon the pleasures
afforded by 'Bird Music in South America,' and relates some romantic tales of white
men in captivity to savages. But it makes very little difference what is the topic when
Mr. Hudson writes. He calls up bright images of things unseen, and is a thoroughly
agreeable companion."—*Philadelphia Ledger*

THE NATURALIST IN LA PLATA. By W. H.
HUDSON, C. M. Z. S., author of "Idle Days in Patagonia," and
joint author of "Argentine Ornithology." With 27 Illustrations. 8vo. Cloth, $4.00.

"Mr. Hudson is not only a clever naturalist, but he possesses the rare gift of interesting his readers in whatever attracts him, and of being dissatisfied with mere observation unless it enables him to philosophize as well. With his lucid accounts of
bird, beast, and insect, no one will fail to be delighted."—*London Academy.*

"A notably clear and interesting account of scientific observation and research.
Mr. Hudson has a keen eye for the phenomena with which the naturalist is concerned,
and a lucid and delightful way of writing about them, so that any reader may be
charmed by the narrative and the reflections here set forth. It is easy to follow him,
and we get our information agreeably as he conducts us over the desert pampas, and
makes us acquainted with the results of his studies of animals, insects, and birds."—
New York Sun.

*THE NATURALIST ON THE RIVER
AMAZONS.* By HENRY WALTER BATES, F. R. S., late Assistant Secretary of the Royal Geographical Society. With a
Memoir of the Author, by EDWARD CLODD. With Map and
numerous Illustrations. 8vo. Cloth, $5.00.

"This famous work is a natural history classic."—*London Literary World.*

"More than thirty years have passed since the first appearance of 'The Naturalist
on the River Amazons,' which Darwin unhesitatingly pronounced the best book on
natural history which ever appeared in England. The work still retains its prime interest, and in rereading it one can not but be impressed by the way in which the pro-
phetic theories, disputed and ridiculed at the time, have since been accepted. Such is
the common experience of those who keep a few paces in advance of their generation.
Bates was a 'born' naturalist."—*Philadelphia Ledger.*

"No man was better prepared or gave himself up more thoroughly to the task of
studying an almost unknown fauna, or showed a zeal more indefatigable in prosecuting
his researches, than Bates. As a collector alone his reputation would be second to
none, but there is a great deal more than sheer industry to be cited. The naturalist of
the Amazons is, *par excellence*, possessed of a happy literary style. He is always clear
and distinct. He tells of the wonders of tropical growth so that you can understand
them all."—*New York Times.*

New York: D. APPLETON & CO., 72 Fifth Avenue.

D. APPLETON & CO.'S PUBLICATIONS.

NEW EDITION OF PROF. HUXLEY'S ESSAYS.

*C*OLLECTED ESSAYS. By THOMAS H. HUXLEY.
New complete edition, with revisions, the Essays being grouped according to general subject. In nine volumes, a new Introduction accompanying each volume. 12mo. Cloth, $1.25 per volume.

VOL.   I.—METHOD AND RESULTS.

VOL.   II.—DARWINIANA.

VOL.   III.—SCIENCE AND EDUCATION.

VOL.   IV.—SCIENCE AND HEBREW TRADITION.

VOL.   V.—SCIENCE AND CHRISTIAN TRADITION.

VOL.   VI.—HUME.

VOL.   VII.—MAN'S PLACE IN NATURE.

VOL. VIII.—DISCOURSES, BIOLOGICAL AND GEOLOGICAL.

VOL.   IX.—EVOLUTION AND ETHICS, AND OTHER ESSAYS.

"Mr. Huxley has covered a vast variety of topics during the last quarter of a century. It gives one an agreeable surprise to look over the tables of contents and note the immense territory which he has explored. To read these books carefully and studiously is to become thoroughly acquainted with the most advanced thought on a large number of topics."—*New York Herald.*

"The series will be a welcome one. There are few writings on the more abstruse problems of science better adapted to reading by the general public, and in this form the books will be well in the reach of the investigator. . . . The revisions are the last expected to be made by the author, and his introductions are none of earlier date than a few months ago [1893], so they may be considered his final and most authoritative utterances."—*Chicago Times.*

"It was inevitable that his essays should be called for in a completed form, and they will be a source of delight and profit to all who read them. He has always commanded a hearing, and as a master of the literary style in writing scientific essays he is worthy of a place among the great English essayists of the day. This edition of his essays will be widely read, and gives his scientific work a permanent form."—*Boston Herald.*

"A man whose brilliancy is so constant as that of Prof. Huxley will always command readers; and the utterances which are here collected are not the least in weight and luminous beauty of those with which the author has long delighted the reading world."—*Philadelphia Press.*

"The connected arrangement of the essays which their reissue permits brings into fuller relief Mr. Huxley's masterly powers of exposition. Sweeping the subject-matter clear of all logomachies, he lets the light of common day fall upon it. He shows that the place of hypothesis in science, as the starting point of verification of the phenomena to be explained, is but an extension of the assumptions which underlie actions in every-day affairs; and that the method of scientific investigation is only the method which rules the ordinary business of life."—*London Chronicle.*

New York: D. APPLETON & CO., 72 Fifth Avenue.

D. APPLETON & CO.'S PUBLICATIONS.

THE DAWN OF CIVILIZATION. (EGYPT AND CHALDÆA.) By Prof. MASPERO. Edited by the Rev. Prof. SAYCE. Translated by M. L. McCLURE. With Maps and over 470 Illustrations. Quarto. Cloth.

This volume is an attempt to put together in a lucid and interesting manner all that the monuments have revealed to us concerning the earliest civilization of Egypt and Chaldæa. The results of archæological discovery, accumulated during the last thirty years or so, are of such a vast and comprehensive character that none but a master mind could marshal them in true historical perspective. Prof. Maspero is perhaps the only man in Europe fitted by his laborious researches and great scholarship to undertake such a task, and the result of his efforts will be found herein. The period dealt with covers the history of Egypt from the earliest date to the fourteenth dynasty, and that of Chaldæa during its first empire. The book is brought up to the present year, and deals with the recent discoveries at Koptos and Dahabur.

SCHOOLS AND MASTERS OF SCULPTURE. By A. G. RADCLIFFE, author of "Schools and Masters of Painting." With 35 full-page Illustrations. 12mo. Cloth. $3.00.

Those who know Miss Radcliffe's previous work will require no commendation of the grasp of subject and thoroughness of treatment shown in this. In addition to her popular but thorough survey of the history of sculpture in all countries, Miss Radcliffe sketches the various American collections of casts, and explains the opportunities for study which we have at hand.

LIFE OF SIR RICHARD OWEN. By Rev. RICHARD OWEN. With an Introduction by T. H. HUXLEY. 12mo. Cloth.

This most interesting biography of the famous anatomist offers a clear, popular account of his investigations in the fields of comparative anatomy and physiology, zoölogy, paleontology, and transcendental anatomy and physiology. In a sense this work offers a history of scientific discovery in these departments for half a century, while in addition it has a constant personal interest.

DEAN BUCKLAND. The Life and Correspondence of WILLIAM BUCKLAND, D. D., F. R. S., sometime Dean of Westminster, twice President of the Theological Society, and first President of the British Association. By his Daughter, Mrs. GORDON. With Portraits and Illustrations. 8vo. Cloth.

The personal charm which invests this biography of the great geologist enhances its interest for the general reader, while his relation to the discussions of religion and science add a peculiar value to a notable biography.

New York: D. APPLETON & CO., 72 Fifth Avenue.

D. APPLETON & CO.'S PUBLICATIONS.

*T*HE ICE AGE IN NORTH AMERICA, and its Bearings upon the Antiquity of Man. By G. FREDERICK WRIGHT, D. D., LL. D., F. G. S. A., Professor in Oberlin Theological Seminary; Assistant on the United States Geological Survey. With an appendix on "The Probable Cause of Glaciation," by WARREN UPHAM, F. G. S. A., Assistant on the Geological Surveys of New Hampshire, Minnesota, and the United States. New and enlarged edition. With 150 Maps and Illustrations. 8vo, 625 pages, and Index. Cloth, $5.00.

"Not a novel in all the list of this year's publications has in it any pages of more thrilling interest than can be found in this book by Professor Wright. There is nothing pedantic in the narrative, and the most serious themes and startling discoveries are treated with such charming naturalness and simplicity that boys and girls, as well as their seniors, will be attracted to the story, and find it difficult to lay it aside."—*New York Journal of Commerce.*

"One of the most absorbing and interesting of all the recent issues in the department of popular science."—*Chicago Herald.*

"Though his subject is a very deep one, his style is so very unaffected and perspicuous that even the unscientific reader can peruse it with intelligence and profit. In reading such a book we are led almost to wonder that so much that is scientific can be put in language so comparatively simple."—*New York Observer.*

"The author has seen with his own eyes the most important phenomena of the Ice age on this continent from Maine to Alaska. In the work itself, elementary description is combined with a broad, scientific, and philosophic method, without abandoning for a moment the purely scientific character. Professor Wright has contrived to give the whole a philosophical direction which lends interest and inspiration to it, and which in the chapters on Man and the Glacial Period rises to something like dramatic intensity."—*The Independent.*

". . . To the great advance that has been made in late years in the accuracy and cheapness of processes of photographic reproduction is due a further signal advantage that Dr. Wright's work possesses over his predecessors'. He has thus been able to illustrate most of the natural phenomena to which he refers by views taken in the field, many of which have been generously loaned by the United States Geological Survey, in some cases from unpublished material; and he has admirably supplemented them by numerous maps and diagrams."—*The Nation.*

*M*AN AND THE GLACIAL PERIOD. By G. FREDERICK WRIGHT, D. D., LL. D., author of "The Ice Age in North America," "Logic of Christian Evidences," etc. International Scientific Series. With numerous Illustrations. 12mo. Cloth, $1.75.

"It may be described in a word as the best summary of scientific conclusions concerning the question of man's antiquity as affected by his known relations to geological time."—*Philadelphia Press.*

"The earlier chapters describing glacial action, and the traces of it in North America—especially the defining of its limits, such as the terminal moraine of the great movement itself are of great interest and value. The maps and diagrams are of much assistance in enabling the reader to grasp the vast extent of the movement."—*London Spectator.*

New York: D. APPLETON & CO., 72 Fifth Avenue.

THE LAST WORDS OF THOMAS CARLYLE.

Including *Wotton Reinfred*, Carlyle's only essay in fiction ; the *Excursion (Futile Enough) to Paris ;* and letters from Thomas Carlyle, also letters from Mrs. Carlyle, to a personal friend. With Portrait. 12mo. Cloth, gilt top, $1.75.

"The interest of 'Wotton Reinfred' to me is considerable, from the sketches which it contains of particular men and women, most of whom I knew and could, if necessary, identify. The story, too, is taken generally from real life, and perhaps Carlyle did not finish it, from the sense that it could not be published while the persons and things could be recognized That objection to the publication no longer exists. Everybody is dead whose likenesses have been drawn, and the incidents stated have long been forgotten."—JAMES ANTHONY FROUDE.

"'Wotton Reinfred' is interesting as a historical document. It gives Carlyle before he had adopted his peculiar manner, and yet there are some characteristic bits—especially at the beginning—in the Sartor Resartus vein. I take it that these are reminiscences of Irving and of the Thackeray circle, and there is a curious portrait of Coleridge, not very thinly veiled. There is enough autobiography, too, of interest in its way."—LESLIE STEPHEN.

"As a study of Carlyle these pages are of very great value ; they were written before he had acquired that peculiar individual literary style which we now know as Carlylese ; although here and there one may distinguish some of the odd and inflated terms in which, in later years, so much of his work was expressed. The romance abounds in passages of great beauty."—*Newark Daily Advertiser.*

"No complete edition of the Sage of Chelsea will be able to ignore these manuscripts."—*Pall Mall Gazette.*

MEN, MINES, AND ANIMALS IN SOUTH AFRICA. By Lord RANDOLPH S. CHURCHILL. With Portrait, Sixty-five Illustrations, and a Map. 8vo. 337 pages. Cloth, $5.00.

"The subject-matter of the book is of unsurpassed interest to all who either travel in new countries, to see for themselves the new civilizations, or follow closely the experiences of such travelers And Lord Randolph's eccentricities are by no means such as to make his own reports of what he saw in the new states of South Africa any the less interesting than his active eyes and his vigorous pen naturally make them."—*Brooklyn Eagle.*

"Lord Randolph Churchill's pages are full of diversified adventures and experience, from any part of which interesting extracts could be collected. . . . A thoroughly attractive book."—*London Telegraph.*

"Provided with amusing illustrations, which always fall short of caricature, but perpetually suggest mirthful entertainment."—*Philadelphia Ledger.*

"The book is the better for having been written somewhat in the line of journalism. It is a volume of travel containing the results of a journalist's trained observation and intelligent reflection upon political affairs. Such a work is a great improvement upon the ordinary book of travel. . . . Lord Randolph Churchill thoroughly enjoyed his experiences in the African bush, and has produced a record of his journey and exploration which has hardly a dull page in it."—*New York Tribune.*

"Any one who wishes to have a realizing sense of actual conditions in the southern part of the Dark Continent should not fail to avail himself of Lord Rando'ph's keen, incisive, good-humored observations."—*Boston Beacon.*

New York: D. APPLETON & CO., 72 Fifth Avenue.

www.ingramcontent.com/pod-product-compliance
Lightning Source LLC
Chambersburg PA
CBHW030625030726
47497CB00006B/1643